HIGH

DESERT

HIGH

Also by Steven Schindler

Sewer Balls

From the Block

From Here to Reality

On the Bluffs

The Last Sewer Ball

HIGH DESERT HIGH

A novel

Steven Schindler

The Elevated Press

FOR INFORMATION AND REQUESTS CONTACT:
The Elevated Press
350 N. Glendale Ave.
Ste. B-240
Glendale CA 91206

mail@StevenSchindler.com
www.TheElevatedPress.com

ISBN-13   978-0-9662408-0-1
ISBN-10   0-9662408-0-4
eBook ISBN 978-0-9662408-4-9

LIBRARY OF CONGRESS CONTROL NUMBER:
2017952792

THE ELEVATED PRESS ORIGINAL TRADE PAPERBACK
FIRST EDITION, NOVEMBER 2017

EDITOR: BRIAN McKERNAN
COVER PHOTOGRAPHY: CRAIG WOLF
COVER DESIGN: CRAIG WOLF
www.craigwolf.com

Printed in the U.S.A.

ACKNOWLEDGEMENTS

THANKS TO JIM SCHNEIDER, PATTY WILLIAMS,
AND RUPERT MACNEE FOR THEIR THOUGHTFUL INSIGHTS AND
COMMENTS.

VERY SPECIAL THANKS TO
BOOK EDITOR, BRIAN McKERNAN
PHOTOGRAPHER/ COVER DESIGNER, CRAIG WOLF
AND MY WIFE, SUE SLATER-SCHINDLER, FOR HER LITERARY
CRITIQUES, LIFE-COACHING SKILLS
AND EVERLASTING SUPPORT

THIS BOOK IS DEDICATED TO ALL THOSE
WHO RUN TOWARDS DANGER,
NOT AWAY FROM IT

Praise for Steven Schindler's novels

Sewer Balls

"Probably the best novel produced by the small presses in 1999" -The Small Press Review

From the Block

Winner- Best Fiction- Indie/ DIY Book Awards

From Here to Reality

"Required reading!" - New York Post
"A very funny Hollywood story told with wit and passion by someone who's obviously been there." -Jay Leno

On the Bluffs

"Schindler could be the male version of bestselling author Nora Roberts, blending the right amount of romance and suspense... a captivating writing style." -Glendale News Press

The Last Sewer Ball

Grand Prize winner -New York Book Festival

ABOUT THE AUTHOR

Steven Schindler was born and raised in the Bronx and has also lived in Washington DC, Chicago, and Los Angeles. Having worked in television for over 25 years as a writer and producer, he has produced TV programs featuring The Who, Anwar Sadat, Michael Jordan, and Vlasta the Polka Queen (among others), winning four Chicago Emmy Awards.
He lives with his wife in Los Angeles and can often be found riding a dirt bike up a rocky trail near Joshua Tree, California.

Chapter One

St. Mark's Lounge, a bar in the East Village, had seen better days. It didn't used to have a hunky bouncer at the door, scantily clad hot-chick bartenders, air conditioning that would keep raw meat fresh for a week, fifteen-dollar shots, and a clientele born in every corner of the country except New York City.

It used to be a dive bar. And for people like Paul Santo, those were the better days. On any given night in the '80s you might see Allen Ginsberg sipping a beer with a table full of fellow beatniks, punks, bikers, Polish immigrants, and Village locals hanging out in this joint on St. Mark's Place, just a little west of Avenues A, B, and C, known as Alphabet City. The bartender was either the owner, Stosh, or one of his sticky-fingered relatives. The jukebox ranged from Woody Guthrie to Richard Hell and the Voidoids with everything in between. On any weeknight you were just as likely to witness a bottle hit over some jerk's head as you were to see a couple of guys with their heads and beards precisely shaved half bald only on one side, performing a perfectly choreographed tap dance routine to Dylan's "Like A Rolling Stone."

Paul Santo waved to the bouncer, walked in, and took a seat at the bar by the large-screen television. He was exhausted after working a double shift and was happy to have the air conditioning set to Helsinki winter, which also made the bar maids look even better in their tank tops.

As usual, it was the end of a long day. He had his guys looking for some good dope in the neighborhood. With orders not to bother with weed or pills, they were only to look for the real stuff. And lately there was nothing. His crew hadn't made a decent collar in days, and that was just a street-corner hustler

1

selling nickel bags of black tar heroin to rich NYU idiots. Most of the big-money action had moved uptown, hidden in plain sight in posh Upper East Side high-rises or Riverdale mansions. Nope, these streets were pretty clean now. And he was damn proud of it.

Lieutenant Paul Santo, NYPD, had just turned fifty, but could probably beat anybody in the bar at hoops, handball, ocean swimming, and downing vodka on the rocks. Five foot ten, one hundred seventy-four pounds, with an afro that would make Lenny Kravitz proud. Like Kravitz, Paul is multi-racial. Paul was multi-racial before it was cool. Or presidential.

Paul may be physically fit, but he's tired. Not tired from his double shift. That's nothing. He's tired from more than two and a half decades of chasing drug dealers, thugs, and armed morons packing heat with the serial numbers removed and trying not to lose his soul in the process.

His father was Italian and Irish, his mother was black and Puerto Rican. And some people in his old Bronx neighborhood said he inherited the best of all four ethnic groups. Or the worst, depending on the situation.

He used to go to St. Mark's Lounge in the '80s with his Bronx buddies because of the exotic atmosphere. It was nothing like the Irish gin mills back in his Bronx neighborhood called Kingsbridge. Those bars were filled day and night with working-class heroes getting kicks and having laughs with their own gene pool; mostly Irish, Italian, Jewish, Puerto Rican, German, and the descendants of whatever else the cat dragged in a generation or two earlier.

But the St. Mark's Lounge in the '80s? That *was* the East Village. St. Mark's Place, like the rest of the city, was out of control. Junkies, street hookers, dealers, and bums were everywhere. Instead of the psychedelic sounds that wafted through the air in the '60s, the soundtrack of the '80s was the sirens of fire engines, cop cars, and ambulances trying to keep pace with the chaos that was everywhere. But in all that chaos there was also a raw excitement that surpassed the '60s and '70s. The Vietnam War and the draft were over. Kids were joyously running amuck. It was pre-AIDS, so everybody was banging everybody. Cops had pretty much given up trying to bust people for smoking weed or drinking beer on the streets and in the parks. There was too much real crime going on. On the average there were around 2,000 murders a year in the '80s; six a day. It was so common to fall victim to violent crime that people stopped reporting them to the police. And that's when Paul became a cop, class of 1985.

A gorgeous twentysomething bartender ignored two sweaty guys in suits clamoring for attention when she noticed Paul.

"Hey Paul! I haven't seen you in a while. Where've you been, honey?"

"I just jetted back from the south of France with Kanye and Kim. They dropped me off at the Lexington Avenue subway and bang, here I am. How are you, Brielle?"

"Fantabulous. The usual?"

"Make it a double."

By the time Paul goes into his wallet, pulls out a twenty, and placed it on the bar, Brielle is back and places his drink on a coaster in front of him. She doesn't pick up his money. She winks at him.

"Thank you, doll, but take the money," Paul said, picking up the drink and taking a swig.

It's hard for Paul to believe this is the same place as back in the day. But then again that's true for the entire East Village. In fact for the entire Manhattan island. It's just the other boroughs that are going to hell now.

"Brielle. Can you please put on the Mets game?"

"It's midnight?"

"They're playing the Dodgers."

Brielle gave him a blank stare.

"On the West Coast. It's only nine there," Paul shouted over the bar chatter.

"Only for you, Paul!"

A drunk in a designer suit, who looks like he just graduated middle school, leaned over. Paul is repulsed by his sliders-and-beer breath.

"I love L.A.! Are you from California?" The drunk asked enthusiastically.

"Perish the thought, junior," Paul shot back.

Paul lost himself in the game while the moronic thumping of the XM radio electronica mix got louder, as did the banter of the amateur drunks who have taken over his hangout. The Wall Street crowd used to get out of Dodge on the various commuter trains to the burbs, or car-service it to Upper East Side brownstones. But these new masterbaters of the universe Uber over from the financial district to their nearby luxury loft mansions in the very neighborhood deemed once too dangerous for the cops to even care about: Alphabet City. Much like the Marines battling apartment-by-apartment and building-by-building in Fallujah, gains against the bad guys were hard-fought with many temporary advancements, setbacks, lost battles, and political quagmires, as the body-bag counts climbed higher and higher. Like many combat veterans Paul prefers not to talk about his days deep in battle with the enemy. He has seen his share of blood, guts, and brains splattered on walls, and was very close on many occasions to having the mess of DNA soup be his own.

It was the bottom of the ninth and the Mets were winning by two. A double by the Dodgers' first baseman Cody Bellinger with two outs and the bases loaded put an end to any glimmer of hope Paul still nursed with every double-vodka on the rocks.

"That game is still going at two in the morning?" Brielle asked while serving the last of the still-thirsty crowd.

"Not anymore. Inning over. Game over. Series over. And probably season over."

"I thought the season ended in October?"

"Not for these Mets. Late August is about the norm for them. Are you staying open until four tonight?"

Brielle looked at the amount of cash on the bar, which wasn't much. These one-percenters rarely leave twenty percent for the servers.

"Nah. Darcy has already started closing everything out. Why? You want me to drive you home again?"

"If you don't mind."

"Let's get a bite first."

"Whatever you want. You're driving."

"It's your car."

"Doesn't matter. You're in the driver's seat."

Paul was close to thirty years older than Brielle. On these neighborhood streets back in the '80s seeing a fiftyish guy with an afro wearing sweatpants walking down the block with a twentyish babe in a tank top might give the appearance of a pimp walking with his ho. But now with all the new-money high-finance swindlers living around here out with their future ex-wife number two or three nobody even gives them a second look.

"Do you want to eat near here, or wait until we're back up in the Bronx?" Paul asked, a little bit slower than his normal rat-a-tat delivery, which is the only indication that he's had a few.

"I'm starving. Let's just walk over to the Brasserie."

"The Brasserie can kiss my ass-ery. That used to be the B&H Dairy. You could get a nice bowl of borscht there. Or potato soup. Or pierogies. You know what *pierogies* are?" Paul asked, playfully.

"Yes. It's like a potato dumpling. I'm part Polish, you know."

"Very good! You know what a *galabki* is?"

"That's a cabbage roll with meat inside."

"You are on a cabbage roll, my dear! Do you know what a *garagshki* is?"

"Garagshki?"

"Garagshki?" Paul said adamantly, stopping his stride and confronting Brielle.

"I give up."

"It's the key to the garage, knucklehead!"

Brielle laughed hysterically as she always does to Paul's corny jokes. Paul was almost old enough to be her father, but he reminded her more of her grandfather. There was something about Paul's no-bullshit bluntness, honesty, and toughness that reminded her of the old codgers who came around to visit her granddad in New Hampshire. Some of that rubbed off on Brielle; she had LIVE FREE OR DIE tattooed on her wrist.

The Brasserie was open late to take whatever leftover cash the drunks had on their way home. The tables were wrought iron with Italian marble tops, accessorized with fine linen napkins and real silverware. But the food was no better than your average Queens Boulevard Greek diner, and the portions half the size.

The place was packed, but they found a booth in the back next to the kitchen door. Hipsters with hillbilly beards and full-body tattoos mixed with the sloppy-suited financiers as they all downed greasy faux French food before they hit their nearby two-million-dollar studio lofts and three-grand-a-month walk-ups. There was laughter, dumb drunk conversations, and too cool for school scowling from some actual French tourists. A waitress, who had the telltale look of a bored, overqualified millennial actress finally approached them.

"What can I get you?" she asked, obviously put out that she had to stoop so low as to work for a living.

Paul was still scanning the menu and pointed to Brielle who ordered first.

"I'll have a small green salad. Oil and vinegar on the side."

"I thought you were starving?"

"I am."

"I'll have two over easy, bacon, home fries, dry whole wheat toast, a side of fruit, and a hot tea. And add a veggie burger to her order."

"I can order for myself!" she whispered as the bored waitress walked away.

"I'll tell your momma on you, back in, where is it in New Hampshire again?"

"You know where it is, you just like to hear me say it!"

"So say it!"

"Dixville Notch"

"Ha, I love that! Dixville Notch!"

The front door bursts open and a diverse group of 20 or so young protesters with signs and banners are chanting.

"No justice no peace no racist police! No justice no peace no racist police! No justice no peace no racist police! From Palestine to Ferguson end racism now! From Palestine to Ferguson end racism now! From Palestine to Ferguson end racism now!"

The protesters are splitting up and going from table to table with stunned diners watching in disbelief.

"Solidarity not sympathy! Solidarity not sympathy! Solidarity not sympathy! Stop police terror now! Stop police terror now! Stop police terror now! Pigs in a blanket! Fry 'em like bacon! Pigs in a blanket! Fry 'em like bacon!"

Brielle looks terrified as she studies Paul, wondering what he might do. Paul reaches over to the next table where a waiter is refilling the salt and pepper shakers, and he picks up a discarded sports section off the table begins reading it.

She taps him on the arm. "Are you okay?"

"As long as my food gets here soon, I'm fine."

It's clear three of the protestors are the leaders. They are African-Americans and look fiercely angry and going right in the faces of the patrons.

"Stand with us! Or you're against us! Stand with us! Or you're against us! Stand with us! Or you're against us!" They scream until the people at the table stop eating and stand with them as they go from table to table, working their way to the back where Paul and Brielle are sitting.

"Paul, we can just slip out the back through the kitchen."

"Why? Is something going on?"

"Paul! Let's just go!"

"I ordered food and I'm going to eat my food."

The three troublemakers are getting closer. "Stand with us! Or you're against us! Stand with us! Or you're against us! Stand with us! Or you're against us!"

A light skinned, mixed race African-American wearing a t-shirt with a photo of a black woman and the name JOANNE CHESIMARD printed underneath approaches Paul. His chant of "Stand with us! Or you're against us!" gets louder and louder. He's holding a large, professionally printed banner that reads, STOP RACIST POLICE TERROR BLACK LIVES MATTER.

Every patron is the restaurant is standing except for Paul and Brielle. She goes to stand, and Paul grabs her arm, pushing her back down in her seat.

"Do you work here?" Paul said coolly to the shouting protester. "I said do you work here? Because if you do, would you please tell our waitress that our food is overdue?"

"Stand with us! Or you're against us! Stand with us! Or you're against us!"

"Do you work here?"

The chant gets louder and angrier. The guy with the banner is yelling louder and louder, his face fraught with anger and violence, getting right in Paul's face.

"I'll take that as a no," Paul said calmly. "I suggest you move on."

The protestor becomes even more vociferous in his chant.

Paul looks at him, steely eyed. "You really don't want to go there, do you? You know what's ironic about this, Brielle?" Paul shouted loudly over the screaming protestors. "This guy here is whiter than me!"

"Fuck you!" yells the protestor. "You ain't black!"

Paul calmly reaches over and picks up the jar of salt on the next table the waiter was using to refill the saltshakers. "Maybe.

But you're awfully white!" Paul yells, throwing the jar of salt in his face, ripping the sign from his hands and violently tearing it to shreds. Brielle jumps up and pushes Paul away from the protestors, who have elevated their screams and yells into an all-out rage.

The lead protester pulls out his cell phone and dials 911.

"Yes. I'd like to report and assault and destruction of my personal property."

"Ha! I like that! Assault with…salt!" Paul said, throwing some salt over his left shoulder. "Funny! He hates cops, but who does he call when his little snowflake ego is hurt, he calls…wait for it…the cops!"

The entire group of protesters is now surrounding Paul and Brielle's table.

"Keep your distance please. And whatever you do, do not touch us. *Capisce?*"

The crowd is emboldened and bordering on out of control, directing all their anger at Paul.

Sirens are heard and four cops burst through the front doors of the restaurant, shouting.

"All right, everybody out! Everybody out! Now!" the lead cop, a sergeant, yells as the three others start steering people out the front door. The sergeant approaches Paul's table.

"This man tore up my sign, assaulted me, and threatened me," the lead protester told the officer.

"Oh, Christ almighty," the sergeant groaned when he saw who the alleged perp was. "Portillo! Take the complainant outside and make a report. Paulie, what the hell is going on here? Assault? Destruction of property? Threats?"

"Wait! Stop everything! Here's my food! Finally!" The waitress places the plates on the table along with the bill.

"I'm off shift in ten minutes. Can you pay me now so I can get my tip?"

"Certainly, my dear. Somebody else might think that's being rude, asking for the tip like that. Not me. That's called honesty. I like honesty. I like being honest," Paul said as he gave her a wad of bills and began eating his eggs. "So Mickey, you're gonna take me in, right?"

The red haired, freckle-faced fiftyish sergeant pulled cuffs off his belt, "I'm gonna have to cuff you, too. Just for looks."

"See? Honesty! Good. But I have to finish eating. Okay?"

"Jesus, Okay, Paulie. Hurry it up, would ya?"

"If I get indigestion, I'm not paying off on the Mets-Yankees bet. Capisce?"

"Just hurry," Mickey said, obviously exasperated as if he's done this before.

"Brielle, here's my keys. The car's in the usual spot outside the precinct. Just meet me there in about, how long, Mickey?"

"An hour."

"An hour."

Paul hands the keys to Brielle. She stands up and shakes her head with her hands on her hips. "I thought being friends with a New York cop would be interesting, but I reckon you are downright mind-boggling!"

"Mickey, only a girl from Dixville Notch, New Hampshire would use *reckon* and *downright* in a sentence, right? See you in an hour. My eggs are cold. Let's go."

Paul puts his hands behind his back and gets cuffed by Sergeant O'Connor. The crowd is chanting outside, "Stand with us! Or you're against us!" awaiting the perp walk of Paul into the idling patrol car. Phones are flashing and videos are being taken

11

as if Jay-Z and Beyoncé were heading for a limo. Once in the car, O'Connor undoes the cuffs.

"You know the Captain is on. He was working late, doing paperwork," O'Connor said from the front passenger seat as they drove down quiet East Village streets.

"Good. I welcome the opportunity to speak my mind with him in person."

"Paulie, please. Just say you're sorry, it'll never happen again, and everybody can just go home and get a good night's sleep."

"Mickey. Come on. Do I have to explain after 40 years of knowing each other?"

"Paulie, I'm just saying. Once in a while you could just make it a little easier on everyone involved if you would…."

"Twist the truth, don't make waves, lie, cheat, what else?"

"You know what I'm saying."

"Yes, I do. And you know what I'm saying."

"Fine."

Paul walked into the ancient Ninth Precinct on East Fifth Street. The building itself is almost a hundred years old, and looks and smells twice that. Its nickname is "The Fighting Ninth," which some say has more to do with what goes on inside the building than out on the streets. As soon as the desk sergeant sees Paul, he gives him a sympathetic head nod towards the captain's door.

"He's waiting for you."

Captain Fernando Vasquez is the second youngest captain currently in the NYPD. At thirty-five his rise has been viewed by some as the personification of the new policy typical of the new mayor; out with the old and in with the new. Or else. And it's not just the NYPD. Fire, Sanitation, Transit, even school teachers with a bit of gray hair poking through are feeling the heat from newly appointed chiefs, superintendents, supervisors, principals, and managers. Although it's quite evident to the grizzled veterans, it's more about the gray matter between one's ears than the gray just above them.

The Captain is more than ten years Paul's junior, but it seems like he's two generations behind him. Paul can name all the original members of The Kinks, Earth Wind and Fire, and The Jimi Hendrix Experience. Paul doubts the Captain even heard of those bands.

"Have a seat, lieutenant." Vasquez said in a strange accent. Strange because, it's not a Puerto Rican accent, or a Bronx accent, it's not even a New York accent. It's like a generic anywhere U.S.A. accent.

"Yes, sir!" Paul said sarcastically.

"Have you been drinking, Santo?"

"I have. I've been off duty for eight hours."

"You could be in big trouble right now Santo, so I'd suggest you simmer down, so we can discuss this professionally. Is it true you tore up a protester's sign and threw salt at him?"

"Yes. A sign that was shoved in my face while I was trying to eat my breakfast with a friend, minding my own business, with a crowd of spoiled-brat NYU and Columbia trust-funders yelling in my face that the police are racist, terrorists, and should be fried like bacon. Yes I did."

"And what about the salt?"

"If I said yes, would I just be throwing salt in the wound?"

"I said simmer down. This is no joke! I'm sick and tired of off-duty guys getting into hot water! It's a disgrace!"

"I'm sorry, sir. You're right," Paul said trying to calm the moment.

"All right. Let's get real here," the Captain said with urgency. "The complainant says he won't press charges if you pay for his sign. He supplied a receipt from a printing shop for 75 dollars. He says it was color, not black and white, hence the extra expense. He'll forget about the assault. No jokes, Santo!"

"Sir, with all due respect, there's cops being ambushed and executed by the week because of the rabble-rousing of these fools. And nobody is doing anything about it. In fact the freakin' mayor came out on their side! Telling the press he had to tell his kid to be careful around white police officers. That's pathetic."

"His son in bi-racial."

"So am I! So what?"

"That's it! You're suspended. For one day. No pay."

"Really?" Paul rose from his chair and pulled a revolver out of the holster in the small of his back. He placed it on the Captain's desk, along with his badge and ID cards. "Well, I think one day isn't enough. I'm out of here. I'm going downtown to the pension office in the morning. I'm through for good. This is bullshit. Consider me retired. You win. Are you happy now?"

"Santo, I suggest you think this over when you calm down."

"I'm calm. I'm done."

"Could you delay it? I've got so many guys on vacation, we're short."

"You could have Ramos or Liu or what's her name? Oh yeah, mother of three, Officer Familia fill in for me. Oh wait. They can't. They were ambushed and executed while sitting in police cars as payback. For what? For what? Never mind. You and the mayor and the press and those downtown defense lawyers and race baiters, you're all to blame. I'm not. I risked my neck for blacks, Jews, Poles, Puerto Ricans, Irish, Romanian, rich, poor, homeless, people in mansions. And I'm the bad guy. No. I'm done. And here's a hundred bucks for the kid's 'let's kill racist cops' sign. Glad I could help," Paul said as he exited the room and softly closed the door.

Paul was worn out. He didn't wave or say goodbye to the guys milling around the desk. He just walked out without looking back. He felt naked as he walked down the street without his gun or badge. It was the first time he had done so since he graduated the academy. He felt vulnerable. Not because he was without the protection of his gun and badge. Because he just left behind the only life he had known as an adult. And that scared him. He saw Brielle sitting in his 1985 Lincoln Continental. He got in the back seat. Brielle started the car.

"Where are we going?" She asked trying to study what was on his mind. "Are you all right?"

"Drop me off at home. Take the car home with you. And pick me up on the way to work tomorrow. I'll tell you all about it. Wake me when I'm home."

This was nothing new for Brielle. She had done this routine with Paul countless times. It got her a safe ride home for free, kept Paul out of trouble, and prevented him from getting a D.U.I. Up the F.D.R., across the 138th Street bridge onto the Major Deegan Expressway in the Bronx, past Yankee Stadium, and exit at Van Cortlandt Park South, about a mile before Yonkers, where she lived. This being a familiar game plan, she knew that before she dropped him off at his home it would save her a few minutes if she first stopped in front of his neighborhood hangout, The Buckeye, at W. 238th Street right under the Broadway elevated line. The steel wheels of the No. 1 train squealed to a stop above them, waking up Paul. Brielle watched him come to.

"You know you snore?"

"Very few women in my life actually know that about me," Paul said, as he shook out the cobwebs and pushed his afro back into position.

"I find that hard to believe."

"There's a lot you don't know about me. But you do know me better than most. Like dropping me off at The Buckeye, even though it looks closed."

"Yeah, most things are at four in the morning. What goes on there anyway?"

"Oh, if you only knew! Beautiful women, Chinese millionaires playing high-stakes pai gow, Johnny Depp and Keith Richards sharing a spliff while playing pool."

"You kill me. What time do you want me to pick you up tomorrow? I have to be at work at six, but whatever works for you."

"You know what? I'm going downtown on the train in the morning. So just take the car to work. Park it in my spot. And I'll pick it up later in the day."

"What are you doing downtown?"

"Gotta talk to some paper-pushers so I can get paid without working until I'm fish food off Rockaway Beach."

"Okay, I have no idea what that means, but I'll see you tomorrow night at the bar?"

"Yes, thank you, Dixville Notch!"

Brielle laughed as she pulled away and headed home. Paul walked over to the window with a GUINNESS sign in it that was switched off and he knocked four times. A curtain opened slightly and a few seconds later the door could be heard unlocking. Paul is greeted by Sergeant Mickey O'Connor, now wearing cargo shorts and a t-shirt adorned with the album art of the Rolling

Stones' *Sticky Fingers*. Van Morrison is singing "Brown Eyed Girl" on the jukebox.

"Paulie, have you flipped your wig? Is it true? You're retiring?" Mickey said to Paul, handing him a pint of Guinness.

"Ah, breakfast!" Paul said before taking a swig. "Mickey, I'm done. This is it. And you know what? I feel good about it. It's time to step aside and let the younger generation take over. Let them deal with these assholes. If you had half a brain, you'd be coming with me tomorrow to sign the papers."

"I got two kids still in college, are you kidding? I'm not the carefree, swinging bachelor."

"Watchoo talkin' 'bout, Willis?"

"Yeah, well you know what I mean."

"Hey Paulie! Come over here! I want to fekking talk business with you!" A raspy Irish brogue shouts from within a cloud of cigar smoke at the end of the bar.

"O'Toole you old fool! I'll be right there," Paul shouted, then put his hand on Mickey's shoulder. "With all this bullshit going on now with this new mayor, and insane cop hatred, it's not the same. At least back in the day, we knew who the hell the bad guys were. Now, we're sitting ducks."

Mickey reluctantly nods his head. "I know. I just can't do it right now. Three more years and I'm out."

"O'Toole, three hundred and sixty four days a year you can break my balls, but not today, alright?" Paul said entering the cloud of smoke. "And why are you still smoking those goddamed ginney dumbwaiter ropes? Here, have a Cuban."

"Really? A Cuban? For me?"

"Sure why not? Castro and Obama said it's okay, so it must be okay, right? What race is this?" Paul said referring to the horse race about to get under way on the television.

The bartender, a small man who looks like he could easily double as a leprechaun in a St. Patrick's Day parade says, "It's Hong Kong."

"Is Bobby Three Shirts here?"

"He's taking a leak."

"Did someone call my name?" An overweight man in his fifties grumbles exiting the men's room. He's got pads, papers and pens in every pocket of his safari vest over three shirts, which couldn't close if he lost a hundred pounds.

"Let's see, it's almost the end of the month," Paul said, thinking aloud.

John Lennon's "Imagine" started playing on the jukebox.

"John Lennon's playing, September's the 9th month, the Beatles, number 9, number 9, put twenty on the number 9 to win."

Bobby Three Shirts goes through some pockets and makes a mark in a small notebook. Mickey took a barstool next to Paul at the smoky end of the bar. They watched in silence as the bell went off at the Hong Kong track, and the British-accented announcer called the race. Once the horses made the first turn, Paul began a slow-building crescendo, "Number nine! Number nine! Number nine! Number nine! Come on number nine! Holy crap, I didn't realize he's a hundred to one!"

Bobby Three Shirts jerked his head towards Paul in a panic. "Very funny asshole, he's three to one."

Paul resumed his chant until it was obvious number nine didn't have a chance at win, place, show, or even appearing like it was in the same race, it was so far behind the pack. "Can you add that to my tab Bobby, or do you want the twenty now?"

"I'll just add it. You want to know your total so far this month?" Bobby said smiling broadly.

"Judging by that smile on your face, no!"

Mickey and Paul have been friends for almost forty years. When Paul moved into the neighborhood when he was ten, he didn't look like most of the kids hanging out on the block. At that time, the neighborhood was mostly Irish, with some Italian, German and Polish thrown in. It wasn't easy being the new kid on the block even if you looked like everybody else. But Paul looked different. Maybe if Paul sucked at basketball, baseball, football, stickball, curb ball, and any other ball you could throw at him, he wouldn't have fit in so quickly. But everybody wanted Paul on their team, once Mickey started choosing him first.

"You really are going downtown to sign the papers tomorrow?" Mickey said sadly. "You're gonna leave me with all those peach-fuzzed kids from the 'burbs who became cops because they think it's like being in an episode of *Law and Order*?"

Paul took a sip of stout. "It's over. From the top down, we are screwed. It's just like the French Revolution."

"The French Revolution? Being a cop is like the French Revolution?"

"This country. This society. It starts out with quote, the people, unquote, demanding power. Overthrowing the status quo. Revolution...."

"Isn't that how we got our own country? Through revolution against the Brits?"

"You've been to Fraunces Tavern?"

"Yeah."

"Well that's where George Washington, after winning the revolution, said good-bye to his troops, and for the first time in history, the military victor ceded power to the elected civilian leaders of a government. He went back to his farm. But in the French Revolution the people overthrew the government and didn't replace it with law and order. No. They went after everybody! Heads were rolling in the streets! You know that. The revolution eats its own! Didn't you learn history in Cardinal Hayes?"

"Apparently not as thoroughly as in Bishop Dubois."

"We're being executed. Our heads are rolling. And it ain't gonna stop with just the cops."

"Come on, Paulie. You're being paranoid."

"That's what they told Marie Antoinette. Next thing you know her curly locks were in the basket. Nah. I'm done. When I think of how we took that rat-and drug-infested shit hole, Alphabet City, and risked our lives every day, pushing those scumbags out of there, making the streets and buildings livable again. Look at it now. It's one of the best neighborhoods in the city. Freakin' A-listers live there. You know. You were there!"

"I was there sometimes. Not like you were."

"You know. You know. I'm did my time. I'm getting out while I can."

Mickey holds his pint out, they clink their glasses. "I'm with you, brother. You know that. And I'm right behind you. As soon as I send that last check to Mercy College, I'm on the next Metro line to sign my papers, too. You want a lift home?"

"Sure."

Mickey drives Paul the few blocks to his apartment on the ground floor of a private home on a tree-lined street of modest houses built in the boom of the 1920s just after the No. 1 elevated line was completed in the Kingsbridge section of the Bronx.

"If I change my mind, you'll be the first to know," Paul said, closing the front door of Mickey's Jeep Cherokee.

"Just get some rest and think about it."

Paul watched Mickey drive towards the northbound Major Deegan and wondered if that was the last time he'd get a ride home from work.

Chapter Two

Paul failed penmanship many times at Visitation Catholic Grammar School, which is one of the reasons he hated paperwork so much. He thought the fallout from barely legible handwriting on forms that he constantly had to fill out during police work would improve once they switched over to computers. But of course, that turned into an even bigger nightmare, because the number of forms quadrupled once they went on-line. That and the fact that he was a hunt-and-peck single-finger typist.

Nevertheless, the retirement forms were to be filled out by hand at the police pension office in lower Manhattan. He had already filled out his forms twice, but each time the clerk found too many mistakes and illegible scribblings, and had him correct his mistakes. Paul handed the corrected stack of forms back to the clerk at her desk for the third time.

"You know, you're worse than Sister Annunciata back in third grade," he said to the friendly middle-aged African-American woman who proofread his forms.

"I feel sorry for the nuns who had to grade your chicken scratchings. Did she pass you?"

"No. But I'm still trying."

"Well, once you complete these forms all nice and pretty you won't have to worry about any more of those crazy police forms. All you'll have to do is press the buttons on your remote control while you sit there drinking your Budweisers, watching the Yankee games 'til kingdom come."

"God forbid! I drink Guinness Stout and I'm a Mets fan."

"Whatever. Choose your poison. And neither team's going anywhere this season."

"And I'm not gonna be one of those retirees that sits in the Barcalounger waiting to die either. I'm finally gonna live my life. Do the things I always wanted to do."

"That's what I love to hear. What?"

"What what?"

"What are you gonna do? After you retire?"

"That, my darling, is a very good question, and something I am going to start trying to figure out on my subway ride back home. Did I pass?" Paul asked nervously as she ran her finger down the last page of his paperwork.

"It all looks good. You passed! Congratulations! You are a free man! Start living your life! I just have to give you the copies and you'll be on your way."

Paul stood there and gazed out the windows of the 47th floor office of the Woolworth Building, which faced west across the Hudson River and New Jersey. From that height you could see many miles into the distance towards the horizon where the sun sets and rest of America sits, still unexplored by Paul.

"Here are the copies," the clerk said, smiling. "And the final paperwork will be in the mail in a day or two. They owe you some time I see, so you can retire immediately." She handed him a packet with all his paperwork and shook his hand.

"Yeah, well, they owe me a lot of time. Like my whole life. Thanks for your help. You would have made a good third grade teacher! Do I get some kind of ID card saying I'm a retired cop?"

"That will be in the packet."

From 1913 to 1930 the Woolworth Building was the tallest building in the world. Now it's not even in the top 20. As Paul exited the building he realized the last time he had been in that neighborhood was the tenth anniversary of 9-11, where he and Mickey and some other guys from the old neighborhood held vigil by the names on the memorial – Johnny Collins and Wally Travers – two close friends who were incinerated on that fateful day. Johnny, a fireman, and Wally, an executive with Cantor-Fitzgerald, were in the wrong place at the wrong time like the nearly 3,000 other poor souls just trying to work for a living. The streets were buzzing this sun-drenched day with tourists, mostly foreigners judging by the men wearing black socks and sandals. Paul felt about as obsolete as the Woolworth Building, which was named for a worldwide retail empire that no longer existed.

Paul had one more stop to make before he considered himself officially retired. He needed to go back to the precinct and pick up his gun, which he left on the captain's desk last night. As he meandered his way north through Little Italy, everything just seemed a little too buttoned up. A little too corporate. But what really blew his mind was how even the Bowery was overrun by franchise eateries and upscale retailers. Mugsy and Satch never would have recognized it. But maybe it was him. Maybe it was his problem that he hadn't changed with the times, and still, somehow, pined for the city that existed 30 years ago, as filthy and crime-ridden as it was.

He looked down Fifth Street and gazed at the precinct with new eyes. Cop cars were double-parked everywhere, with cops rushing in and out of cars and into the ancient doorway. He remembered the day he stepped into that doorway for the first time. It was raining like hell on that first day in September, just like it was when he reported for his first day at Visitation grammar school. But his last day going through that door would be a glorious sunny afternoon.

"Johnson, you're out of uniform!" he said to a young black officer as he pointed to one of his shoelaces being untied.

"Hey, Lieutenant! Is it true? Are you retiring? For real?"

24

"What's real? What isn't real? I don't know. Do you?" Paul said bounding up the steps into the building.

"Can I talk to the Captain?" he cheerfully asked the desk sergeant, busy on a phone call. The sarge looked towards the office and nodded it was okay.

Paul knocked on the door.

"Come in."

Paul entered and smiled broadly. "Good afternoon, sir. I was just downtown signing my papers and…."

"You're serious?"

"Dead serious, sir. It's time."

"I'm going to miss you," Captain Vasquez said, rising and reaching out to shake hands.

"Thanks. Sir, I came by to pick up my gun. I'm sorry about mouthing off."

"Right."

Vasquez took out some keys, unlocked a drawer in his desk and handed Paul his .38 service revolver. "You have enough time saved up to start immediately I assume?"

"And some," Paul said placing the revolver in the holster he keeps in the small of his back.

"All I can say, is…," Vasquez paused as he fished for words, "thank you and good luck."

"Thank you, sir."

Paul exited the office and waved to the desk sergeant. He saw a group of cops he knew to the right, and turned a quick left. That was it. He was done. He looked at the spot where his car was usually parked and it was empty. He took out his phone and punched in some numbers.

"Brielle! It's me, Paul. Give me a call back so I know what time you're driving my car to work. If it's too much later, I might just take the train home. I'm walking over to St. Mark's Lounge now. Talk to you soon."

Paul didn't know what to expect as he got further and further from the police station. But once he turned the corner and started walking up Second Avenue, it became apparent that he had a bounce in his step. It was more than a bounce, he was bounding. If he had a basketball he'd be dribbling with both hands through the defense, even going between his legs and doing a no-look behind-the-back pass like he did on the Bailey Park courts. If he was playing ice hockey, he'd be deeking-up ice, doing ring turns around those clumsy d-man goons, and going five-hole on the flummoxed goalie. He felt so good, he actually gave a drunken bum in a doorway five bucks, which he knew would go for some MD 20/20. He usually only gives out McDonald's gift cards, which he kept in his wallet for just such occasions.

There wasn't much of a crowd at St. Mark's Lounge in the afternoon. It was strictly an after-work hang out. The beautiful barmaids didn't work the day shift. It was usually some out-of-work actor. He took a seat by the TV, which was turned to *Judge Judy*. The bartender, who looked like he could star in any number of the silly superhero movies Paul wouldn't be caught dead at, plopped a Captain Morgan coaster in front of him.

"You're Brielle's cop friend, right?"

"Not anymore."

"You're not her friend anymore? What happened?"

"I'm not a cop anymore."

"Oh shit, did you get fired or something?"

"Yup. I got caught stealing quarters from the parking meters on Fifth Avenue in front of the Met."

"Oh, okay. What can I get you?"

"Guinness. Pint. What time is Brielle on?"

"I'm not sure. She might be off tonight."

"Hey, could you change the channel to SNY channel 639?"

"The Mets don't play until later."

"That's okay. Anything is better than *Judge Judy*. I've had my fill of courtrooms for a lifetime or two."

Paul took a sip of his Guinness and overheard the bartender telling the old guy fixing the beer tap he was busted for breaking into parking meters in front of the Met. Through the old guy's laughter he heard him say there were no parking meters on Fifth Avenue in front of the Met. The bartender walked over to Paul smiling. "Very funny. There aren't any parking meters in front of the Met. Ha ha."

"I'm not a cop because I'm retired. In fact, I just signed my papers this morning," Paul said proudly.

"Retired? Already? You look like you're in your forties!"

"Not quite, but thanks anyway."

"Man! I want that deal!"

"They're giving a test next week. You want the website for information?"

"Nah. I don't think so. I've got some auditions coming up."

"Lots of cops become actors."

"Like that Steve Buscemi guy."

"He was a fireman. That's part-time work. Cop is full-time."

"Fireman is part-time?" the clueless bartender asked.

"That's a joke."

Paul liked jerking people's chains. Especially about the fire department. Why? Who knows? But all the different departments constantly break each other's chops. Cops, firefighters, sanitation, corrections, court officers, bridge and tunnel guys all make fun of each other. But since 9-11, when so many lives were forever destroyed, and people are still dying of assorted cancers from days, weeks, and months digging through "the pile" for anything – bones, teeth, laundry labels, anything from those pulverized in the inferno – everybody knows somebody who died. And almost everybody lost somebody near and dear to them. The kidding had taken on a new significance, a way to express a teasing kind of camaraderie with no hint of pathos.

Paul's flip phone rang. "Dugout, Casey speaking. I'm here with…," Paul motioned towards the bartender.

"Dylan," the bartender said.

"I'm here with Dylan waiting for you. Okay, see you in a little bit. Yes, I'm officially retired. You don't have to ask me twice. Yes, a dinner celebration would be great! P.J. Clarke's? No, that's fine. I'll see you over there in an hour. Bye."

Paul hadn't planned on celebrating his retirement with anyone. Both his parents were gone. He wasn't even talking to his brother somewhere in Arizona. And letting his ex-wife know wasn't a remote possibility. He knew she was in a bad way, because Mickey's wife gave him unsolicited updates on her, which were never good. It hurt Paul that he was a lousy husband, but that was his first year on the force. He was working non-stop and she was taking drugs and drinking non-stop. Thank God she took a breather while she was pregnant. She divorced him fast. Soon after the baby was born.

P.J. Clarke's was not one of Paul's favorite places. Okay, he hated it. Yeah, it's been around for over a hundred years, but it has been a yuppie hangout for at least 90 of those years. He decided he'd walk there even though it was over 50 blocks away. It would take about an hour and would give him time to transition.

It's been a while since he had made such a long walk through Manhattan. For the past several years the only path he had worn was from his car to the precinct, the precinct to St. Mark's Lounge, and back to Kingsbridge. Oh, he loved walking, but not through the concrete canyons of the city. He preferred the tree-lined streets of Riverdale, or the cross-country running trails of Van Cortlandt Park. He still went for horseback rides at the stables in Vannie once or twice a year. And when he really wanted a long run or bike ride, he'd go up the bucolic Bronx River bike trail that went for a good 20 miles. Those were the places he preferred to walk, run, ride horses, and ride bikes.

Manhattan had lost its charm for him a long time ago. With everybody and everything madly rushing by or in your face, he couldn't relax. Every questionable-looking character was a potential criminal and every tourist a potential mark. He couldn't even count the times he was out with a date or a buddy having a beer or a cup of coffee at a sidewalk café and the next thing you know, he was chasing some skel purse-snatcher through traffic with his gun out. Then there was P.J. Clarke's. Sure, it was a fine establishment; beautifully old-school in décor, friendly wait staff, decent food, clean bathrooms. But the clientele? No thanks. Despite that fact that Paul was one of NYPD's most decorated lieutenants, there was something about the Scarsdale/East Hampton/Harvard/Yale/Wall Street/City Hall vibe there that made him uncomfortable. Those one-percenters had no idea how many guys like him either lost their lives or their sanity beating back the scum that once ruled the dark corners of this city, which is now crowded with Disney Stores, Olive Gardens, Applebee's, and gazillion-dollar condos built on landfills. But maybe now he wouldn't care about those people. Maybe he could just enjoy the food, the pleasant atmosphere, the polite servers, and the harmless clientele of P.J. Clarke's. Just for tonight at least.

As he walked through the east thirties, Paul remembered dating a girl who lived just off Lexington Avenue in a walk-up. Back in the 1980s, as soon as the sun sank over Hoboken and the streetlights came on, there were more hookers walking the streets than law-abiding citizens out for a stroll. Then after a few dates, he realized there were no more hookers on the block in front of his date's building. She told him that a guy across the street in one of the apartments started shooting at them with a BB gun. Okay, maybe they were still hooking, but not on that block. That was before Paul was a cop, but it was a lesson in criminal justice 101.

There are no street hookers now in the east thirties. In fact, street hookers aren't seen anywhere in Manhattan anymore. Oh, there's still plenty of prostitution. More than ever. But now it's all done on the internet: Tinder, Grinder, Craigslist, and who the hell knows what else is being invented in some Silicon Valley social media lab to perpetuate the world's oldest profession.

Paul took a seat at the end of the bar next to the where the servers get their drinks for the tables. He liked to eavesdrop on their chit-chat to get a read on what was going on; who the A-holes were, A-list celebrities trying to hide, D-list celebrities trying to get noticed, guys who needed to get cut off, and the women trying to prevent it. He got a tap on the shoulder. It was Brielle but he almost didn't recognize her. She didn't look anything like the quasi Hooters/Vegas Strip bartender she dressed up like while serving drinks at St. Mark's Lounge. She looked...amazing! If she was wearing makeup, he didn't notice. Her raven hair was pulled back and then draped across one shoulder. She wore a faded jean jacket over a black t-shirt and a white cotton skirt that went below her knees and ankle-high cowboy boots.

"Wow!" Paul said taking it all in. "You look...great! I like that look. Is it like a cosmic cowgirl thing?"

"I guess. How are you? Congratulations!" She said, leaning over to give Paul a peck on the cheek. "Let's get a table." She waved to a waitress across the bar, who smiled and made a beeline towards them.

They were seated at a tiny table for two by the window, which looked out onto Third Avenue, and Brielle ordered drinks. She didn't drink alcohol when she worked, but she was pounding Margaritas down like they were San Pellegrinos, and Paul took notice.

"Where'd you park my car?" he asked, nursing the first Guinness he had ordered while waiting for her at the bar.

"In your usual spot. I took the bus up from there."

"I'll take the keys."

"You don't trust me with them?"

"I want you to have a good time, so I'm driving," he said, taking the keys from her and stuffing them in his pocket.

"You're the boss," Brielle said as she finished off another Margarita.

Several plates of assorted fried appetizers came and went, as did salads, and the main entrees. It was dark outside, and the bar was so crowded that people were bumping into the table as they stood there babbling away.

"I can't believe it!" Brielle shouted, noticing a thirtysomething guy wearing a pink polo shirt, pleated khaki shorts, leather shoes, no socks, and two of those earlobe-stretching plugs in his ears. "Todd, come over here!" she said, planting a sloppy kiss on his cheek. "Pull up a chair."

Brielle was kind of drunk. Okay, pretty wasted. Todd looked to be on something, but he was holding bottle water.

"I am so stoked to see you, Brielle," Todd said, slurring his speech slightly as he sat down. "I haven't been to St. Mark's Lounge in a while. I'm back to the Connecticut office. It's so boring there."

"Todd, this is my good friend, Paul. We're celebrating his retirement tonight."

"You look young for retirement. You must have made a killing in something! What was it? Hi tech? Currency? Hedging?"

"I had a different line of killing," Paul said, not very friendly like. "NYPD."

"Oh." Todd said flatly. "So how are things at St. Mark's Lounge, Brielle? Any of my old gang there?"

"Not lately. None of them."

"Yeah, we've had some troubles. Hedge funds aren't performing like they were. What's your name again?"

"Paul."

"Paul, maybe you heard of my uncle, Lance Beaumont? He was in the New York State Assembly and City Council for years."

"Hmmm. Not sure. Doesn't ring a bell," Paul lied.

Damn right Paul knew the name. He was a scumbag politician that somehow managed to avoid jail time despite enough indictments to make a Tammany Hall crook proud.

"What did you do? In the NYPD, I mean." Lance said still bored.

"Just about everything. But mostly undercover narcotics on the Lower East Side."

"In the Eighties and Nineties?" Lance said suddenly perking up.

"Yeah, why?"

"Can I shake your hand?" Todd said sticking out his puppy paw.

"Sure. For what reason may I ask?"

"Well, you and your people, were sort of, how can I put this? Were instrumental in making my father a very rich man."

"Go on, you've got my interest now."

"Well," Todd said, leaning in, trying to keep his voice down. "My uncle on the city council kept my father abreast of what was going on in your 'hood. He worked closely behind the scenes to make sure, um, the streets were safe, but on a particular schedule. My father bought blocks of real estate at ridiculous prices, and now, oh my God, don't even ask!"

"Brielle, you know what? It's time to go. Are you coming with me, are do you want stay here with Todd."

"What's the rush?" Brielle asked, disappointed, as she had just started another drink.

"Don't go! I want to buy you a drink for your efforts!" Todd said holding his water bottle high.

"Just for me? Or for my dead fellow officers who helped you and your uncle get rich through the scumbag city council cabal?"

"Now wait a minute!" Todd said, just getting the insult. "Nobody talks to me – "

Paul reached across the table and grabbed him by his rubber earlobe ring. "Listen junior, you better take your Great Gatsby shtick to some other table. Because I'm about to pop a champagne cork right up your ass."

It got quiet in their section and people were staring at them.

"Paul, stop!" Brielle said, grabbing his arm. "Todd's an old friend."

"I'm not feeling well," Paul said releasing Todd and standing up. "It must have been the clams casino. Too rich," he said glaring at Todd.

"I'll go if you want, Paul," Brielle responded.

"Let's go. I'll pay at the bar."

Of course Paul wasn't sick from the clams. But he was sick. There were always rumors that certain powerful politicians used sweeps of targeted neighborhoods in complex real estate flipping rackets, but you just ignored those conspiracy theories. You were sworn to duty. You did your job. Even if it meant going into burnt-out abandoned buildings to root out junkie squatters. Or raiding basement fortresses where heroin dealers were holed up. Paul was lucky. He was alive. But he attended funerals too many times for cops in his precinct who weren't so lucky. He carried their caskets, and cried with their kids and wives and parents and other cops. Was it really just so scumbags like the Connecticut Beaumonts could get even filthier rich?

He handed the bartender his bill and the cash and looked over at the table where Brielle was sitting with Todd. He was leaning in to her and getting a little too close either for Paul's or Brielle's comfort. "Keep the change," he yelled to bartender as he rushed over to the table. "Hey, Todd, I think it's time for you to go," he said lifting Todd's hand off of Brielle's shoulder.

"Hey man, what are you going to arrest me, or something?" Todd said incredulous but slurred.

"I'm not a cop. But you don't want to find out what I might do next, so just go away. Come on, Brielle, the bus is leaving. Now."

Todd left in a huff as Brielle stood up and stumbled slightly.

"Thank you for saving me. Todd is such an ass. But you've got to control yourself."

"I don't know; how do you beautiful women put up with such jerks?" Paul asked, leading her out to the avenue and quickly whistling a yellow cab to a halt. "Fifth Street and Second," Paul told the cabbie.

"Oh, we learn. Just like you learned to fend for yourself when you were a rookie cop."

"I don't know what's more dangerous: junkies or Toddskies?"

"Toddskies? I like that. Fits in with the garagshki," Brielle giggled. "Where are we going?"

"We're taking a cab to pick up my car, then I'm driving you to your house in Yonkers. And thank you very much, for celebrating my retirement night with me. It means a lot to me. Really."

Brielle studied Paul's face. He was tough to read. Figuring out the difference between sarcasm and honesty was not an easy task where he was concerned. "Really?"

"Yes, really. What?" Paul asked, mystified.

"I can't tell when you're being serious."

"I'm being serious. Thank you."

She wasn't convinced.

They arrived at Paul's Lincoln, got in, and headed north to Yonkers. Paul only had one Guinness the whole night, and he couldn't wait to drop off Brielle at her place so he could have a few nightcaps at The Buckeye. He looked over at her as she gazed out the passenger window when they passed Yankee Stadium. Sometimes Paul wished he was a Yankee fan. He could be there in ten minutes if he wanted to go to games. But his old man was a New York Giants fan, then a Mets fan, and that's just the way it was.

"Paul, I forgot to tell you I can't go back to my house."

Paul looked at her, trying to figure out what kind of female conundrum was about to unfold.

"And why is that?"

"My roommate's boyfriend is visiting from out of town, and I promised her I wouldn't be home tonight."

"And where were you planning on staying?"

"I meant to ask you earlier, but can I stay over at your place?"

Paul smiled as he shook his head. How many times in his life did he fantasize about moments exactly like this?

"Of course."

Paul parked on the street in front of his house. He rented the downstairs of this home for the past 20 or so years. It was on a tree-lined street just a couple blocks from the Broadway No. 1 elevated line, a few blocks from the much tonier and more expensive neighborhood of Riverdale.

They entered Paul's apartment, which was tidy, clean, and furnished à la Sears furniture department circa 1985.

"Well here it is. Sit on the couch. Can I get you something to drink?" he asked Brielle.

"Just water, please."

Paul grabbed two bottles of water from the fridge, handed her one, went to a closet, pulled out some linens and a pillow and placed them next to her. "This is a pullout. Here's some clean bedding. Do you want to turn in now? Or watch TV? Because I was going to head over to The Buckeye."

"Paul, come over here and sit next to me."

He complied. "Brielle, look, I like you a lot. You've been a great friend to me...."

Brielle sidles up practically on top of him. "Paul, you know I like you. It's a special night. It won't change anything."

"Brielle, I can't."

Brielle pulled back, terribly embarrassed. "Oh my God. Paul, if you're gay, there's nothing wrong with that...."

"I'm not gay."

"Then what is it?"

Paul stood up, took about five steps in a circle and sat back down. "Brielle, you're gorgeous. But...."

"But what?"

"When I look at you, I see my daughter."

"You have a daughter?"

"Yes. I don't get to see her much, and it's really complicated, but I see my daughter when I look at you. And I just...couldn't. In fact, ever since I saw you, I thought, hey, maybe this is what Tracy is like. Like you. And it gave me some solace."

"Why don't you see your daughter?"

"Guess."

"Your wife."

"Ex-wife. Triple X wife. Tracy has been trained like a ninja warrior since birth to hate me. It's just the way it is. I don't blame her. I'm hoping that now that she's a woman, she'll grow out of it. But if she doesn't I don't blame her. My wife has problems. Let's just leave it at that. You should probably get some sleep. I'm going to see who's over at the bar, okay?"

"Okay," Brielle said as she gave him a soft peck on the cheek. "I'll make up my own bed. Thanks."

There was a wisp of autumn cool in the late-night air as Paul walked the cracked slate and concrete sidewalk towards The

Buckeye. Quite a few leaves were already on the ground even though summer still had a few weeks left. He didn't look forward to winter. It was the snow and ice he abhorred more than the cold. In fact, the colder the better because it kept of lot the bottom-feeder criminals off the street. But the snow? The worst. Especially when you had to park on the street every day. You'd spend a couple hours digging your car out, shoveling the snow into the middle of the street – where the hell else is it supposed to go? – and next thing you know a snow plow comes down the block and puts all the snow right back onto your car. And if you do dig out your car so you can drive to work, when you get home, some slob is in the spot you broke your back clearing out. Then there's the worst kind of jerk, the one who digs out his car, goes to work, and while he's gone puts some garbage cans and old chairs in his spot so nobody parks there. And if you dare move the junk and park there, chances are when you wake up, you'll have four flat tires. If you're lucky, they're only deflated, not slashed. No, he had it with winter. Who knows? Maybe he'll be a Florida snowbird?

It was before closing time, so there was still a small crowd in the bar. A couple played pool, two guys were throwing darts, and there was the usual assortment of neighborhood characters who'd rather be there than in an early 20th Century walk-up apartment, guaranteed to have roaches, peeling paint, bad plumbing, and noisy neighbors.

"Seamus, I'll have a Guinness. Have you seen Mickey?"

The diminutive bartender, who always wore a white apron, white shirt, and black bow tie, put a little extra elbow grease into cleaning the pint glass for Paul. "No, I haven't, lad. Maybe he's already home with the little lady."

Bobby Three Shirts was there as usual, but Paul didn't want to strike up a conversation because it would quickly evolve into being informed how much he owed him. The rest of the crowd were semi-regulars, but Paul didn't like engaging them either. He knew a couple of them were meth heads, and kept his distance. As long as they didn't bring any of that or any other hard drugs into the bar, he and Mickey didn't mind. Seamus made sure everyone knew that little code of conduct. Violators were swiftly dealt with.

On this day, more than any other, Paul wanted to hang with Mickey. Only another cop would understand. They both watched too many cops retire then quickly drop dead. Mostly suicide by Seagrams. A slow, painful and sometimes bloody death usually preceded by divorce, excommunication, and large payments to Bobby Three Shirts.

He was bored watching horse racing from Hong Kong and infomercials on green pots and pans. "What the hell is the big deal about green pots and pans? Do you only use them on St. Patrick's Day?" Paul shouted to no one in particular. "Seamus, if you see Mickey, tell him I went home."

He opened the door quietly to his apartment and Brielle was fast asleep on the pullout bed. He thought it was cute that she snored slightly. He tiptoed to his bedroom and shut his door. No sooner did he kick off one of his New Balances did his flip phone ring.

"Mickey! You didn't have to call.... You're outside the door. Now? Okay, here I come."

Paul walked past the pullout bed and stubbed his toe on it. He tried his hardest to stifle every bad curse word he knew as he opened the front door.

"Be quiet. I have a guest sleeping," he said to Mickey, leading him through the living room and into the bedroom.

"What's a babe like that doing out there sleeping?"

"It's a long story. So is something up?"

"Yeah. It's bad. You better sit down."

Paul knew Mickey wasn't kidding. They've told each other about too many accidents, shootings, cancers, and deaths to fool around at times like this.

Paul looked stone-faced. "Let's hear it. It's about Marcy, isn't it?"

It wouldn't be the first time Paul heard bad news about his ex-wife Marcy. She had her share of car accidents, DUI's, drug busts, hospital stays, and – yes – jail time to keep Paul aware of her lifestyle, even though she lived way the hell upstate and wouldn't let him near her or Tracy, their daughter.

"Yeah, it's Marcy. I'm sorry. It looks like an overdose. Probably suicide."

"What? Jesus Christ. Who discovered the body? Tracy?"

"No. She was alone in a motel room. The cleaning lady found her."

"Christ almighty. I thought she was clean. She swore to me she was. I talked to her a few weeks ago. Tracy was going to start classes at a college up there. Things seemed to be looking up. I can't fucking believe this...." Paul's voice trailed off as he wept.

The way Mickey sat next to him on the bed and put his arm around him, it was clear it wasn't the first time one or both of them wept together in the middle of the night after some terrible news.

"Pam phoned me as soon as she heard." Mickey said, referring to his childhood sweetheart and wife of 25 years. "A friend of Marcy's called her as soon as she heard. It happened tonight, actually. Do you want me to do anything? Call anybody?"

"Yeah, call the job…oh wait. Shit. I don't have a job. Can you believe it, I'm not even retired one full day and this happens. Yeah, my number for Tracy isn't good. Can you ask Pam to get me her number? I'll call her in the morning. Maybe I'll drive up. I don't know."

"Do you want me to stay? I will."

"Nah. I'm okay. Thanks. I'll walk you out in case the princess wakes up and sees a crazed red-headed Irishman in the room."

Paul let Mickey out and as soon as he shut the door a light was switched on and Brielle was sitting up.

"What's going on?"

"It's okay. I'll tell you in the morning."

"No you won't. You'll tell me now," Brielle demanded, not drunk anymore.

He took a seat across from her. "My ex-wife died."

"Oh my God! Illness, car crash?"

"It looks like an overdose. Maybe suicide."

"I'm so, so sorry, Paul." Brielle got up from the bed, a sheet wrapped around her nude body, and comforted Paul.

"Yeah, it's bad. I'll deal with it in the morning. Get some sleep. You're a good kid, Brielle. You should get out of that bar. Away from boozers and druggies. So should I. Good night."

He went into the bedroom, closed the door, turned off the light, and laid down in his bed. He did something he hadn't done since his mother died, five years earlier; he said Hail Marys until he fell asleep.

Chapter Three

Brielle was gone by the time he was up, at nine. She left a note saying she Ubered it home. It took Paul almost an hour on five different phone calls to finally get details on what happened, what the arrangements were, and where his daughter, Tracy, was. He packed a gym bag for the trip, got in his '85 Lincoln and headed over to the Major Deegan northbound towards Utica, New York, about four hours away.

It didn't take long for the high-rise apartment buildings of the Bronx and Yonkers to fade in the rear-view mirror, and the thick, lush greenery of the northern suburbs of New York City to take hold. Even with the windows closed and the air conditioning on, he could start to smell the change in the damp air thick with forests, ponds, lakes, and rivers.

Before they were married, Paul and Marcy loved getting out of the city. Group vacation homes were all they could afford, but it was Hampton Bays in the summer, Hunter Mountain in the winter, Stones, Springsteen, or Who concerts and weekend getaways to Mets or Jets away games. Paul organized those epic trips with crazed neighborhood fans venturing into the enemy territories of Philadelphia, Boston, and one time all the way to Wrigley Field. He was the one who put the deposit on the bus, bought the tickets, and ordered the food and beer for the bus ride. It was always a mad scramble to try and break even, but no matter how much he lost over the years, he and several hundred of his closest friends had unforgettable times. That's where Marcy fell in love with him. Paul was a doer. A risk-taker. A leader. And he knew his classic rock. Marcy was a drifter, literally and figuratively.

Marcy Hastings was born in the Bronx neighborhood of Kingsbridge, but moved to somewhere near Utica when she was six. But as she grew up, she spent a week or two with relatives in the old 'hood and wound up closer to her cousins and their friends on Bailey Avenue than she did to her classmates upstate. As soon as she was eighteen she shocked her parents by moving back to the Bronx, the very place they wanted their child not to wind up.

Marcy was a wild child. She liked to party and have bad-boy boyfriends. Paul wasn't a bad boy, but he liked to have fun. And with lots of friends. That drew Marcy to Paul from the very first bus trip she went on to a Jets/Patriots away game. After her bouncing around from boyfriend to boyfriend, from crowd to crowd, from thrill to thrill left her feeling empty, Paul was her rock.

Paul never had a problem with females. He had his share. But he didn't go for relationships where they expected him to change his lifestyle of hanging with the boys, and having fun with busloads of people. Marcy bought into his lifestyle and Paul fell for her. What started out as just hooking up after mad parties and adventures morphed into more and more excursions between group trips. Paul thought this was it; Marcy was the girl for him. And she was. Marcy got pregnant and they were married. Marcy went clean for her pregnancy, but after Tracy was born, the old wild child Marcy was reborn. Was it some kind of strange postpartum reaction? Who knows? All Paul knew was that he had to put a limit on Marcy's drinking, staying out all night, leaving the baby with her cousins, and even visiting old boyfriends. Paul laid down the law. Either she changed or he was out of there. Tracy wasn't even two when she and Marcy were on the next Greyhound out of town. He figured it was Utica. They were divorced shortly afterwards.

She wouldn't take his calls. Wouldn't return his letters. But she did cash all the checks. Paul knew a lot of the money he sent was going up her nose, but he didn't want his child to be destitute. He was relieved when he worked out a system to send money directly to Marcy's mom, Grandma Greta, for Tracy's care and Catholic school tuition, from pre-school through high school.

Paul knew this drive to upstate New York pretty well. He used to drive up for weekends, hoping he could see Tracy, which was a real balancing act because Marcy's drug and alcohol abuse never subsided and only got worse. But he did manage to see Tracy a few times a year, even if sometimes it was just from the bleachers at one of her softball games or in the background at a large gathering. Thank God for Marcy's mom, Greta. She saved Tracy's life. And his.

If Marcy's mom wasn't there to take in Tracy when times were bad, Paul might have done something drastic. He always thought about going after custody of Tracy through the courts, but knew what that would involve. And with the courts biased towards the mother, and him being a single cop, he knew his prospects weren't good. He didn't even want to think about what he might have done if Marcy's mom, Greta, hadn't come to the rescue.

Greta grew up in the old Bronx neighborhood, when it was almost like a resort area. She was born on Corlear Avenue in 1931, just a few blocks from where Paul now lived. There were a couple of kiddie amusement parks nearby, a skating rink, and pony rides. Not to mention the wonders of Van Cortlandt Park, one of New York City's largest parks, more than double the size of Manhattan's Central Park. And being from the neighborhood, naturally, she was a tough cookie.

It was Greta who initially reached out to Paul. She knew that Marcy was having problems with drugs and alcohol, and she was more than happy to take Tracy in, to raise her as her own for weeks, and months at a time and – eventually – for good. Not that it was easy, but she had some insurance money after her husband died, and the house in Herkimer, about 20 miles from Utica, was paid for. Plus it had a separate basement apartment. That's where Marcy and Tracy lived, rent-free. And of course Tracy was up and down the stairs from one household to the other seamlessly from the time she could walk. Greta was sympathetic to Paul's concern for Tracy's welfare, so without telling Marcy she handled the extra money he sent for tuition, clothing, food, and whatever else Tracy needed. Greta made it look like it came from her. Both Paul and Greta knew that if the money went straight to Marcy, it would be spent on Marcy's destructive lifestyle, which is where most of the alimony checks went.

It was almost magical when you were about 90 minutes out of the city. The suburbs and exurbs were behind you, and rural America began to unfold in a tapestry of rolling hills, farms, and small towns in the distance. Yes, even in New York State. Paul thought many times about quitting the NYPD and moving near Tracy, but there were no guarantees he could make the kind of money he did in the city. He also feared what he might do if he was witness to Marcy's shenanigans on a daily basis.

The thought of Marcy taking her own life haunted him. Maybe he should have ditched everything to live nearer to her and Tracy? Maybe it was his fault for being too demanding of her? Maybe everything was his fault? But deep down, he knew otherwise. He saw too many friends crying over their kids and spouses and parents with drug and alcohol problems. All of them from good, hard-working families where people tried to do the right thing. Yeah, nobody's perfect, but these were people who cared deeply and were desperately trying to save a loved one. They loved unconditionally.

Sometimes when people hit rock bottom, they can turn it around pretty late in the game. But too often, rock bottom for them is when they're zipping up the body bag. He loved Marcy. Unconditionally. He always would.

The miles were flying by and radio stations came and went as he sped along the highway. He was well on his way, traveling west towards Utica, when his car suddenly sputtered, shuttered, and made a terrible noise like a subway car that just had its emergency brake pulled in a tunnel. He put on the flashers and coasted onto the wide right shoulder and onto some grass.

"Shit," Paul said scanning his dashboard. All the warning lights were on, including the idiot-light temperature gauge. He knew he was screwed.

"Come on, T-Mobile, don't fail me now," Paul said as he opened his flip phone and punched in some numbers.

"Yes, thank goodness, Triple A, saves the day! I'm stuck here on Interstate 90 at, ah, let me see, Can-a-joe-hairy? What the hell kind of name is that? Canajoharie, yes. My car is DOA. 45 minutes? I ain't goin' nowhere."

Paul took a catnap in the expansive back seat of his 1985 Lincoln Town Car and dreaded the thought that it might well be a goner. He bought it new after getting on the force, and had many a good time in that very same back seat, from Myrtle Beach to Cape Cod and all dark beach roads in-between. It was only about 20 minutes and the tow truck was there.

They decided to take the car to a nearby Ford dealership where they service Lincolns, and after about an hour of waiting in an oversized closet with a coffee maker, sitting on a folding chair, the verdict was in: Seized engine. Dead.

The bearer of the bad news was the service manager, a polite thirtysomething with a pressed shirt and a slightly askew clip-on tie. "What would you like us to do?" He asked, clipboard and pen at the ready.

"I think I better talk to a salesman. You have used cars on the lot, too?"

"Yup. I'll walk you over to the sales department."

The dealership had obviously just gone through major renovations to make it look like every other Ford dealership in the country. Nevertheless, the cars on display and salesmen greatly outnumbered the customers, which was exactly one: Paul.

"This is Mr. Santo," the service manager said to an eager fiftysomething bald-headed man. "Randy here will help you out."

"How can I help you, Mr. Santo?"

"Call me Paul. I have an '85 Town Car I brought in DOA. Seized engine. I need two things: First, how much will you give me for the Town Car? And, second, can I drive out of here in less than two hours with a car?"

"How about we look for a car first? New or Used?"

"Used. Two or three years old. Under 30,000 miles."

"I like a man who knows what he wants!"

"I hope you feel that way a half hour from now. Waddyuh got?"

"Let's go out to the lot."

Paul had no time to hunt for the best deal on the perfect car, which is the reason he kept the Lincoln for all those years. Every time he thought of buying a new one, he'd tire himself out researching and shopping for perfection. But today, he pointed at a small SUV that had a placard stating 30K MILES and $13,999. He asked what it was.

"It's an Escape."

"I'll take it. What'll you give me for my trade-in?"

"It says here, zero," the salesman said, finger firmly on a Kelly Blue Book printout.

After signing enough forms to give him writer's cramp, the salesman asked how he'd be paying.

"Credit card," Paul said, looking through his wallet.

The salesman's eager demeanor scrunched into worry. "Oooh. I'm sorry, the most you can put on a card is $5,000. You know, like a deposit."

"Are you kidding me? Come on, cut me some slack here."

"I'm sorry but those are the rules. I don't make them up."

Paul sighed and collapsed back in his chair. "Look. I need this car. I'm on the way to a funeral from New York City, heading to Herkimer."

"I don't know," the salesman said, now terrified he might lose this sale.

Paul didn't like to pull the cop card on people, especially these days with all the heat all over the country against cops. He figured it was his last resort. "I don't know if it makes a difference, but I'm a retired cop."

"Let me get the finance manager," the salesman said abruptly, leaving the small glass enclosed cubicle. Paul watched as a broad-shouldered, fit, middle-aged African-American man with a lot of gray in his hair approached. He felt like he was about to get caught in the middle of a classic good cop/bad cop sales smackdown.

"Mr. Santo," the finance manager said officiously, "I'm Glenn Williams," and took a seat. "You're a retired police officer?"

"Yes, sir, in fact just yesterday I signed my papers."

"NYPD?"

"Yes, sir."

"My father was a New York cop. Transit police."

"Really! That must have been back in the day when they were two separate departments."

"Exactly! He was a detective sergeant, District 1. He passed a while ago."

"I'm sorry. How did you wind up here? I mean, so far upstate?"

"We lived in the Bronx, by Arthur Avenue, Little Italy...."

"I eat there once a week, at least. Safest neighborhood in New York. The mob protects its own."

"No question! But as soon as he retired, he said we're getting out of Dodge, and somehow we wound up here. It's really beautiful. You know, I feel for you. When I was growing up, my mom and dad always said if you have trouble in the street, go find a cop. And if you have trouble in your soul, go find a priest. And today? Neither of those professions are at the top of the list anymore. Anyway, you'd like to pay by credit card for the total amount?"

"If possible. My ex-wife passed away, and I'm on the way to the funeral."

"Man, you are going through some changes. I am sorry. But no worries. Your credit card is fine. And let's up your trade in value from zero, to $500. Randy will take care of you."

"Thank you, Mr. Williams."

"Glenn."

"Glenn, can I ask you something personal?"

"Shoot."

"How long after your father retired did he pass away?"

Glenn hesitated. "Eighteen months. We had just settled in up here, and he had a massive heart attack."

"Thanks. For everything."

Paul was back on the road in an hour with his Ford Escape, and headed back to the Thruway for Herkimer. He thought about the stories of guys who dropped dead soon after retiring. And not just cops. He read somewhere that most men get their identity in life from their work. Everything is tied up their job: self-esteem, pride, usefulness. And when that goes, what's left? He couldn't remember who said it, but he remembered the quote, *If you kill a man's dreams, you kill the man.* He wondered if he had any dreams left. Any goals. Organizing bus trips to Mets away games were a great distraction from the stresses of being a cop, but not a way of life. And as a famous cartoonist, and an ex-Beatle, both said, *Life is what happens to you while you're busy making other plans.* This was his exit, Herkimer.

Paul had a theory about downtowns; if there were thrift stores like Salvation Army and Goodwill right in the middle of downtown, it was a depressed town. But if it had antique boutiques, it was a successful town. Same used junk, different pricing and packaging. Herkimer had a Goodwill.

He had discovered Crazy Otto's Empire Diner a few years ago, and that was always his first stop. A classic railroad car diner filled with locals, license plates on the walls, and posters of Elvis and old movies. Pork chop on an English muffin was his favorite dish. Herkimer is about 20 miles from an old rust-belt city, Utica. Just another town that once had vibrant industry and manufacturing jobs, and now gets by due to some crazy scheme where people who work in one store buy stuff from other stores and somehow that's an economy. Herkimer's a small town, only about 7,000 people and is dependent on Utica for jobs, so as anyone can see, things aren't going so great.

After lunch, Paul used landmarks to navigate to Greta and Tracy's. He smiled when he passed the Mudville Softball Complex, where they held national softball tournaments. Some of his favorite memories of watching Tracy from afar were when he sat in the stands during her softball tournaments, from grade school through high school. He was so proud of her athletic ability. Maybe some of his genes actually came in handy.

He pulled in front of the house on Jefferson Avenue. It was an old wooden two-story clapboard building separated from the homes on either side by narrow driveways built for Model-Ts. He didn't know what to expect from Greta or Tracy at this horrible time. Everyone feels guilt when a loved one commits suicide. What he did know was that it wasn't going to be easy. Five times he had told families that their cop husband or son was dead. But even the closest blood brother of a friend isn't the same as this. He rang the bell and waited.

The door opened and there she was. For a nanosecond he thought it could be his wife, Marcy, she looked so much like her. But Tracy was even prettier. She still had some baby fat around her cheeks and eyes. And she had gained a few pounds since he last spied on her.

"Hi, Tracy. I'm so sorry."

Tracy just stared at him. Paul could see the wheels spinning. Her right hand had a tight grip on the front door and he thought he saw her flinch as if she was going to slam it shut on him.

"Come in," Tracy said flatly.

They were in Greta's living room. It had a slight scent of Pine Sol in the air.

"Where's your grandma?" Paul asked, scanning the room and hall for any sign of her.

Tracy turned slowly, her head slumped, a little girl again who began to weep as she trudged toward Paul.

"Grandma's in the hospital. It was so awful. I was with her when she collapsed and I called 911. It was too much for her. But she's going to be okay."

She melted into Paul's arms and he hugged her for the first time since she was still in big-girl Pampers. Paul felt the years of neglect and distance dissipate as her tears flowed down his neck while she lost it.

"Greta is the best," was all Paul could think to say.

"I don't know what I'm going to do."

Paul sat her down on the dark-green velvet sectional and sat next to her. "Don't worry. Things are gonna be fine. We'll get through this."

"We? We? Since when is it fucking 'we?' " She screamed hysterically and ran up the stairs.

Paul made some tea and found some graham crackers in the pantry. The kitchen was chock-a-block with magnets, photos, and even yellowed pieces of papers with drawings by maybe a first- or-second grader. It was all Tracy and Marcy mementos. Not one clue that Paul even existed. He walked over to the door that led to the basement apartment where Marcy lived and flipped on the light. He took three steps down and stopped. It looked like an episode of *Hoarders*. Clothes, boxes, and empty cans and bottles everywhere. At least it didn't smell. Greta probably cleaned it up. He went back to the kitchen table and sipped his tea.

Tracy appeared in the doorway.

"I'm sorry. I shouldn't have said that."

"Want some tea and crackers?"

"Yes, please."

Paul got up and was somewhat relieved. *She apologized and said "Yes, please."* That was a good sign. He felt there was hope.

He poured her a cup of tea, put a cracker on a small plate, and stirred his own absentmindedly. "First things first. Where's grandma?"

"Saint Elizabeth's."

"Is anybody checking in on her? What's the prognosis?"

"Her sister. Aunt Peggy. At first, they thought it was a heart attack, but now they say it was just stress."

"What are the arrangements with your..." Paul stopped cold. Their eyes met. He braced himself, like those five times he told families about their dead loved ones. "...Your mom."

"She's being cremated. Tomorrow."

Paul wept, but not much. He fought back the tears. "Honey, you'll understand some day. Your mom and I...we...."

Tracy reached across the table and touched his hand. "It's okay. I know. I'm all cried out I think. For now, anyway. Let's go to the hospital and see grandma."

St. Elizabeth's was a lot different from the many hospitals in New York City that Paul had frequented as a cop. Unlike the mayhem at just about every hospital in the New York City, here at St. Elizabeth's there was a clean, quiet professionalism in the air.

Paul hadn't seen Greta in a few years, but the last time he saw her she was a robust late-seventies babe who wore make-up, always had her hair done, and wasn't above making a flirty remark to a handsome young waiter. Of course now, here, under these awful circumstances she looked every bit of an old woman. Tracy and Paul stood in the doorway a few seconds taking it all in.

"I don't know if I can do this," Tracy said, her voice trembling as she stared at her grandmother.

"Come on," Paul said, softly leading the way.

They stood next to the bed, and Tracy leaned in. "Hi grandma. It's me, Tracy."

Tracy and Paul were awestruck when Greta's eyelids popped open and a large smile beamed across her face.

"Tracy! I was wondering where the heck you were! Let's get out of here!" Greta said, happily.

"I'm so glad you're okay!" Tracy said leaning in to kiss her. "Look, Daddy's here."

"I knew you'd be here, Paul."

"Of course. You look great, Greta!" Paul said, all smiles.

"Fiddlesticks! I need some makeup and my hair done before I go anywhere!"

In the doorway, Aunt Peggy, Greta's sister appeared. A handsome woman in her seventies who dressed as if she still might shop at Forever 21.

"Sweetheart! Oh, Tracy, I'm so glad you came by. Paul? Oh my God, you are a sight for sore eyes! We knew you'd come. Greta and me, I mean."

Hugs and kisses were exchanged all around.

Peggy leaned in, "Honey, you look good right now! Your baby is here, and her daddy and everything is going to be all right, so don't worry yourself. I just checked at the nurse's station and you're being released in a little while, so let's start getting you presentable. You need to be back out to Country Joe's for Wednesday night line dancing!" She turned to Tracy. "This is the best she's looked since you know when."

After a half hour or so in the cafeteria, Tracy and Paul were summoned back to the room. It seemed miraculous that Greta, with a little makeup, and Peggy's skill at fixing-up her hair, looked like she was good to go.

Paul drove Tracy home and Grandma drove back with Peggy. After dinner and cookies, the photo albums came out. Everyone marveled at how much Tracy looked like her mom at the same age. And what a beautiful couple Paul and Marcy made. The photos where Marcy and Paul were partying drunk with throngs of similarly blasted friends were ignored.

Paul slept on the couch, and Tracy and Grandma in their upstairs bedrooms. They knew tomorrow would be tough.

Unlike the funeral homes in New York City, this funeral home actually looked like a home. A house, that is, on a neighborhood street. It made sense to Paul, who was only used to funeral homes that were boxy buildings on busy city streets that could have just as easily been a garment factory or dental offices.

Greta stayed home. She didn't think she was ready for a visit to the funeral home. Tracy and Peggy didn't want a service, just the lowest priced cremation. It wasn't totally because of the expense. It was also because of the circumstances. They didn't want all the obvious, invasive, dumb, and more than likely offensive questions and comments that would arise from wake attendees because Marcy committed suicide by overdosing.

Tracy, Peggy, and Paul sat in a wood-paneled office with Christian and Jewish religious paintings and sayings on the walls. An elderly man in a dark pinstriped suit came through a door holding a plain cardboard box about the size of one that would contain a Christmas fruit cake.

"You are the family of Marcy Santo?"

"I'm her daughter, my name's Tracy, this is my aunt Peggy, and this is my dad, Paul Santo," Tracy said stepping up and acting totally pro.

"I'm so sorry for your loss. Here are the remains. You can stay in here for as long as you like, if need be. Thank you."

He handed the box to Tracy, smiled, turned around and went back out the door.

"So that's it. The end. Let's just go," Tracy said, carefully handing the box to Paul. "Please hold on to this."

"Want to get a bite? How about Crazy Otto's?" Paul suggested.

"It figures you'd find Crazy Otto's," Peggy said. "Let's go discuss the future over pork chop sandwiches."

Paul placed the box of remains in the back of the SUV and put it in a compartment underneath where the spare tire was stored. He'd figure out what to do with it at a later time.

Peggy and Paul ordered the pork chop sandwich and Tracy ordered a salad with no eggs, cheese, or meat.

"Oh, are you vegetarian?" Paul asked, proud that he picked up on it.

"Vegan."

"What's the difference?"

"I don't eat any animal products."

"No eggs, dairy, cheese?"

"Nope."

"Where do you get your protein?"

"Legumes."

"Legumes?" Paul asked mystified.

Peggy tapped his arm, "That's hippie talk for beans."

"Okay, whatever works," Paul agreed. "Waitress!"

The waitress came back to the table. "Yes, hun?"

"Can I get a beer? Waddyuh got? Anything dark?"

"Sam Adams is the darkest."

"I'll take it."

Peggy and Tracy became quiet and shot each other subtle looks that could mean something, but what?

"What? Just one beer? Is that an issue?" Paul asked.

Tracy bowed her head. "Grandma doesn't allow alcohol or drugs in the house or in our lives. Due to something that runs in the family, I've been told," she said pointedly looking at Paul.

"Whoah. Okay. I'll keep that in mind. But if you don't mind, I'd like to have a beer with my meal."

Tracy bit her lip.

Peggy chimed in, "Paul, just do what you want. But keep it in mind, please. It's been something that has caused a lot of pain…." her voice trailed off.

Tracy looked upset, angling her head in an uncomfortable position.

The waitress returned with the opened bottle and a glass.

"I'm sorry, dear. Put it on the bill, but I changed my mind," he said softly to the waitress.

"No problem, no charge. I'll drink it. But don't tell!" She said chuckling as she walked away.

Tracy forced a smile and reached for a glass of water. When she did, Paul noticed a tattoo on the underside of her wrist. It looked like a small black triangle.

"Is that a tattoo?"

"Oh, that? Um, yeah."

"Why a pyramid?"

"Oh, it's just a symbol, of…." She struggled to find the words and nervously looked at Peggy "…of the ancient Indian spirits. That kind of thing," Tracy said, not wanting to reveal the actual meaning of the black triangle's significance in the LGBT community.

"I'm just glad there weren't tattoo shops on every corner when I was a kid. I'd probably have a Mr. Met tattoo on my neck. Excuse me, I have to go the men's room," Paul said sliding out of the booth. He walked over to the hall on the other side of the long counter and got the attention of the waitress, well out of the sight of Peggy and Tracy.

"Excuse me, let me have that Sam Adams. I'll just drink it here."

"Here you go," she said as she winked.

He downed it in three long gulps.

"Thanks. Just between us friends," Paul said, returning the wink.

There wasn't much talk during the meal. It was as if each knew that once the food was eaten, the plates removed, and the coffee was finally served there would be a "discussion." There had to be. Paul couldn't remember ever having a family discussion. Oh, there were screaming matches and curse words thrown around, both growing up and when he and Marcy were married, but not any "discussions." There were threats and challenges and doors slammed. And things happened. But they usually weren't good. He was hoping that having Peggy at the table would force father and daughter to be a little more civil.

"Do you have any plans, Tracy?" Paul asked tentatively, breaking the ice after his second cup of coffee.

"Yeah, I do, actually. I have some definite plans," she said slowly and confidently.

"Great. Let's hear it."

"I want to move to the West Coast. California," she said as she studied Peggy and Paul. Both of them had poker faces.

"Are you sure, honey? It's a big move," Aunt Peggy said reaching out and putting her hand on top of hers.

"I'll need your help, Aunt Peg."

"Anything for you sweetie."

Tracy sat up straight, brushed back her hair, and readied herself for her "discussion." "Well, it would all depend on grandma. She has to be one hundred percent."

"You know something, Trace? Your grammie and I have been talking about me moving in to her place for a few months now. Sometimes these things have a way of just working out in God's time, not our own. And now's the time," Peggy said tenderly.

"But why California?" Paul asked. "Do you even know anybody out there? I mean, come on, it's the land of fruits and nuts, you know? La-la land?"

"I really need a change. A complete change. And my friend moved out there a while ago, and loves it."

Paul perked up a little. "Well, a friend? Good! A guy friend?"

"No. A girl friend. A good friend. You know Heidi, right, Aunt Peggy?"

"Oh, that's the girl with who worked for the ambulance company, right?"

"Yes. She's out there and loves it."

"Where in California? It's a big place," Paul said, starting to take on an air of a concerned father.

"It's in southern California. Outside L.A. near Palm Springs."

Paul's cop intuitions began to kick in. He felt Tracy was being slightly cagey about something. But like an experienced cop, he knew not to rush into something, especially just a hunch, too quickly. You could blow the whole thing. "Oh, Palm Springs. That's nice. For nine months out of the year. The rest of the time you need a freaking space suit. It's like Baghdad on the Fourth of July!"

"People have air conditioning. Like in Florida or Phoenix," Tracy said, answers at the ready.

"What would you do out there? What does your friend Heidi do?" Paul said falling slightly into interrogation mode.

"She drives an ambulance. She said she thinks she could get me a job."

"Sounds kind of tentative."

"Dad, I'm ready for this. This kind of move. As long as I know grandma is well, and won't be alone."

"She's doing great, and she won't be alone, honey," Peggy said reassuringly.

"Do you have any money, Tracy? This is serious stuff, moving thousands of miles away." Paul said, getting more stern.

"You tell him about the insurance money, Aunt Peggy."

"Paul, Greta took the insurance money and your secret payments and invested wisely. All in Tracy's name. It's a decent amount."

Tracy looked like a little girl as she pursed her lip and looked to Paul. "Secret payments? I…I…you…."

"Don't even mention it. I just thank God it worked out the way it was supposed to. Well, not exactly, I mean…."

"I know what you mean," Tracy said, smiling through a few tears that were quickly wiped away.

"You know, I could drive you to California if you wanted. I've got nothing else to do."

"Really?"

"Really. I'll go pay the check," Paul said, heading to the cashier.

Peggy and Tracy stirred their coffee.

"Do you really think grandma will be all right?"

"I really do, sweetie. I don't know why, but I do. You should go to California. You need to start your life."

A week went by, and Grandma Greta got stronger every day and was back to her frisky self. It was clear that Tracy's plan to finally leave home and head west would happen, knowing that her grandma would be living with Aunt Peggy.

With things under control in Herkimer, Paul went back to his Bronx apartment to pack some things for the extended cross-country trip. It was becoming clearer with each passing day that he and Tracy would be heading for California.

He made arrangements for Brielle to stay at his apartment, which she was thrilled about, since she would have her own place for a while, at least. He figured a trip out west would do him good. He could bond with Tracy, and – who knows? – maybe he'd like it out there as well. He doubted it. There was nothing about the West Coast that appealed to him. He didn't like the people, the terrain, or the sports teams...despite the fact he had never been there.

Chapter Four

Tracy didn't want the trip to be a sightseeing extravaganza. As far as she was concerned, they were going from point A to point B. Eating, sleeping, and whatever other bodily and mental functions needed to be addressed would be done on an as-needed basis. Now that grandma was back home, feeling well and living with Aunt Peggy, she could finally live her own life. She didn't want to think that it was through the death of her mom that she finally felt free. She wouldn't let herself think that. But deep down in the place where thoughts and urges are buried – sometimes only with the help of addictions that provide the overwhelming distractions necessary for keeping those thoughts and desires under wraps – she knew she would never have been able to leave her mother while she was alive. Not in that state of desperate dependence on alcohol, drugs, and chaos. She knew she'd forever have the guilt of losing someone to suicide. But she was strong. She was taking action. She could start to live her life on her terms.

"Okay, here's the deal," Paul said, putting Tracy's bags and boxes in the back of the Escape and on the roof rack as Tracy sat on the front steps of Greta's house while she and Peggy sat on a porch swing chair. "This is my first time doing something like this. I've never been west of Chicago, so if something looks amazing, we might take a little detour to check it out. I know you have your license, but I like to drive. I could drive for hundreds of miles without stopping if need be. I enjoy driving. When I've had it, you can take over. Have you had any accidents? D.U.I.'s or anything?"

"I don't drink. And no, I've haven't had any accidents," Tracy said, annoyed but keeping her emotions in check.

You couldn't fit a box of Girl Scout cookies in the back of the Escape or on the roof rack. Paul admired his extreme packing skills as he stood hands-on-hips in the driveway. He looked over and saw that Tracy was now squeezed between Greta and Peggy on the little swinging porch chair built for two. She was bigger than both of the elderly ladies, who were shrinking and turning paler as the years pushed them towards their last days. There were hugs, tears, and whispers among the three that Paul knew he would never hear. That was okay. He was an outsider. Yeah, he was the father, he got Marcy to the hospital, and home, and changed a few diapers until he was kicked out. But these two ladies and Marcy gave life to Tracy. And now she was on her way. Seeing the love on that porch made Paul feel good. When he wasn't distracted by chasing bad guys, or planning bus trips, or betting that month's rent on a game, he worried deeply about Tracy. Greta assured him that she made sure she was taken care of, but he always had doubts. One always does. But now he knew.

"The train's leaving the station," Paul said, leaning down to give Peggy and Greta a peck on the cheek.

"I'll call often," Tracy said, waving and getting into the SUV.

Paul loved it when there was no traffic. He felt he could drive forever, and he almost did. One hundred, two hundred, three hundred miles went by like stops on the IRT subway express line. At first he thought for sure it would be like in Kerouac's *On the Road*, with Dean Moriarty and Sal Paradise cruising across America, going where the wind blows them, with stops to check out whatever curiosities beckoned just beyond the interstate chain-link fence. Instead it was more like the Kerouac passages where they made a mad dash across America just to get "there." To the other side. As quickly and madly as possible.

There was some small talk, but once it was dark, Tracy put her seat back all the way and slept. Or maybe just pretended to sleep. Paul pushed on and on until he couldn't any longer. He had clocked 575 miles, got off the interstate, and got two rooms at a Motel 6. And that was the routine for the next four days interrupted only by truck stops for bad food, worse rest rooms, and overnights in cheap motels. They made a couple of touristy stops for snowballs in the Rockies and vista lookouts in Utah and Arizona, but they were both anxious to keep moving forward, leaving their past in the rear-view mirror as quickly as possible.

They were at the crossroads. After taking I-40 through Flagstaff, Arizona, into Needles, California and onto the I-15 south towards southern California, they had to make a decision in a Barstow truck stop.

It was lunchtime and the place was jammed with truckers, tourists, bikers, and commuters. There were some cowboy hats, but not as many as the stretch through New Mexico and Arizona. There was a smattering of hipsters, probably on the way back to L.A. from Vegas, who somehow have taken on the garb and look of backwoodsmen, with their bushy beards and knitted skullcaps, despite the upper 90's temperature outside. There were also some toothless walking and talking zombie meth-heads looking to buy or sell their poison. It reminded Paul of what he was leaving behind in home sweet home.

"Hopefully, once we get closer to Los Angeles it will be easier for you to get some of your hippie food. I don't know how you've survived on rabbit food and garbanzo beans. I can't stand those things! They taste like…dirt."

Tracy chuckled and she struggled to get four garbanzo beans onto the tines of her fork. "Should we go to Los Angeles? Or just head out to Palm Springs?"

"I don't know, what do you want to do?" Paul asked, between bites of his rubbery, dry burger.

"I mean we've come this far, it might be a good idea to at least check it out."

Paul knew he would hate L.A. Every television show from *TMZ* to *The Real House Wives* of anywhere added to his disdain of plastic land. Watching Dodger Stadium draw four million fans every single year even pissed him off. Doesn't anybody have to work out there? Plus the fact that they just got two NFL teams after something like a quarter of a century of not having even one, was just further proof that the city was insignificant. Even Green Bay, Wisconsin, a town in the middle of the tundra with less than a hundred thousand people, has enough gravitas for a football team. L.A. has a hundred thousand people stuck in cars at one Starbucks drive-up window. "Well, if you really want to…," Paul said, reluctantly.

"Yeah. Let's go to Los Angeles first," Tracy said, showing the first glimpse of a smile in several hundred miles.

Paul thought the Grand Central Parkway was bad trying to make a Mets game on a Friday night. But it was nothing compared to the ten lanes of highway hell that lay out before them as they approached Los Angeles. "How can there be ten lanes and nobody moving? It's unreal."

They were on the I-10 about 20 miles east of the city and heading west towards downtown L.A. With each exit they passed, traffic was slower and slower. It even came to a dead stop at times. But something struck Paul. No one was blowing their horns, and for the most part, people were pretty much staying in their lanes, windows up, A/C cranked, and just dealing with it.

"I don't know," Paul said gripping the wheel tightly, "I think if this was New York, there'd be road rage and horns honking all over the place. I guess after a while you just get used to it out here."

"Look, I can see the skyline!" Tracy said excitedly.

"Yeah, what do you know? They have a skyline. Not too bad, but looks like about 12 blocks of a skyline compared to Manhattan's 12 miles' worth."

"You're not in New York anymore."

"You're right. I'm not. This ain't New York. Honey, do me a favor. Do that for me?"

"Do what?"

"When you have an observation like that. Let me know."

"You're kidding, right?"

"No really. Be honest. I can handle it."

"Okay. You asked for it."

"Should we go downtown?" Paul said as they approached the exit for downtown L.A. "It looks a lot like New York."

"This highway ends at Santa Monica, let's go to the end of the road."

"I like that. Take it all the way."

The highway dumped them a few blocks from the Pacific Ocean in Santa Monica just as twilight was approaching. Paul was paranoid about parking the Escape on the street with the car and roof rack filled with luggage so he pulled into a parking lot with an attendant.

"Do me a favor," he said to the middle-aged Hispanic man wearing a pressed white shirt and black trousers, "Can you please keep an eye on my car while we walk around? I'll give you an extra ten dollars."

"Of course. But no extra charge, señor! Park right here. Let me move this cone."

"Gracias, mi amigo!" Paul turned to Tracy and whispered, "We are definitely not in New York anymore."

The attendant gave them walking directions to the Santa Monica Pier, only a couple blocks away. There it was, with its retro neon sign archway welcoming all to SANTA MONICA – YACHT HARBOR – SPORT FISHING – BOATING – CAFES. There was also a Route 66 sign that read END OF THE TRAIL.

"Man, I could just see Sam Spade walking down here in the Forties, going to grab some oysters and a boilermaker," Paul said, feeling the wooden planks creak under his feet on the pier.

"Boilermaker? What's that?"

"A shot of whiskey with a beer chaser. You never heard of that?"

"Nope."

"Actually that's a good thing. I knew what a boilermaker was when I was fifteen. Don't ask me how I knew, either. Wow, check out this merry-go-round!"

Paul and Tracy went on the carousel, played some carnival games, and went on the Ferris wheel. He couldn't help but feel a certain sadness that he was doing this with Tracy when she was pretty much a grown woman, not eight or nine. They were quiet as the giant Ferris wheel rose to its zenith and probably a hundred miles of coast line was in view, with the sun setting into the ocean. Paul could still see the little girl in her that he mostly saw in photos and fleeting moments over the past 20 years. He could also see her mother in so much of what she was. The mysterious look on her face as she gazed silently into the distance. He wondered if she also would snap one day, and become a stranger to everyone around her. An uncontrollable whirlwind of bad choices and self-destructive behavior. All he could do was hope. And pray she wouldn't.

"What else do you want to see? Hollywood, Beverly Hills, Dodger Stadium?" Paul asked as they maneuvered through the crowd on the Third Street Promenade, a busy pedestrian mall of bars, restaurants, and street performers a couple of blocks from the beach.

"I'd really rather hit the road, and get to where we're going."

"Sure, babe. Whatever you want. Do you mind if we just go in here, maybe grab a quick bite?" They were in front of a bar with crowded sidewalk tables and television sets turned to sports.

"Okay," Tracy reluctantly agreed.

Paul wondered how she subsisted on lettuce, energy bars, and bottled water. He needed a burger and fries and maybe a beer. Or two. Maybe a few.

On the way back to the car after dinner, Paul could sense Tracy was mad. She stared straight ahead and he could see the tension in her jaw as she clenched it tightly. He figured it would blow over once they got on the road.

"Give me the keys!" She demanded, stopping a few feet from the lot entrance.

"What?"

"I'm driving!"

"What's this all about?"

"You've been drinking!"

"I had three Coors Lights. Are you serious? You can just simmer down and – "

"What happened to me being brutally honest with you?"

Paul did the simmering down. He figured what the hell. "Okay, you are correct. Here are the choices: you drive in the dark a hundred miles and get into Palm Springs late at night, or we get a room near here and get a fresh start in the morning."

A slight crooked smile appeared on Tracy's face. "Let's spend the night and start in the morning. I still want to drive to the hotel."

Paul dropped the keys into her outstretched palm.

The garage attendant was thrilled at the extra ten bucks Paul gave him, and they were on their way. Paul was shocked to learn from Yelp that the cheapest motel they could find nearby was $200 a night at a Best Western a few blocks away, but that would have to do.

After a good night's sleep they were already backtracking on the I-10 eastbound, headed for the southern California desert, which they knew absolutely nothing about. Once they passed downtown L.A., the eastbound 10 reminded Paul of the Long Island Expressway after emerging from the Midtown Tunnel and into Queens. Miles of industrial parks, shopping malls, and tract housing. But just like the L.I.E., once they traveled around 50 miles things began to change drastically, although in a very different way from what you'd see on Long Island. Huge mountains seemed to appear out of nowhere. And suburbs transitioned into rural landscapes with rolling hills and horse farms, with the occasional cluster of housing developments and mega malls. But at the 90-mile mark, they were in awe at the sight fast approaching.

"Oh my God! I think we're being attacked by the Transformers! I mean look at this! It's like something from outer space," Paul said amazed at the gargantuan field of windmill turbines that stretched for miles in front of them and on both sides of the freeway. "I heard of these things, but up close, they are startling! And ugly!"

It was a bizarre welcome to the Coachella Valley, home to Palm Springs and other desert cities. Like a futuristic forest of gigantic spindly robots, they gazed at the ginormous turbines slowly turning like some alien pasture of giant robotic pinwheels.

"It's really otherworldly," Tracy said, slowing panning across the landscape.

"I expected desolation out here, and we're in the middle of a freakin' Futurama nightmare!"

And while they were enthralled with this spectacle of human technological wonder, or perhaps blunder, they didn't notice that the exterior temperature gauge on the dashboard had crept up to 109 degrees.

"What's our exit?" Paul asked, while Tracy checked the map on her phone.

"Gene Autry Trail."

"What? Gene Autry Trail? Should we watch out for Indians?"

"Who's Gene Autry?"

"Who's...? Never mind, I keep forgetting I'm a hundred five years old. He was a cowboy actor in old movies, and the original owner of the Angels," Paul said, noticing the blank look on Tracy's face. "The Angels are a baseball team. The Los Angeles Angels. But they don't play in Los Angeles. It's a long story. And he sang "Rudolph the Red Nosed Reindeer."

"Now that I heard of!"

"What happens after we exit the freeway?"

"Oh, Heidi said take it for a while, until Dinah Shore Drive, make a left, and...."

"Don't tell me, make a right on Frank Sinatra Way."

"No, make a right on Frank Sinatra Drive. How did you know?"

"You're kidding me, right?"

"No. I'm serious."

"By the way, where are we going exactly? Whose house and what are you doing there?"

"Heidi and some friends rented a condo. There's a big festival this week in Palm Springs, and Heidi took a few days off so we could hang out."

"Okay, then what?"

"Then what, what?"

"What are you doing again?

"I'm going to room with Heidi at her place in Twentynine Palms and she's going to help me get settled and find a job. She said I could probably work where she works."

"Driving an ambulance?"

"Not right away. Something else with the...company."

Paul let that go. He wasn't going to pry or pull daddy rank on her. *She's twenty-one,* he thought to himself. *She can do whatever the hell she wants.* "Damn, this street is like going through the Sahara! Look at this! A freakin' tumbleweed. An actual tumbleweed, tumbling across the road on Gene Autry Trail. Nobody at The Buckeye would believe this."

After a mile or two, suddenly there was green everywhere. Lawns, trees, shrubbery, and even an emerald golf course. On both sides of the road were housing developments with high walls and manned security gates to enter the property.

"Is it one of these?"

"It's called the Desert Sky Resort. There it is! What are you going to do for the next few days, dad?"

"I was wondering when that would come up. I'm not sure. Isn't Joshua Tree around here?"

"Oh, that was that U2 album!"

"Very good! Something we both can share! Yeah, it's Joshua Tree National Park. Maybe I'll kick around there a few days, and we'll decide later what we'll do."

They pulled into the driveway of the Desert Sky Resort, which looked like all the other developments built around a golf course for the surrounding ten square miles or so. The guard gave them directions to the house. They passed tennis courts, an outdoor café, people on bike paths, golfers in carts, and a swimming pool.

"Is it me, or is it like 90 percent women around here?"

"This is it, I'll text her!" Tracy said excitedly as she thumbed her message outside the unit they were looking for.

The door to the house flew open, and a young African-American woman in camo cargo shorts and a green tank top came running down the walkway towards Tracy. Paul didn't really pay attention, because he had work to do. He had to find Tracy's luggage, boxes, and stuff she had left scattered around the car.

Had he been paying attention, he would have seen Tracy and Heidi in a joyful, sweet, embrace. Not of just two good friends meeting after a few months of separation. But the reunion of two people very much in love.

Paul looked over from undoing the bungee cords on the roof rack just as they were walking towards the vehicle.

"Dad, this is Heidi, and Heidi this is my dad," Tracy said, trying to dampen the emotional temperature in 109 degree heat.

Heidi was a solid young woman. Five foot five, a good 140 pounds, with a short, neat afro cut. Heidi's grin was wide, her teeth gleaming white, and her smiling eyes clear and bright. "Pleasure to meet you, Mr. Santo, sir."

"Call me Paul," he said shaking hands. He immediately noticed a firm handshake. She was wearing a tank top and he noticed her defined muscles. She reminded Paul of some of the fine woman he had served with on the police force. "Nice to meet you! I can't believe how hot is here! Man, I've been outside for a minute and I'm sweating like a pig outside a bacon factory. Here, start taking this stuff inside. You're from Herkimer, Heidi?"

"Yes, sir. Born and bred. I moved out here a few years ago after high school," she said, taking hold of a large box. "You get used to the heat. I don't think I could take another upstate New York winter."

"Heidi, I wanted to check out Joshua Tree? Is that worth doing?"

"Absolutely, sir! That's the high desert. Only about 45 minutes away, but it's magical."

"Magical? I thought it was rocks and cactus? Why's that?"

All three had armloads of boxes and bags and walked towards the house.

"Well, there's the amazing sky, the quiet, the hidden desert life, the ancient Native American spirits, the mystery of it all."

"What mystery? Like Agatha Christie mystery? What?"

"Don't worry dad. You're not going there as a detective."

"Just go up there and explore. You'll see," Heidi said, winking. "Stay at the Joshua Tree Inn. Stay in the Gram Parsons room."

"Gram Parsons? The Flying Burrito Brothers guy who hung out with Keith Richards and overdosed, then they stole his body and cremated it in the desert? They made a movie about that."

"That's it. There's a lot to explore. It can expand your mind," Heidi said, with the look of someone who knew what she was talking about.

"Where can we get something to eat?" Paul asked, after putting down the last of Tracy's boxes.

"Do you like Jewish delis?" Heidi asked.

"You're kidding, right? Let's go!"

Sherman's Deli wasn't exactly Katz's on East Houston Street near Paul's old precinct, one of the best Jewish delis in New York, but it wasn't too far off the mark, albeit this was 3,000 miles west of Houston Street. Tracy and Heidi were catching up with things and Paul kept his distance throughout the meal. He realized that he had just entered Tracy's life in the last five minutes and to try and influence her at this point would probably just tick her off. So he listened to their small talk about old friends, and of course about Tracy's mom, grandma, and aunt. Paul's cop skills were honing in fast. He knew that Tracy and Heidi were tight. Tracy was opening up to her like she hadn't done with him. But still he knew there was something that both were holding back. He didn't care. Heidi seemed like a good kid. Better than that; she seemed great. He felt Tracy made a good choice of friends and felt a little better about this whole crazy adventure.

"Well, I'll drop you guys off at the house and be on my way," Paul said after signing the credit card bill. "I'm heading to the high desert. You know what they say, adventure before dementia!"

The mention of Gram Parsons by Heidi a little earlier caused Paul to do some deep brain digging. He was a fan of The Byrds and the Flying Burrito Bros., and knew that Keith Richards and Gram were tight at one point. But after Gram's death from an overdose, his legend morphed into myth. Paul saw the movie based on the aftermath of Gram's untimely death in a high desert motel room, where a friend stole his body from an airport prior to being transported to New Orleans for burial. The friend claimed that Gram had stated he wanted to be cremated in Joshua Tree at the very spot where they used to camp while waiting for UFO's, Indian spirits, and a myriad of hallucinogenic drugs to take effect. The movie was a strange one, but it added to the mythology of Parsons. He remembered shortly after the movie was released he went out and bought a CD that had two of Gram's solo albums, *GP* and *Grievous Angel*. He pulled the car over on a sandy shoulder on the long stretch of two-lane blacktop that led back to the interstate. He was sure it was in a box he hastily threw several dozen of his favorite CD's into that he thought could get him through just about anything, and there it was! He hadn't listened to it in ages, but something told him the right time to play it would present itself. Like throwing a Swiss army knife in a backpack before a trip. You don't know why you would need it, but you know you are going to. He slid it into his dashboard CD player and the unmistakable sound of fiddle and classic country rock blasted out of the speakers to the tune of "Still Feeling Blue." It struck Paul that this was why he had thrown the old CD into his box.

His Escape threw a cloud of dust behind him as he spun his tires getting back onto the road towards the interstate. He headed west on the 10 towards the 62, which would head north around the western edge of Joshua Tree National Park. The 62 was also called Twentynine Palms Highway, which led to Twentynine Palms, which was also one of the nation's largest Marine bases. The desert was a natural training environment for those destined for the Mideast wars of Afghanistan, Iraq, and wherever the hell else barbarians trying to turn the clock of civilization back a thousand years rear their ugly heads and start beheading infidels, which happen to be mostly other Muslims of a different variety. You know, kind of like how the Lutherans and Baptists argue over who has the better music programs during service.

Back in the middle of the Futurama world of ginormous windmills, with only about a third of them slowly spinning, he took the exit off the I-10 and headed north on Twentynine Palms Highway towards Joshua Tree. The windmills disappeared behind him, and then there was just hardscrabble, dirt, dust, and the occasional yucca tree. In the distance he could see small cabins on top of rocky hills seemingly in the middle of nowhere and he wondered why the hell anybody would live in such a remote, desolate, God-forsaken place?

Straight ahead a few miles he could see formidable mountains. And as he approached them it became clear that the mountains weren't the verdant sort, like the Adirondacks of upstate New York. Nor were they like the hills above Los Angeles dotted with many varieties of trees. These were mostly covered with just small shrubs and dirt. But the mountains themselves looked more like something out of the *Flintstones*. Giant brown boulders piled on top of each other and huge stone slabs shooting up at angles. And suddenly the flat highway veered into a steep mountain pass worthy of any John Ford western where the Indians look down on the wagon train from high above the pass. The road kept winding and climbing and snaking up and around and his ears popped, so he knew he was gaining some serious altitude. He felt sorry for the cars in the opposite direction, going downhill, with giant big rigs too close behind. In addition to the increasing altitude, he noticed that the temperature was dropping with every mile or so; it was 109 when he last checked on the flat land, and now it was down to 101. On both sides of the steep two-lane was nothing but rocks: big rocks, gigantic rocks, small rocks, tiny rocks, and mountains of rock.

Paul opened the window when the temperature dropped to 99, and a *woosh* of hot, dry wind swept through the vehicle. It had a dusty smell to it, as though the air was filled with microscopic-sized rocks. He was making a sharp swooping upward turn around a bend when suddenly he saw things growing out of the dirt and rock. They looked familiar. Yes! Appearing all at once was a small forest of Joshua trees, just like the one on the U2 album cover. He wondered why they appeared so suddenly: Was it the air? The dirt? Or something magical?

After about ten miles on this incline he could see he was coming to the top of what must be a plateau. There were businesses on both side of the highway every few hundred feet. A gas station, a feed store, a tire-repair shop, an Indian-themed junk store, and it seemed between almost every business there were these small abandoned sheds in various stages of disrepair and decay. And up ahead there was yet another long and winding road that went up and up and up probably another thousand feet higher. The Joshua trees were almost everywhere. Growing like those weedy "Trees-of-Heaven" that grow all over New York City, sometimes even out of the sides of brick and concrete apartment buildings.

The temperature was down to 92 and at the top of this hill there was a round sign that read WELCOME TO YUCCA VALLEY. Paul was surprised how many businesses were on this stretch of road: motels, motorcycle shops, the Route 62 Café, antique stores, and several more feed stores. But like that last stretch of commercial properties, these were also separated by abandoned sheds, dilapidated homes, and dirt roads that led to other rocky hillsides. Most of the other vehicles on the road were huge pickups, 4x4's, motorcycles, or steaming beaters held together with duct tape and spit. Even though just about every strip-mall franchise was represented, from Applebee's to a Walmart Superstore, in between those cookie-cutter behemoths there were also businesses like Vern's Auto Repairs (with a half a Model-T sticking out from the front of the roof, complete with its wheels spinning), Alexandra and Farquar's Magic Crystals and Gold Mining Emporium, and Billy Bob's Feed and Tack Store (with life-sized statues of a horse, a steer, and a sexy woman dressed in a traditional Dale Evans-style cowgirl outfit with a rigid lasso above her head). Plus, dirt bike repairs, a gun shop, and a pawnshop, so you knew that although civilization was creeping in, they still couldn't smother the Wild West nature of this part of the world. Not yet anyway.

After passing the Walmart Superstore and a Home Depot, there was a stretch of road with just sand and Joshua trees on both sides, then a sign that read WELCOME TO JOSHUA TREE. So apparently there was a town of Joshua Tree in addition to the national park. There were little strip malls, but mostly with mom-and-pop stores (a liquor store, a Chinese restaurant, a used book store) and then the landmark he had been looking for: A wooden sign, with non-professional lettering that read JOSHUA TREE INN, the motel where Gram Parsons breathed his last breath. He pulled over at the end of property and parked his car. His New Balance running shoes crunched sand and gravel as he walked across the parking lot to the office. In the window there was a black felt letter board behind glass with white interchangeable letters, like the kind you might see in the lobby of a funeral home listing which room held which deceased person. This one read WELCOME TO THE JOSHUA TREE INN, OFFICE HOURS 3PM-8PM, THE HOME OF GRAM PARSONS' SPIRIT. Paul realized things were different here.

Physically, the inn was really just a cinder block horseshoe-shaped motel, probably built in the Fifties, but it was easy to see this was no longer an ordinary desert motor lodge. The windows had dainty curtains, wind chimes hung off the porches, and artistic Mexican tiles accented walkways and walls. He meandered around back and saw an odd collection of empty bottles, dead flowers, and rocks around a 3 ft. by 3 ft. stone slab with SAFE AT HOME written on it. He knew it had to be a tribute to Gram, but he wasn't sure exactly what it meant. He noticed there was a door gilded in gold; room number 8. That must be it. The room where he made his final transition from artist to legend.

A young white dude in a hoodie and dreadlocks down to his waist came out of the room and approached him. Paul thought the guy must be sweating his ass off in this desert heat, but he didn't seem to have a bead of sweat on his brow.

"Can I help you?" the soft-spoken man asked politely.

"Is that the room where Gram Parsons died?"

"Yes, room 8. I guess you've never been here before?" he asked, reaching down to pick up an old trampled cigarette butt. "You can stay there tonight. The folks in there are checking out later on and we had a cancellation."

"Really? How far is the national park?"

"About a mile up the road make a right, and it's about ten minutes down the road. Stop in the visitor's center for a pass and information."

"Yes, I'll take it. How much?"

"One twenty four a night."

"That's a deal," he said as the man led him to the office. "What's this Safe at Home thing?"

"That was out in the park where Gram's body was burned at Cap Rock. It got a little out of control and the park was going to remove it and destroy it. We're the custodians of it now."

"Cap Rock? Can I go there?"

"Sure. It's in the park. We have some maps."

They entered the office. Incense was burning from a Buddha's belly, tapestries and artfully framed vintage posters of The Byrds, Gram Parsons, The Rolling Stones, The Eagles, Emmylou Harris, and Donovan were on the wall.

"Did all these people stay here?"

"Yeah pretty much and more. We try to downplay the current visitors. Here's your key to room 8. How many nights?"

"Do you need to know now?"

"It gets booked fast."

"Let's say two nights."

"Okay, and you can stay longer because of the cancellation."

"Great. Are there good hikes in the park?"

"Mind blowing."

"Are there any bars within walking distance?"

"The Joshua Tree Saloon is a about a mile that way," the dreadlocked host said with a grin as he flicked his head east.

"Thanks."

In any other motel, room number 8 would just be another small, cinder block walled room for tired truckers and low-budget hookers. But from the moment Paul opened the golden door he sensed something. Maybe it was the hippie-themed décor, the posters of vintage rock icons, and the pictures, drawings, and photos of Gram himself, or just being aware of its infamous backstory. He didn't want to unpack his suitcase for just two nights, so he just placed it on the canvas straps of the folding suitcase holder next to the bathroom door.

It was in the nineties in the middle of the afternoon, too hot for a hike in the desert park, so he decided he would do it first thing in the morning. He stopped at a café, Crossroads, and ordered a non-antibiotic, hormone-free, free-range buffalo burger, no sprouts, please. He wondered if the buffalo had been slaughtered or died of natural causes. It reminded him of the hippie health food restaurants that cropped up in the East Village back in the Eighties, like his favorite, *Sightless in a Savage Land Sandwich Shoppe*.

Every worker and most of the patrons in Crossroads looked like they could be from central casting for a remake of *Hair*, which was strange since that was almost 50 years ago. But the vibe was more hippie than the current white bro hipsters who had taken over Manhattan and Brooklyn, which to Paul looked more like Hitler Youth with their shaved heads. Next door to Crossroads was a store stocked with rock climbing and camping gear that looked like it was made for pros climbing Everest. And listening to the multi-lingual conversations at nearby tables in Crossroads, he began to realize that this wasn't just a mecca for hikers, campers, and rock climbers from SoCal, but from the entire world.

The Joshua Tree National Park visitor center was teeming with tourists. He purchased a day pass for the next day, and some guides, maps, and brochures. Although he had been to the majestic mountains and forests of the Northeastern U.S., most of his time was spent drinking beer in a lodge and watching sports on television with several dozen of his closest friends. This was going to be something different for him. He was solo and he was going to let his feet and his mind do some wandering in a totally unfamiliar and alien environment. He had been exposed to every earthly terrain and type of body of water imaginable, except for the desert. This would be something entirely new.

After leaving the visitor center Paul realized he was exhausted and headed back to his room for a quick nap. He kicked off his shoes, laid down on the cowboy and Indian bedspread, and before he could say three Hail Marys he was nodding off into dreamland. But each time he was ready to get some serious REM deep sleep, the sound of an acoustic guitar in the next room awakened him back to reality. It happened three times, but it was only 7 P.M. and he couldn't in good conscience complain about somebody doing some tasty finger picking in their room on the other side of a cinder block wall at this totally acceptable time of day. He just waited until it stopped and then fell back to sleep again, until it happened a fourth time. Then he gave up trying to nap, and decided to see what a neighborhood bar was like in the middle of the high desert. He put his shoes on, headed out the door, and paused to lock it. And just as he turned the key a Mexican cleaning lady exited the room next to his with her cart of cleaning supplies.

"Hello, sir," she said, her chubby cheeks smiling wide.

"Hello, señorita," Paul replied.

Weird. He thought that was the room where the music was coming from. Perhaps it was the room on the other side. A less-than-a-mile walk would take only around 20 minutes at the most. He couldn't imagine this gin mill would be anything like The Buckeye, back in the Bronx.

The sun was setting fast and once in the twilight zone where day became night, he realized two crucial things about his walk. One: no street lights. And two: no sidewalks. Soon the mesh in his running shoes was letting all kinds of rocks and sand in, and cars and trucks were moving fast, really fast, just a few feet to his left. He wasn't wearing light-colored clothing and probably the only thing that made him at all visible to the vehicles coming up fast behind him were the small reflective strips on the back of his shoes. Whenever a big rig blew by, it kicked up a tornado of dirt and debris that got in his eyes and mouth. He thought about the 100-year-old elevated trains that passed next to The Buckeye on Broadway and figured these trucks that went rumbling past would probably also become just an invisible part of the landscape that you eventually got used to as time wore on. But then again, an elevated train wasn't about to come flying off the tracks and kill you. One of these big rigs easily could.

He could see the bar in the distance, lit up like a Vegas casino with a floodlight and neon sign illuminating it, the only structure visible in the darkened desert town. The front of the bar was like something out of western: worn wood, hand-painted signs, and even swinging doors. In fact, it reminded Paul of a photo hanging on a wall inside of The Buckeye that showed what that Bronx bar looked like in the early 1900's. The resemblance between it and the Joshua Tree Saloon was uncanny.

He entered the bar and was hit with another familiar sensation: that smell of decades of beer, wine, and liquor infused into the walls, floors, and ceilings. There was a long bar on the right, with about a half-dozen folks, another half-dozen or so scattered at tables, two people throwing darts, and different baseball games on three TV sets. Paul took a seat at the corner of the bar, under the Dodger game, and put a twenty on the bar. At the other end, the bartender was talking to a young woman and noticed Paul.

Like a lot of New York hipster bartenders he was twentysomething, white, bearded, tattooed, and had an earring. But unlike city hipsters, this guy had a rough-around-the-edges toughness; more like a biker than the guy behind the counter in a mid-town Manhattan Apple Store.

"What can I get you?" he asked, placing a coaster in front of Paul.

"You don't have Guinness on tap, do you?"

"No sir. Want to know the beers we got?"

"Nah. Stoly on the rocks. Make it a double."

"No problem."

So far that was the only difference between here and the Bronx. No Guinness. And it only took two double doses of Stoly for the other revelations to kick in. He was alone, didn't know where he was going, didn't really know where he was, his ex-wife was dead, his daughter was no longer estranged but was still a stranger, he had no job, no friends, and no bookie. Paul wasn't going to allow himself to be depressed. So the doubles kept coming, and with each trip down the bar to deliver his drinks he would ask the bartender questions that became more personal as the evening wore on: "Where do people work? What do people do? Did you grow up here? What's the deal with the Gram Parsons room at the Joshua Tree Inn?"

The bartender, Dwayne, was indeed a biker. He was also pretty wise for a young man. Unfortunately, as time and the Stolys wore on, Paul was drunk when he got to the important issues and could only remember three things by the time he left his tip on the bar: the Marine base in Twentynine Palms was important to the local economy, watch out for rattlesnakes in the dirt, and there's weirdness in the high desert air.

Paul had walked home from bars drunk thousands of times. His Bronx apartment was less than a half-hour walk from probably a dozen bars and five diners. There were times when he didn't touch his car for the entire time he had days off, whether it was just a single day, or a two-week staycation. He loved to walk and didn't think this under-the-influence trek would be much of a challenge.

Exiting the bar put him in the bright glare of the lone floodlight that illuminated the entrance, but once he crossed the street the only lights visible in front of him were the scattered homes in the hills and the occasional cars whizzing past. It was hard enough not tripping on the relatively even Bronx sidewalks, but not having any sidewalk at all was a real challenge for an intoxicated stranger 'round these parts. After a few hundred feet he recognized the lit sign of the Joshua Tree Inn, which gave him some relief. But it was still a good ten-minute walk away, bobbing weaving, and trying not to become road kill on Highway 62. Whenever possible he leaned against a signpost, but soon realized even that could be dangerous when he leaned against a tall object that turned out to be a gigantic cactus.

"Ahh! My hand's on fire!" he shouted into the darkness.

He knew that removing the prickly spines would have to be a project for later-on that evening, and continued on his way. A big rig going way too fast swerved slightly into the shoulder of the road he was next to, and the draft from the truck almost sucked him into the street. But the motel was now only a few steps away. He gave a sigh of relief, paused, and felt something welling up inside him; he then puked into some tumbleweeds. Like a pro, after hurling, he barely missed a step and walked around the back of the motel to look for his room. The U-shaped patio was dark except for the single votive candle that sat among the empty bottles and dead flowers on the Gram SAFE AT HOME slab. He flashed on the many times when, as a kid in Catholic grammar school, he would light a candle for a dead relative in the vestibule of the church. He also flashed on his days as an altar boy when he was an acolyte, which meant he held the large candles at funeral masses as the priest sprinkled the coffin with holy water and the family members wept. A wave of dizziness suddenly enveloped his head as he struggled to focus his eyes, find his key, figure out where he was, *Oh yeah, room 8, the gold door.* He managed to get into his room, push the door closed, make it to the bed, and immediately fall into a drunken, deep, black-out sleep."

KNOCK KNOCK KNOCK.
    "Housekeeping."
    KNOCK KNOCK KNOCK
    "Housekeeping."
    Paul shielded his eyes from the shards of morning sunlight slicing through the drapes right into his face.
    "No thanks. Not now. Come back later, please," Paul mumbled from his bed, still trying to figure out where the hell he was and what was going on. He looked at the clock on the end table: 11:37 A.M.
    "Okay, thank you," a female voice said from behind his door.
    KNOCK KNOCK KNOCK!
    "Shit," Paul whispered. "What does she want now?" He got up from the bed, and looked in the bathroom mirror. "Christ, look at me," he grumbled. He almost lost his balance as he opened the door. "Yeah, can you come back a little...oh, excuse me."
    It wasn't the cleaning lady this time. He thought maybe he was still dreaming and there was a vision, an apparition at his door. The sun was shining behind her, making it difficult to see facial

features. But it was a woman, with wide, wild hair, spreading down like it was creating a pyramid, huge silver loops dangling from her ears, and a large medallion of silver and turquoise reaching down into her cleavage.

"I'm sorry to disturb you. I'm Kate. I'm working the desk. Is everything all right?"

Paul stepped across the threshold and was taken aback at the sight of this beautiful woman at his door. She could have been thirty-five, or maybe fifty-five. There was a serenity about her, even though she was obviously acting as security and checking on the drunken asshole in room number 8.

"Yes, um, everything is fine," Paul stuttered as he collected his thoughts, trying to remember if he did anything stupid the night before. "Is there a problem?"

"No. Can we step inside, please," she asked politely.

"Sure. Yes. It's a little messy. I had kind of a rough night," he said opening the door wider to let her step in. "You know, after a cross-country trip and all."

"A guest in a nearby room thought she heard some kind of disturbance in your room at about 4 A.M. But it was brief and she didn't think it was an issue. She told me about it this morning, and I just wanted to double check."

"That's very nice of you, but no. I don't recall anything. But ah, I have been known to have nightmares," Paul explained, knowing full well he had more than nightmares on a regular basis. In the world of alcoholics, it's called *the horrors*; waking up screaming gibberish in the middle of the night and sometimes jumping out of bed, still asleep, and crashing into things.

"That's what we thought. Where did you come from?"

"Oh geez. Let me think. Oh yeah, the Joshua Tree Saloon."

"No I mean, where are you traveling from? On your journey?"

"My journey? Oh yeah, New York. City." He was having trouble concentrating as his eyes and head began to clear and he could see that this woman was a special kind of beauty.

Most real hippies had long disappeared from the New York scene. The Bernie Sanders/Occupy Wall Street/black lives matter/no GMO/climate change/alt whatever crowd certainly contains an element of hippie-ness, but it always seem to be tinged with an angry, demanding, hard edge. But back in the day, being a hippie was more about peace and love and mellowness, free love, and great live rock concerts. At least in Paul's mind. Kate had that hippie vibe from the tip of her Birkenstocks to the top of her thick salt-and-pepper hair. Paul noticed an aroma. Could it be patchouli oil? And there was an earthy fragrance wafting around him as a warm desert breeze blew in from the open doorway. Was it incense, weed, witch hazel? It reminded him of when the great record stores in the Village like Bleecker Bobs and Second Hand Rose started selling rolling papers and would light incense to attract customers. Kind of like how throwing a piece of bacon on a bar grill gives drinkers an appetite. He hated having to breathe in incense while going through the rare record bins looking for Beatles, Stones, and Hendrix bootlegs, but Kate's mixture of fragrances brought back a whirlwind of pleasant sensations.

"I've never been to New York. I'm an army brat. Mostly west of the Rockies. My dad was a missile silo tech during the Cold War. While I was flashing peace signs and marching against Viet Nam and Nixon, my father was actually someone with his finger on the Button. It was a job to him."

That was a lot for Paul to take in, in light of his current head full of cotton and chaos. He couldn't tell how old Kate was, even though sizing-up people's ages, weight, ethnicity, hair color, and distinguishing characteristics was a prerequisite in his former line of work. His mind rushed to calculate; if she protested Viet Nam and Nixon she had to be at least fifteen in 1974, the year Nixon resigned, which meant she had to be close to sixty.

"You were at protests during Nixon?" Paul asked, trying not to be too overt in figuring her age.

"Actually I was only around five. My big sister who was fifteen took me along with her."

That put her somewhere in the fiftyish range, which pleased him, because there just was something about her. That something that may not hit one for days, weeks, months, or in Paul's case, years. But he felt it. Was it the aroma she exuded, her caring demeanor, or maybe just his damaged condition?

"My older brother took me to a bar when I was five, but never to a protest," Paul said, smiling.

"You start early in New York."

"Yeah, and we finish early, too. Look I'm really sorry to cause concern and a disruption...."

"No cause for concern. No disruption. Don't forget you're in room 8. There's a certain…sensitivity for strange occurrences in this room."

"Oh, right. I didn't even think of that. Again, my apologies. By the way, is there coffee in the lobby office?"

"Yes, and some breakfast pastries. Stop by, won't you?" She asked, with a soft smile and went on her way.

"Thank you, I will," Paul said, watching her as she glided away, the dirt crunching under her Birkenstocks.

He felt like he already blew it. Here she was, looking in on a hung-over stranger, who probably reeks of saloon, admitting to screaming nightmares and hanging out in bars from the age of five. And in the infamous room 8 of death, no less. Just wait until she finds out that he's a former narc. That's probably worse than having your finger on the Button in her book.

After breakfast and a shower, Paul's head began to clear and he decided to call Tracy. He didn't want to appear to be prying into her life, but that is what he wanted to do. He thought how ironic it was that he, an undercover narc most of his life, was sitting on the bed where a rock star had overdosed and died at the age of 27. Was it worth it? He could have just as easily died at the same age as Gram Parsons from drugs. Not from ingesting them, but from chasing drugs just the same. His life had been spared by dumb luck on more than one occasion. There were chases, stings, breaking down doors, busts that went terribly wrong, but the most dramatically nightmare-inducing incident was the time a gun misfired while a bad guy pulled the trigger with the barrel inserted into Paul's mouth. Luckily, his backup arrived in the nick of time, but the ensuing struggle broke several teeth, which still pisses him off since one of the molars was still a jagged reminder.

He punched the numbers into his cell and called Tracy.

"Hello," Tracy's voice could be heard over a crowd of people enjoying music outdoors somewhere.

"Hi, hon, it's your old man."

"Hi, I can hardly hear you. It's a little crazy here."

"Is everything all right? Are you okay?"

"Yes, everything is fine. We're just relaxing by the pool."

"Do you want me to come down and…do anything for you? Do you need anything?"

"No, we're really busy with planned events for a couple more days. This is a big week in Palm Springs. I'll call you then. Take care."

"Yes, you too."

He had no right to think that Tracy would suddenly accept him into her life as a normal father might be at this point in time. He was well aware that she probably had no concept of the pain he suffered being forced away by her mom, and the certain brainwashing his ex had laid on her. Thank God Greta occasionally put in a good word for him. But here he was, in the middle of nowhere on a dead man's bed, pondering his future. Without his elaborate support group of neighborhood friends, he felt more alone than ever. And as he looked out his window, across the patio, he could see the hills of Joshua Tree National Park in the distance. Maybe that's just what he needed to clear his head. Maybe he needed to be in the middle of nowhere. Far from everything he was used to. Everything that made him what he was up until that moment. No bars and buses filled with pizza, kegs, and friends. No back-up units busting through tenement doors to save his ass. No girlfriend-of-the-month hookups.

He put on his most comfortable sneakers and a pair of shorts. He was ready for a long hike in the park. Clear the head. Get a new perspective. He loved long hikes at the beach and in Van Cortlandt Park in the Bronx. Never once did he say after a long hike, well that sucked.

Kate was behind the counter in the office reading a magazine. She hadn't seen him through the window, so he could have just gone on his way unnoticed. But he decided to stop in.

"Any more pastries left?"

Kate looked up from her magazine and smiled. "No more pastries. But there's some fresh coffee. How are you feeling?"

"Like forty bucks. I'm going for a hike in the park. Any suggestions?"

"Where's your water?"

"Water? I need water?"

"You always need water. The desert will suck everything out of you. And with any exertion at all, it can be deadly." She walked over to a small refrigerator and pulled out a bottle of water. "Take this with you. Do you have a protein bar?"

"I'm not really hungry."

"Take this," she said handing him a protein bar from under the counter. "Do you like the ocean?"

"I love the ocean."

"Do you fear the ocean?"

"Hmmm. Yeah, I guess I do."

"Love the desert. Fear the desert. Try a marked trail at first," she said, pulling out a map of the park and laying it out on the counter. "Try this Lost Horse Mine trail. It's a good newbie hike."

"I'm in pretty good shape, you know?"

"I can see that. Just start slowly," she said, softly putting her hand on his.

"Duly noted. Thanks."

"Stay on the trails, and watch out for rattlesnakes."

"Seriously?"

"Seriously. And take my number in case you run into any trouble," she said, writing down her number and handing it to him. "Just punch in my number on your phone."

Paul complied. "I don't know what kind of help I could need, but I appreciate it. Bye."

He left the office and thought that perhaps that was just a subtle way of her giving him her phone number. That made him smile and think to himself that he still had it.

The road to the park entrance was longer than Paul had anticipated. All around him were rocky hills, hardscrabble, Joshua trees, yuccas, and the occasional house or horse ranch in the distance. The park entrance was a proper gate and park ranger kiosk. Paul showed his pass and noticed the friendly female ranger with the Smokey Bear hat was not carrying a firearm. *How dangerous could it be?* He thought to himself.

It was almost 1 P.M. and he noticed the temperature had risen over 15 degrees from the morning and was now sitting at 95 on his dash temperature gauge. *Not too bad. It's a dry heat.* Paul didn't realize it, but he was experiencing a common affliction many drunks go through the morning after a bender: hangover euphoria. That's where one convinces oneself that despite blacking out, throwing up, having the horrors and a splitting headache, and swearing off alcohol forever, things were starting to look up and a cold beer would go great right about now. But first he needed to go on this hike to prove to himself he could do it. Hiking up a trail in desert heat? So what. It's nothing compared to running up a dark stairway chasing a perp in 100 degree heat and 100 percent humidity on the Lower East Side. He had to deal with life-and-death situations on the job with worse hangovers and less sleep than this.

He followed the signs for LOST HORSE MINE and parked his car in a dirt lot where there were two other vehicles parked. He switched off the ignition and could immediately feel the cabin heat up. He opened the door and a rush of hot, dry air enveloped him, causing him to gasp. He stepped out of the vehicle and the only sound he heard was the dirt crunching under his feet. He closed the door and paused to take in the silence. He closed his eyes and could feel the hot air pressing on his skin as if he was in some kind of pressure chamber. He heard a hum in the distance and opened his eyes expecting to see maybe a model airplane or a kid with one of those radio-controlled drones, but saw nothing. The hum became a buzz and at the other end of the lot, coming between two large rock piles, was a dark cloud, changing shape as it got closer to him. *What the hell is this?* He thought, frozen as it came towards him, increasing in volume and intensity.

"What the hell?" he said aloud. "Holy shit! It's a bee swarm!"

Suddenly the black cloud of what seemed like a billion bees darkened the space and totally surrounded him. Some touched him, poked him, and went right up to his ear hole, scaring the bee-Jesus out of him. But just as suddenly as this cloud of buzzing bees appeared it was gone. Floating away, across the lot and into the open desert, disappearing in the distance. He never imagined such a thing. A small car pulled into the lot and parked by him. Two twentyish females emerged and began putting on their backpacks.

"Did you see that?"

"See what?" the girl on the driver side asked.

"That swarm? The billion or so bugs. I mean bees. It was a huge black cloud. Of bees."

"Uh, no. Missed that."

Paul could tell they thought he was a nut. The two hikers took off up the trail, peering back at him as they briskly walked ahead. He figured he'd wait a few minutes so they wouldn't think he was stalking them. He walked around the parking lot just to check out the lay of the land from the other side, and in each direction as far as the eye could see there was the same landscape he had been seeing since he arrived in the high desert: dirt, sand, tumbleweeds, rocks, boulders, Joshua trees, and yuccas leading to rocky hills and mountains in the distance. It all looked the same.

Like one gigantic empty lot. There was nothing there. No tall trees, no green grass, no lakes, rivers, ponds, swamps, meadows, critters scurrying, or birds squawking. What was the point? He could look at this Joshua tree in the parking lot, or hike for an hour and see a few more. Paul walked back to the Escape, and from under a pile of rags pulled out a pint of Vodka. He took a long gulp. Then another. Maybe that would help liven up his journey.

He was a few hundred yards up the trail and the two hikers that preceded him were nowhere in sight. The trail took a turn through some giant boulders that must have been 40 feet high and gave him some welcome shade for a few minutes. But when he emerged at the other end of the boulders he saw the real trail: a steep rocky incline that switch-backed up a mountain of rock and boulders. The sun was beating down on him and the heat was being reflected off the rocks and dirt. He picked up his pace to conquer the obstacles that were ahead. This was nothing. As the trail got steeper he began bounding up the path. It was for tourists, right? Probably on the weekends there were Cub Scouts trooping up here with little old lady den mothers. Maybe even church groups with pastors pushing seniors in wheelchairs. He wasn't a senior citizen, despite the mailings he got monthly from the AARP since he turned fifty.

Higher and higher, faster and faster he went. He paused at a switch-back about half-way up and gazed at the vista laid out before him. He noticed he was breathing more deeply. He could control that, right? He was light-headed, but that was normal under these conditions. It's hot, he's jogging up-hill. He can do this. He remembers the time he was playing in little league on a hot and humid summer afternoon. That was the hottest he had ever been in his eight years on the planet up until that moment.

He was in right field. No shade. A long inning. Sun just beating down on him. *Should I keep going? Yes.* Up, up up, the vistas were amazing, as far as the eye could see, no cars, no people, no buildings, no structures of any kind. The horizon goes on forever with nothingness. Just miles and miles for 360 degrees of sand dirt rocks boulders hills mountains. *Should I wave to my coach, Mr. Paccione, and tell him I don't feel well? That I think I'm going to be sick. I, might, faint….*

At a sharp turn in a switch-back, Paul for a moment thought he was seeing another black bee swarm, but no. It was black spots, getting larger and larger as he collapsed like his bones had turned to Silly Putty and he fell backwards down an embankment. He rolled down ten feet or so and landed on a flat surface of soft dirt, missing a large boulder by inches. He was unconscious.

Kate was registering a guest at the front desk when her phone rang. She looked at the number. It was a New York number. She swiped to answer.

"Excuse me," she said to a young German couple signing in. "Hello, is this Paul?"

All she heard was a whispering wind blowing through something…a mesquite tree, cypress? Is that someone breathing? "Hello? Hello? Are you there? Did you butt-call me? Hello?"

"Eez everyting okay?" asked the German man.

"Excuse me. Someone will be here in a minute to take care of you."

After getting another worker to take over, Kate grabbed two bottles of water and headed to her 1989 Bronco. She checked the cargo area for her emergency first aid kit, retrieved it, and put it on the passenger seat. The spinning tires threw dirt and rocks behind as she sped to the park road. Her mind raced, *If he just butt-called me and he's walking up the Lost Horse Mine trail, I'll make some excuse as to why I'm up there. Hopefully that's all it is.*

She showed her yearly pass at the kiosk and sped to the lot closest to the trailhead for Lost Horse Mine. She saw Paul's car in the lot, looked in the window, and saw his bottle of water still on the front seat next to his park map and energy bars. *What a knucklehead!* She double-timed it up the trail, scanning the areas next to it. Two female hikers came towards her.

"Have you seen a man hiking? Fiftyish. Olive skinned."

"No."

"Thank you," Kate said as she rushed passed them.

Am I panicking for nothing? Am I being ridiculous? Butt-calls happen all the time. It doesn't mean someone is having a medical emergency!

She stopped suddenly when she smelled a strong scent that usually emanates off a Creosote bush after a rainfall. But there wasn't a cloud in the sky. She turned slowly, and down the embankment next to the turn in the switchback there was a grouping of Creosote bushes about 20 yards down.

"Paul!" She shouted as she adroitly negotiated the rocks and loose dirt towards the shoes she saw between two bushes. *How did the hell did he get in that position?*

"Paul!" She went around the bush to where his head was situated. He was breathing. "Thank you, Lord!" She began her routine. Pulse? Normal. Body temperature? Above normal probably. Injuries? Blood? Nothing obvious. She began pressing on his arms, shoulders, and feeling his head. A nasty bump, but no blood. She opened her bottle of water and caressed his head so she could put some water on his lips. His eyelashes fluttered and he moaned.

"Paul. Paul. Can you hear me?"

He slowly opened his eyes. "Oh. Yeah. My. Head. Where am I? Marcy? Is that you?"

Paul had woken up from being unconscious many times. On the job there were two car accidents, three times falling or pushed down stairs, one time hit over the head with a frying pan, and one time falling one story down an abandoned building's elevator shaft. Not-on-the- job unconsciousness included getting sucker-punched in a bar league football post-game rumble, a car accident, trying to break up two bar fights, and waking up several times in various apartments, hotel rooms, and subway cars after drunken blackouts.

"It's Kate. From the Joshua Tree Inn."

"Shit. Don't tell me room number 8 killed me?"

"No, you collapsed. Probably a light case of heat stroke and dehydration from a heavy dose of booze the night before."

"Oh. How did you find me?"

"You butt-called me?"

"I did? People always tell me I'm talking out of my ass, and for once it paid off I guess." He began to come to and sat up. "But how did you find me here?"

"I got lucky, I guess."

"*You* got lucky?

"Take it easy and take little sips," Kate said still caressing his head gently.

"I feel like a jerk. My first hike in the high desert and it almost kills me."

"Respect the desert."

"Right, you said that didn't you? But tell me what happened. How on God's green earth, I mean brown earth, did you find me?" Paul said, sitting a little straighter and starting to look more like himself. He began to pat his hair, causing dirt and some pebbles to fall out.

"You butt-called me, I guess. My phone rang and all I could hear was the wind whistling and what I thought was breathing."

"But doesn't a butt-call require a butt to call?" He reached into the front-buttoned pocket of his shirt and pulled out his phone. "How do you butt-call from your chest?"

Kate took the phone from Paul, examined it and pushed some buttons. "That's crazy."

"It must have hit the dirt just right," Paul said, putting the phone back in his front pocket. "Stranger things have happened. Oh, yeah, when I parked my car, a black cloud surrounded me and it was a bee swarm. It was like I was in a tornado of bees. The buzzing was overwhelming. Then they disappeared into the distance."

"A black bee swarm?"

"Yeah."

"I've been here for years, I've never seen one."

"Stick with me, who knows what you'll see. Let's get out of here."

"Are you sure you're okay?"

"Yeah. Just a damaged ego. You probably think I'm a bum. Hung-over, know-it-all, reckless, foolish city boy."

"True. But maybe there's hope. Let's stop at my house. It's on the way and I'll fix you up. Let's leave your car in the lot and we'll come back for it later. I don't want you to drive alone just yet."

"One of the only times I almost got in a fist fight with my best friend Mickey O'Connor in over 40 years of friendship was when he wanted to take my car keys from me because he thought I was too drunk to drive."

"Were you?"

"Of course."

"Did you drive your car?"

"Nope. But I didn't talk to him for a week."

"Then what happened?"

"Nothing. We never mentioned it again. Let's go in your car."

Kate watched Paul in the rear-view mirror, sprawled out in the back seat of the Bronco trying to rest. She was used to dealing with substance abuse. It was only two years since she lost her husband on Christmas after a night of eating, drinking, and secretly taking the drugs that would kill him as he slept on the living room couch. She hasn't had a drink since. Yes, she still has the occasional bowl of weed, and yes, she had a medical marijuana card. In her eyes marijuana is another natural substance that has existed since Mother Nature sprinkled the earth with natural remedies. She also believes that pre-historic ape-like creatures made a quantum leap of self-awareness and consciousness after ingesting certain hallucinogenic fungi and plants.

"We're here, Paul," Kate said as she stroked his forehead tenderly, while also trying to determine if he had a fever. He didn't. "I think you should stay at my place for a little while until I think you're out of the woods. Heat stroke is a funny thing. And we're still not sure if that bump on your head did any real damage."

Paul straightened himself onto the seat, and still had a look in his eyes that told Kate he wasn't 100 percent just yet. She knew that a bump on the head could lead to a brain bleed and it wasn't smart to be alone for the next little while.

"I'm fine. Ouch," he said grabbing at the back of his neck. "Okay, doc, I'm with you. Just give me the word."

Paul felt a little woozy once he stood outside the vehicle, but his eyes widened noticeably as he looked around. "Where the hell are we? Am I in Bedrock?"

"Bedrock?" Kate laughed.

"Yeah, you know. Where the Flintstones lived? Look at that pile of boulders! It's like somebody balanced them there!"

"Well somebody did. Come inside," she said, leading him across the dirt driveway.

There wasn't another house in sight. The massive front yard was a mini park with Joshua trees, cacti, and several larger trees. In the nearby distance was a rock pile of boulders and rocky hills littered with more Joshua trees and also boulders, and clumps of prickly green vegetation.

Paul stopped after a few steps. *"Ssshhh."* He stood motionless for close to a minute.

Kate studied him; eyes closed, head slowly turning, nostrils widened, his face relaxing with each breath.

"I hear it."

"What?"

"What I've been longing for. Dead. Silence."

Paul inhaled the dry, hot air. He could smell that strange, heady aroma he noticed once he was in the land of Joshua trees. The ringing in his ear, that sound ingrained in his brain of growing up in the shadow of the elevated subway line and across from the Major Deegan Expressway. A hum in the ear caused by a lifetime of shouts and cries and curse words and screams and cheers and rock concerts and juke boxes of New York City began to ever so slightly dissipate and let the total nothingness of silence began to creep into his head.

"What is that smell? That fragrance?" He asked, his eyes still closed as he stood, his arms folded in front of him, hand on his chin, like a Jack Benny yogi.

"That's the creosote bush. When it rains, it exudes an intoxicating aroma that blankets the high desert. It makes me high. It could you, too."

"Which one is that?"

"See that bush there? It's a creosote bush. Some say that a bush around that size could be close to 500 years old. A bush twice that size could be a thousand or two thousand years old."

"You mean to say, that that bush over there, that large one, could have been alive when Jesus walked the earth?"

"Yes."

"This is a lot for me to handle, right now. I think I need to sit down, cool off and have a large drink. Of water." Paul said walking towards the front door of the house.

From the outside, the house seemed ordinary. A covered front porch with a wooden table and two chairs. The walls were stucco painted nearly the same color as the dirt, sand, and rocks that seemed to be everywhere, whether small like the ones in the driveway or gigantic like the boulders in the distance.

As soon as Kate stuck a key in the door, it became apparent that Kate had a large dog.

"Don't worry. He doesn't bite if he knows I like you," Kate said with a wry smile.

Paul still felt woozy, but nevertheless began trying to analyze that statement from Kate. *Likes me how?* He wondered. Then he flashed on being in sixth grade and realized how that mystery of girls liking boys was yet to be solved. He followed her into the front room and a medium-sized mutt wagged his tail energetically as he jumped back and forth between Kate and himself.

"I guess you like me," Paul said, patting the dog's head.

"That's Chunky. He's part pug, part German Shepherd and part raccoon."

"I see that around the eyes. Does he wash his food?"

"Only if he doesn't trust who opened the can. Sit over here, and put your feet up. You're under my care for the next little while."

As plain and nondescript as the outside of the house seemed, the inside was anything but. The ceilings were vaulted with rough hand-hewn timbers. Hanging in the middle of the room was a chandelier made of an old wagon wheel. The walls were adorned with paintings, etchings, drawings, and artifacts of Native American Indians and cowboy scenes. The colorful Mexican tile floors were covered with assorted area rugs placed throughout. A large table in the middle of the large room, which also served as a kitchen, was constructed of actual limbs and branches of trees with an oval-shaped glass tabletop. On tables, shelves, and on the floor were various statues of Buddha, Jesus, the Virgin Mary, St. Francis of Assisi, and some others he didn't recognize.

"Wow. This place is amazing. I feel like I'm in some sort of cosmic cowboy and Indian chapel."

She guided him to an overstuffed upholstered chair, sat him down, and placed his feet on an ottoman.

"This is a great room!" Paul said, finally feeling comfortable.

"Actually it is a *great* room. That's what it's called in many indigenous cultures, from Eskimos, to Native Americans, to Caribbean Islanders. There was always a room where meals were prepared and families gathered to eat, relax, and socialize. Like a combination kitchen, living room, and family room."

"I don't know. Kind of sounds like the Bronx bar I used to hang in, and I wouldn't call that so great."

"See! Commonality is everywhere! I'm making you some special tea. Are you hungry?"

"I'm not sure. I still feel a little bit light-headed."

"We'll hold off on the food."

Kate walked over to a table that had a Bose radio/CD player, picked up a CD and placed it into the slot. Strange hums and long tones began emanating from the player and filling the room.

"What is that? The sounds of the humpback whales thing?"

"No. Tibetan singing bowls. Have you ever heard of them?"

"Nope."

"Every rub your finger over the lip of a crystal wine glass and it makes a humming sound?"

"Oh, yeah. Many times. Too many times."

"Same principle, only with large crystal bowls, and various amounts of oils in each one. Here's the CD cover."

The image on the cover looked like a UFO. But it was anchored to the rocky landscape, which looked like it could have been Kate's backyard or anywhere in the local vicinity.

"I'll bite. What's this?"

"The Integratron. It's a few miles from here. It's built over a vortex of earth energies and was designed by a Venusian to attract UFO's."

"Venusian? You mean someone from Venus? The planet?"

"Yes, and they give sound baths to the accompaniment of this music made by Tibetan singing bowls."

"I think I must have hit my head harder than I thought because now I think I'm hearing things. Sound baths? Aliens from Venus? UFO's? I think I need a nap."

"You do need a nap. Here, have some tea, close your eyes, and just relax. I have some things to do around the house. Give me a shout if you need anything."

It didn't take long for Paul to fall fast asleep after just two sips of tea. His head tilted slowly from right to left almost in time to the slow vibrating sounds emanating from the speakers, bouncing off the walls, tile floor, and rafters. From the expression on his face he looked at peace, with Chunky at his feet and Kate quietly tending to little housework chores around the home. Until suddenly Paul's eyes popped open and he grabbed at his throat.

"Where's the bathroom?" he shouted into the empty room.

"Over here!" Kate replied from down the hall.

Paul followed her voice, rushed into the bathroom and knelt in front of the toilet. He hadn't eaten much, so it was mostly dry heaves and some water he was throwing up. Kate held his head until he stopped retching.

"Are you done?"

"I wish I knew the answer to that," he said, standing slowly.

"Those are clean towels, new toothbrushes in here, and everything you need if you want to take a shower and clean up."

"You know a shower would be great."

"Do you need any help?"

Paul did something he doesn't usually do. He enabled his mouth filter. He found Kate very attractive. He didn't know many women like her in New York, the earth-mother type. Oh, he saw them around in the Village, but didn't really know any. Unfiltered Paul might have said, *Yeah, I could use some help scrubbing my back.* Instead he said, "I'm fine. But thanks."

"You're sure? I don't want you falling in the shower and hitting your head. I'd have a hard time explaining this scenario to the police."

"I was thinking the same thing!"

Kate smiled as she closed the bathroom door.

The force of the water was much stronger than the weak showers at the string of motels he had stayed at for the past several days. He turned the showerhead to the massage position and pointed it at the back of his head and down his neck and spine. He hadn't felt this good in a while. Days? Weeks? Decades? He wasn't sure. He heard the door open and for a split second thought he might have a visitor coming to join him in the shower for a splash.

"Here's a robe," Kate announced, as she placed it on the sink.

"Thanks," Paul shouted over the noise of the flowing water.

It was a man's robe. Paul's detective mind kicked in and he began examining the robe after he stepped out of the shower. He felt slightly weird putting on what was probably her boyfriend or ex-husband's robe, but after talking about aliens, UFO's, and singing bowls, he figured a lot of weird was in his future. He was wearing the robe and drying his hair with a towel when Kate knocked.

"Do you need anything else?" She asked from behind the closed door.

"Do you have a razor and some shaving cream? I have to shave my legs."

"Yeah, right. I'll get them."

The door opened and Kate stuck her arm in with a disposable razor and a can of Barbasol.

"You can come in. I'm wearing the robe."

Kate stepped through the door.

"It's a little big on you."

"The guy who wears this is about six-two, 250 pounds, left-handed, smokes cigarettes, and probably likes his weed in a pipe."

"Jesus, don't spook me like that. It was my husband's. Are you a medium?"

"No, I'm half-baked. Some psychics claim to be detectives. Most detectives have the same skills that psychics use," Paul said, moving his hands gracefully in the air in front of his face. "It's called deductive reasoning. Husband?"

"Yes, he passed away. A couple years ago," Kate said, reaching out and touching the worn sleeve on the robe.

"I'm so sorry."

"Thanks."

"Well, it's a few sizes too long for me, especially the arm length. The cloth belt is a little frayed about six inches past where I would tie it. On the left cuff there's still a slight smell of cigarette ashes and a burn mark that didn't come out in the wash. The left pocket has a hole in the bottom, perhaps from something in there that he nervously gripped tightly, as though he didn't want to part with it. Am I being too personal?"

Kate pushed the toilet lid down and sat on it. "Yes, you are. No you're not. You're spot on. He puffed a lot. And did coke. And his cholesterol was terrible. Was overweight and had diabetes. And...."

"I'm sorry. I shouldn't have...."

"No, it's okay. That was amazing how you pieced that together. You must have a very analytical mind."

"Enough to get by. I'm a cop. Was a cop. Detective. Lieutenant."

Kate stood up and her mood switched abruptly from pity party to full attention. "A cop? A New York City cop? A lieutenant?"

"Oh yeah. I just retired."

"A detective?"

"Well, for the last ten years. Before that, I was undercover."

"Undercover?"

"Narcotics."

"A narc?"

"10-4."

Kate sat back down on the toilet lid. "Wow. A narc. A New York narc. That blows me away."

Paul gathered himself, as he tried to explain. "I mean, really, when you came in to the bathroom, I thought I was just going to tell you I was just kidding about shaving my legs. It all just kind of came out. Unfiltered. Sorry."

"I need that. Sometimes I think I'm too filtered. I puff on occasion."

"So do a lot of my friends. Not an issue."

"Do you?"

"No. Never."

"I'm going to prepare some food," Kate said somewhat absent-mindedly as she left the bathroom.

Well I probably just loused up everything right there, Paul thought to himself.

Chapter Five

Although Paul had showered and shaved, he didn't feel comfortable in his clothes, which were still sweaty and dirty from his foolhardy foray deep into the desert, unprepared. There was a kitchen island with several large bowls of food and two table settings upon it. Kate motioned for him to take a seat as she began doling out portions onto the plates. Paul had an inkling as to what the food was, but by no means was he certain. One bowl looked like it had shiny, curly seaweed with ground-up bacon bits on it. Another looked like a bowl of sour cream. And another looked like a mush of something orange with green blobs in it. That last bowl did not smell familiar or tasty.

"I take it you're a vegan?" Paul asked, leaning in to take in the aromas emanating from his oversized plate now filled with the colorful foods.

"No, just a vegetarian. I'm addicted to yogurt. I'm also gluten-free."

"You know, I didn't realize how tasty gluten was, until I tasted food that didn't have it. Oh, I'm sorry. I'm sure this gluten-free food is the exception. And, um, what are these dishes? They look great, by the way."

Kate explained that the bowls consisted of non-fat Greek plain yogurt, pumpkin puree with whole Brussel sprouts and kale, not with ground bacon bits, but with ground flax seeds.

"I hope you don't mind eating my food. It's what I eat. Every day."

"Every day? Like 365 days a year every day?"

"Yes. It saves me a lot of time. And I enjoy it."

Paul felt hungry, but still a bit nauseated, so he treaded carefully as he tasted the small amounts of food on his plate. "Do you have any bread?"

Kate went to the refrigerator, retrieved a bag of bread, removed two slices, and placed them on Paul's plate. "Would you like some almond butter?"

"Sure," Paul said, looking forward to biting into something he was familiar with that would have a solid consistency. He noticed the bread on the table was Ezekiel brand, with quotes from scripture on the bag.

"Is the bread okay?" Kate asked, taking a slice for herself.

"It's good. Very…."

"Health-foody?"

"Yes. Good description. I like it, but it's just a little different from what I'm used to."

Paul liked the almond butter, and put a good amount on his bread, of which he had already eaten four slices. He didn't like the yogurt, or the pumpkin puree with Brussels sprouts. The kale wasn't too bad, after he created his own French dressing by combining some ketchup, mustard, and mayonnaise and plopped a good amount on top. But he kept the displeasure to himself.

"If you're finished, why don't you relax in that chair while I clean up," Kate said as she put a CD in the player.

"No, I have to help clean up. I earn my keep."

"Great. Nice."

Paul followed Kate's lead, washing, drying, putting things away, as they listened to the music that seemed strangely familiar to him. He picked up the CD cover, and was surprised to see it was Ry Cooder playing with Indian musicians.

"Wow. Ry Cooder on Indian music. Weird. But I like it."

"That kind of sums up the high desert for lots of us."

"What?"

"Weird. But I like it," Kate said with a slightly crooked smile and a wink.

Paul didn't eat all that much and was feeling a little bit queasy as he sat in a comfortable chair with his feet up. But he didn't refuse when Kate offered some gluten-free brownies.

"You know, I don't even miss the gluten in these. Excellent!"

It didn't take long after the brownies were consumed with gusto that Paul was snoring away in the chair while Kate went about her business.

Paul was in the same chair that her husband used to nod out on. But usually that was from too much alcohol, or weed, or harder drugs. Yes, even heroin on occasion. She wouldn't be telling Paul about the heroin that ultimately killed him, yes, in that very chair. Kate had always hoped that by her example over the past 20 or so years her husband would notice her eating healthfully, exercising, improving her mind, and abstaining from alcohol and most drugs. Maybe it was because she shared the occasional bowl of weed with him that he thought everything else he did was okay. Like staying out all night getting high and jamming rock-and-roll with a bunch of twenty- and thirtysomethings. He just wouldn't accept the fact that he was on the wrong side of fifty and his organs weren't working like they used to. In fact, whenever Kate was successful in getting him to go to the doctor after a few brutal months of abusing his body, the proof was in his lab work. She always thought it was ironic that he – who believed in UFO's, aliens, ghosts, chem trails, and every other conspiracy spread by every all-night radio wacko – wouldn't believe the red numbers, arrows, and letters so plainly warning him of his imminent demise on the doctor's lab report. He paid dearly.

Kate suspected that's what she liked about Paul. Even though she didn't really know him, she had a feeling that he was a pragmatist. Here was a guy who spent his life making choices between good and evil. That's what a cop does, right? But there are bad cops. How did she know he wasn't one of them? She thought that Paul's snoring was even louder than her husband's. That could be an issue later on. Maybe. She hoped.

"I think I should go home," Paul said, after being awakened by one of his own explosively loud snores. "Could you take me back to the motel?"

Kate thought for a moment. *Should I offer spending the night here? I would have 20 years ago. What would he think of me? And how do I know I can trust him?*

"Sure, I'll take you now, before it gets too late, if that's okay with you?"

"Definitely. I'm ready. I'll pick up my car from the park tomorrow."

Once they were in the car and driving down the washboard dirt road, Paul didn't feel so good. He didn't say anything to Kate. He just wanted to sleep it off in private. He couldn't remember a time when he threw up twice in front a potential date, but that doesn't mean it didn't happen.

Kate dropped him off, and once room 8's door was closed he made a beeline for the bathroom, where he began throwing up again. He was glad he didn't barf in her car. As he put his head on his pillow with only his shoes kicked off, the room began to spin. He was worried. His mind raced. He didn't know Kate from Adam. Or Eve. Who knows what she really gave him to eat and drink? Or what was in that tea. Then it hit him. *The tea! The brownies. They were probably full of marijuana! How could I be so stupid?*

He calmed himself down by breathing slowly. He began to say a string of Hail Mary's, his go-to meditation chant for a Catholic kid. Once he knew his heart rate was down, he looked at the time, and picked up the phone.

"Hi, Tracy? It's your father," he said to his daughter's voice mail. "Listen, when you get a chance, give me a call. Okay, thanks."

He didn't really want to trouble her with his problem. He wasn't going to overdose on a little bit of weed tea and brownies. But he needed to talk to someone. Then the phone rang.

"Hi, it's me, Tracy. Is everything okay?"

"Yeah, um, listen. Do you know anything about pot brownies and stuff like that? I think I may have ingested something. I'm felling kind of ill."

"Yes, I do. But it shouldn't make you really sick. Unless you had like a bunch of them. Like five or six."

"No just one. And possibly some tea."

"And tea? Where did you get that stuff? Are you experimenting in the desert already?"

"No, I wasn't feeling well, and this woman from the motel, well long story short I think she slipped me this stuff without telling me. I was hiking in the desert and collapsed and she sort of rescued me, and I think I might have had a touch of heat stroke, and ate some weird food, like yogurt and kale...."

"Dad. You had heat stroke. You weren't feeling well. You ate weird stuff. And now you feel worse. Are you very high?"

"As a matter of fact, um, no. Just kind of sick."

"I doubt she slipped you anything. Ask her."

"Ask her?"

"Duh, yeah."

"By the way, what's going on with you? What's happening?"

"Oh, we're still just hanging out and relaxing. We think we'll be heading up your way in a day or two or three on the way to Twentynine Palms, so I'll let you know."

"Great. Thanks."

"Ask her."

"I will. Goodnight."

He didn't know what to do. Should he ask her? Wouldn't that pretty much destroy any hope he had of possibly pursuing this as a relationship? *But I'm not even high! I feel sick!* He thought to himself. *What a paranoid jerk! What a moron. What's wrong with me?* Paul was soon fast asleep.

KNOCK KNOCK KNOCK

Paul woke up and looked at the red numbers on his bedside clock. 10:15! He still had his clothes on, and it took him a minute or two to realize he felt pretty good. Just thirsty. He picked up the half a bottle of water from the table and answered the door. There she was. Kate looked even more beautiful than before. Her thick hair was tied back and her fully exposed face, neck, and eyes made her look like a teenaged hippie chick.

"How are you this morning? Did you get enough sleep? I only have a minute, I'm due back on the desk," she asked, earnestly.

"I feel surprisingly good. Thanks so much for last night," he said almost whispering, as a middle-aged couple passed by the doorway on the patio. "By the way, I meant to ask you, what kind of tea was that. I really liked it."

"Shit, I should have told you," Kate said, her hand swiftly darting up to her chin.

Paul was frightened. Would she really slip him pot without him knowing?

"It was that St. John's Wort. It's all-natural and it's supposed to help you sleep. But some people don't react well to it."

"I feel great. Thanks. I'll stop by later."

He closed the door and leaned against it. Once a cop always a cop. Case solved.

Tracy wasn't ready to face her father. She knew she would have to eventually tell him the truth about her West Coast trip. And it terrified her. Yes, she knew her mom poisoned her from an early age against Paul. But the nastiest, most vile descriptions of him always seemed to come from her mom when she was the most wasted. When she was very young, around four or five, she thought that when her mom talked about her father in such awful ways, it was what made mommy so mean. Just the mere mention of her daddy made her mommy loud, angry, and disgusting to the point where she would fall asleep, sometimes next to her own vomit in bed. And it was always her grandma who would come to the rescue, clean up the mess, and explain to her that her mommy was very sick, and her daddy was actually a nice person. It wasn't daddy who was making mommy sick. And some day she would understand.

It only took her to about the age of seven or eight to realize that her mother was an alcoholic and abused drugs. In fact it was easier to figure that out from watching TV shows than it was to realize that there was no such thing as Santa Claus. Once that became a fact of life, Tracy and her mom began to switch roles. The daughter worried about the mom, took care of her, went to the store, cooked meals, and cleaned up after her. By the time Tracy was a teenager, she and her grandmother talked about her mother as if they were her parents. Rehab became a running joke. If she was so messed up that she actually agreed to it, she usually managed to come out of it with some new junkie boyfriend or drug dealer connection.

But then she realized her father wasn't Satan in the flesh. After years of Al-Anon meetings as a family member of an addict, she knew that sometimes a spouse has to leave. And knowing now through her grandmother that Paul footed the bills, kept close tabs on her from a distance her entire life, and even secretly drove hours from New York City just to observe her from afar, she realized that he was a special man. But that wouldn't make it any easier to tell him that she was a lesbian. And on top of that, she was going to marry her girlfriend and join the Marines so they could both be in the Corps together. In the meantime, sitting by the pool, playing softball, working out, playing golf and volleyball were excellent ways to keep her mind off the day when she would tell him the truth about herself. If he disowns her again, then that's his life choice, not hers. She was ready for whatever happens.

After taking a cab to pick up his SUV in the parking lot, Paul drove to the Frontier Café for breakfast, and sat alone at an outdoor table. It was late morning and about 90 degrees, but it didn't feel hot to him. He didn't even mind the piping hot cup of black coffee, and spicy huevos rancheros. There was something about the heat and the air and the dust that made one slow down. Even breathe a little slower. The cars in the desert were dirtier, and it was easy to pick out the local desert rats, as opposed to the tourists from L.A. or Europe. Desert rats had that dark brown tan with creased leathery lines across their faces, the moisture having been sucked out of their skin and organs after decades of exposure to the sun. But they still had a glint in their crow's feet-lined eyes, full of stories to be told if you were bold enough to ask and patient enough to listen. As he got a third warm-up on his coffee he wondered about Kate. Was she telling the truth about the tea and brownies? Maybe she was setting him up for next time when she really would put some pot in his tea and brownies, like people who poison their spouses by putting a pinch of arsenic or a few drops of anti-freeze in their morning coffee. Or tea. But why would she do that? Her husband died from drugs. Maybe she blamed cops or the drug war or the government for his death? After all Paul wasn't just a cop. He was an undercover narc. Then Paul stopped himself. He was still thinking like a narc. Looking for clues in everything. Noticing things like a bulge in a waist band – *a gun?* – a drop of sweat on a brow – *why so nervous?* – or an eyeball looking at something nearby – *what's he up to?* – could mean the difference between life and death. He never wore a wire while undercover, so he knew very well that all he had to rely on were his own senses and gut instincts.

After breakfast he finally felt good. Whether it was the food, the coffee, the five glasses of water, or just being fully recovered from his heat prostration episode he wasn't really sure. Maybe it was the St. John's Wort.

There was an envelope on the floor inside his room. It was from Kate. *If you'd like, meet me at the Integratron later today. I have two reservations for a sound bath. Text me if you can make it.*

Paul pulled out his phone and texted, *Yes, I'll meet you there. Let me know when. Do I need to bring my bathing suit?*

Immediately she responded, *No. Just your birthday suit.*

Paul laughed, then stopped. What if she meant it? What if it was a nudist thing? What if it was with other people? Paul had gone skinny dipping a couple of times with girls, but that was when they were in their early twenties and it was a just a big old drunken late-night party with friends at the beach.

Paul laid down on the bed, kicked off his shoes, and instructed himself that he wasn't going to let this experience frighten him. Here he was, 3,000 miles and a lifetime away from his past. From the time he was in first grade he wore a uniform of some kind, whether it was the uniform of Catholic grammar school and high school, or the police force, or the uniform of jeans and sports team t-shirts worn while hanging out with friends in the same old neighborhood bars where fathers, uncles, and grandfathers used to hang out. It was time to start thinking differently. Stop being suspicious of everything and everybody, and start seeing the world with new eyes. Listening with new ears. And a sound bath is a perfect place to begin. Nude or clothed.

To his left, the red rubber ball of a sun was just beginning to drop behind the rocky hills as Paul drove on the two-lane blacktop called Old Woman Springs Road. On the right, the mountains were becoming purple mountains majesty. With every mile the landscape became a little more barren, the fences fewer, and the abandoned ramshackle sheds more prevalent. He passed through Flamingo Heights, a curious name since the closest wild flamingo was several thousand miles away and the heights were a good five miles to his right and left. He made a right onto Reeche Road, the first side street that was not a dirt road in quite a while. And after another turn and five miles later, there it was!

It certainly looked like a UFO, sitting in the middle of a dirt lot behind a wooden and wire fence. It was bright white, sort of like a geodesic dome, but not quite. It had windows on the top portion and some sort of cylinders every few feet protruding outward as if they were remnants of some sort of propeller. It was futuristic yet had an ancient air about it, as if it was one of those drawings unearthed in a cave that revealed the earth was invaded by aliens in prehistoric times. He saw Kate's car in the lot and parked next it.

He walked over to the only door, which was quite ordinary for an intergalactic space ship, and just as he knocked a bunch of floodlights turned on and illuminated the structure brighter than a Vegas Strip fountain. The door opened and a hippie guy with a tie-dye shirt, white cotton pants, and long gray hair appeared. The smell of marijuana surrounded him like the dust cloud around Pig Pen.

"I'm here for the sound bath with Kate."

"Welcome! Are you a virgin?"

"Excuse me?"

"Is this your first sound bath?"

"Yes, I'm a virgin," Paul said as he stepped inside and hoped that it was a clothing-required event.

"I'll get Kate. She's upstairs," the hippie dude said as he bounded up a rickety set of stairs that was more like a ladder that might lead up to an attic.

The room was circular, all wood, with wires strung across from one side to the other just above his head. On the wall there were pictures portraying the construction of the building throughout the years. There were magazine and newspaper articles, diagrams, graphs, charts, and even maps of the solar system. He turned to the staircase when he heard it creaking with footsteps.

Kate was resplendent in her long white cotton dress, which seemed to have thread made of silver. Her hair was tied back and she had a narrow silver headband that was almost halo-like.

"I guess you met Ranger?" Kate said walking across the room.

"Oh, is he a park ranger? Paul asked.

"No. That's his name. Ranger. He'll be down in a minute to give us a short history lesson."

"Looks intriguing? Who else is here?"

"A friend of mine from meditation class and her friend."

The ladder shuddered with more feet descending. Ranger was first, backing down, followed by a woman in yoga pants, and a guy wearing black leather pants, which is not exactly something you normally see just after a 98-degree day in the high desert. At the bottom of the stairs the woman came towards Paul. She was about ten years younger than Kate and resembled her. Same calm, friendly, natural, demeanor. A new-age hippie. The guy, however, looked like he was wearing a costume rather than an outfit. His 50 pounds of extra weight made his leather pants look like they were the outside skin of a lumpy kielbasa. He had a three-day beard, a cracked front tooth, and a tattoo on his neck of some Chinese characters. Paul's plan to not look at the world like a cop was already falling by the wayside.

"This is Jasmine, and this is…."

"Ash," the guy said, with a voice made deep possibly by decades of booze and weed. "Thanks for letting me join in here with you."

Kate, Ash, Jasmine, and Paul waited for Ranger to begin his tour, as he was busy doing some kind of meditation underneath the center wooden pillar, where all the wires converged. His arms reached up and his index fingers touched two of the wires that were strung across the room. His eyes darted back and forth like he had just stuck his finger into an electrical outlet. Then he stopped and acted as if nothing happened.

Ranger didn't faze Paul in the least. He reminded him of the old hippies who frequented the streets and park benches of the East Village back home. As long as they had their weed, food to eat, and a roof over their head – in that order – they were harmless enough. But Ash? That was another story. Paul was getting a vibe from him similar to the harder-core dudes in the Village who supplied the Rangers of the world with weed and whatever else the market demanded, from cocaine cut with assorted poisons to pure black-tar heroin and the latest synthetic mishmash of hallucinogenic amphetamine-laced concoctions brewed-up in some Mumbai lye factory sure to make you want to bite your girlfriend's face off. He didn't know exactly why he sensed it, but he learned about three weeks into being a cop that it was better to be wrong about hunches and get your ass chewed-out by your captain, than to be chewed-up by rats as you rot in a Staten Island landfill. He'd stood at attention in his dress uniform behind a family all in black too many times to make those kinds of mistakes.

Ranger wasn't a bad tour guide at all. He explained the history of the Integratron. How the builder received the plans from a Venusian – yes, the kind that come from Venus – and was built on the convergence of energy forces that emanate across the universe and go through the earth like lasers of WiFi, and that all of this energy would be magnified through this structure to extend the human life form indefinitely and also attract visitors from other planets in their flying saucers. He also mentioned the nearby Giant Rock, and a brief explanation of the relationship between the Integratron and the people who holed up inside a cave at the Giant Rock and were thought to be Nazis during World War II, and how it somehow got blown up…but that was all lost in a marijuana coughing fit.

They were told how the upstairs of the Integratron was an acoustically perfect space so unique that no less than Moby himself recorded there. *Whoever the hell that is*, Paul thought to himself as he took up the rear position on the way up the rickety ladder right behind Ash's leather-clad rumpled ass.

Upstairs was impressive. It did have a feeling of being churchlike even though it was essentially devoid of any furniture or décor. At one end of the round room was a pile of yoga mats. At the other were six large clear glass bowls with varying amounts of liquid in them. Behind the bowls were large pillows. They were instructed to take a yoga mat and choose a spot where each of them would lie down on their backs and get "as comfortable as possible," as Ranger put it. Paul wondered if that meant to get naked. After going up the ladder behind Ash he hoped that wasn't the case. Apparently it wasn't. Kate put two yoga mats next to each other, as Jasmine and Ash put two together on the other side of the space. Ranger instructed them to be still and try not to make any sounds, or have sexual fantasies about anyone in the room. Which of course caused Paul to immediately think of what it would be like if they were naked in this spaced-out space as they lay on their backs on the yoga mats with their eyes closed.

Ranger took a seat on the pillow behind the six large bowls, and picked up two large mallets that were covered with thick cotton-like fabric at the top. He then began circling the top edges of the bowls, two at a time, and the bowls began to ring and vibrate at different frequencies. At first it seemed silly to Paul. He even secretly opened an eye to peek at Kate who kept her eyes shut tight and had a look of total peacefulness across her face. As the bowls rang, the vibrations seemed to be bouncing off the rounded walls and ceilings and continuing to reverberate around and up and down as if they were gaining strength as the seconds and minutes passed. Five minutes must have gone by, and the different frequencies seemed to be gaining strength as if they were joining together into one great vibration instead of hundreds of little ones.

With eyes closed, breathing slowed, and total relaxation taking him over, Paul could feel a tingling going through his body. He felt a lightness. Almost as if he was floating. He was imagining the frequencies entering through the top of his head, and creating swirls of colors as they traveled through his skin, muscles, bones, and organs, down to his legs, and exiting through the tips of his toes. He also began to see something behind his eyelids. It made him think of those times when he was clocked in the head, with a baseball or a low doorway or a fist – those things depicted as stars in cartoons – that you see just before you black out. But he wasn't blacking out, and those tingly things he was seeing with his eyes closed were swirling around his head as if it was hollow and were reverberating back and forth just like the sounds ricocheting around the space they were all laying down in. He discovered that he could send those sounds and images down out of his head and into other parts of his body, and that those parts became more alive, or at least he felt he was aware of every tiny little part of his body that the sounds and images were willed to travel to.

Paul did something he hadn't done in a long time. With all the times he had been high or buzzed or drunk on booze, or having sex, or running up a darkened stairway chasing somebody with his gun out, with adrenaline surging, it was always an exhilarating rush. But this was different. He was having some kind of a high, but he didn't understand where it was coming from. Was it coming from this place – the convergence of energy life forces shooting through the universe, the planet, the desert, this crazy UFO-attracting building, the good vibrations from the mysterious bowls – or from the inside of his head? So he just let himself go, to see where all this would take him. His mind was drifting, lost in the waves of sound energy going into, around, under, over, through his blood, bodily fluids, eyeballs, intestines, hair…then out of nowhere:

ZZZKKKRRROOOPPPPPPKKKKKKZZZZZZKAAAA GH!

Someone snored loud enough to rattle the tie-dye off a Grateful Dead t-shirt. Paul looked over and there was Ash snoring like an English bulldog with asthma. Ranger was so startled he stopped ringing the bowls with his mallet. But the snoring continued. Paul, Kate, and Jasmine looked at each other and just rolled their eyes. Ranger started it up again, but the moment was gone. After all that, Paul began worrying about Tracy, whether he needed to go to Walmart for anything, and what he might want for dinner; monkey mind was back, eyes closed or not.

Five minutes later, the sound-bath session was officially over as Ranger's vibrations ceased and he asked for the yoga mats to be placed neatly away. But Ash continued to snore away until Jasmine gave him several hard finger pokes in his chest.

"Wow that was great!" Ash said, rubbing the sleep from his eyes.

"I'm surprised you didn't wake yourself up. You couldn't hear a bunker-buster explode if *you* were napping nearby," Paul said.

"Do I snore?"

All laughed and began to put their yoga mats away. Jasmine approached Kate and asked if she and Paul would like to join them for dinner at her place, only a few miles from there. Kate discreetly pulled Paul aside and asked him.

"Is Ash going?" Paul whispered. Paul looked over and saw that Ash had heard his whisper, which had bounced off the perfectly acoustic dome and into his ear. He didn't want to seem like a dick so he agreed with a big smile and a nod on his face. "Sure. I'll leave my car here in the lot."

"If everybody drove on the left side of these washboard roads, it would help smooth them out," Kate said, driving down the bumpy dirt road in the dark.

"Even at night? In the dark? Seems dangerous to me," Paul said with his right hand holding the handle above the passenger-side door as he bounced in his seat. "Watch it!" Paul yelled, grabbing the wheel and pulling it to the right as Kate slammed on the brakes, barely missing a huge jackrabbit that darted across the road and into the darkness.

"Oh my. That happens a lot. I forget sometimes about the things that come out of nowhere. Especially at night," Kate said, rattled.

"Are you okay?"

"Yes."

"Do you want me to drive?"

"No. I'm fine. We're almost there," Kate said, concentrating on the road ahead.

Paul wondered how anybody could find their way around these pitch-black dirt roads at night. Even the darkest corners of New York are illuminated by the glow effect from billions of light bulbs across the city, bouncing off buildings, bridges, and the atmosphere itself.

Kate drove off the road and into what appeared to be merely another empty lot. The ride got bumpier, and after going over a berm or two, there was a small house that looked like one of the many abandoned sheds in various stages of decomposition throughout the desert. But this one was a survivor. A square building of concrete blocks and a flat roof, lit up by Kate's high beams.

"Here we are," Kate said, turning off the car and the headlamps.

Paul exited, closed his door, and looked up. Paul had never seen a sky so bright with stars, particularly the mushy mix of stars and lights across the moonless sky. "I don't think I've ever seen the Milky Way so clearly. It's amazing! In New York you're lucky if you can see the moon on a clear night."

Kate walked across the front of the car to stand next to him. "There are so many kinds of pollution. Even light pollution. That's why it's so important to get away from it. Even just temporarily. Just listen."

They stood next to each other, the house still a hundred or so feet away, in total silence and darkness. Much like the sound bath, Paul could feel his breath traveling into his nose and through to his lungs. He could also hear Kate's breathing and as he inched towards her. He was almost certain he could hear her heartbeat as well as his own.

Was this something new? Was he always able to hear his own heartbeat and breathing, and that of someone standing next to him, but didn't because there was too much noise, light, tension, and bullshit bombarding him constantly that made it impossible to see and hear those sensations?

From the outside, Jasmine's home looked like a bunker: concrete blocks, a plain steel door, small windows, a flat roof. But upon entering, it became an enchanting abode of silken fabrics streaming across walls, large unframed landscape watercolors, and funky thrift-store furniture. It was a single room: a kitchenette off to the right, complete with an antique stove, looking like something from a Laurel and Hardy movie; upholstered chairs constructed for small frames a hundred years ago placed to enable conversation, not television viewing; faded Oriental rugs strewn throughout the room over a simple concrete-slab floor.

"Come in! Have a seat! Would you like some tea?" Jasmine said as she welcomed Paul and Kate into her home.

Paul immediately noticed what wasn't in the room: Ash. "Yes, I'd like some tea. But not that funny kind."

"I'll have some!" Kate replied, hoping Paul wouldn't immediately go into an anti-weed routine.

"No, just plain old Earl Grey or herbal," Jasmine said, as the red teakettle sputtered. "Has Kate been giving you the funny stuff?"

"Funny *sounding*," Paul said, "St. John's warts!"

"*Wort* not *wart*," Kate said laughing.

Dainty cups of tea on saucers were served. Paul felt odd in the overstuffed chair, balancing a saucer and teacup on his lap. The conversation wound around the décor, the night sky, the washboard road, the sound bath, but no mention of Ash.

"By the way, where's Ash? I thought he was coming," Kate asked.

"I thought so, too," Jasmine said, surprised but not disappointed. "He mentioned he had a few deliveries to make and would try to come by later."

Kate studied Paul. She knew the *deliveries* mention would get his narc radar going and hoped it wouldn't surface in an uncomfortable way. Paul just nodded, took a sip of tea, and smiled.

"That guy's quite the window rattler," Paul said.

Kate and Jasmine looked quizzically at each other.

"His snoring. It rattles the windows."

In the distance the sound of loud motorcycle pipes could be heard approaching. The noise increased until it was parked next to the house, and in fact did rattle the open windows until the engine stopped. Jasmine looked outside. "It's Ash."

Paul looked at Kate as they were both trying to gauge each other's reaction to the arrival of Ash. He entered the house and stomped his feet on the concrete floor, knocking sand off his boots. Reaching inside his leather jacket he pulled out a bulky envelope and handed it to Jasmine.

"Here ya go," Ash said, handing her the envelope and taking off his jacket. "Do you have any beer?"

"Anyone else want one?" Jasmine asked.

Paul though for a moment, but decided against it. He didn't know why. He actually really wanted one at this moment, on this warm, cozy evening, but something told him to stay clear-headed. "Not me, thanks."

Ash drank the can of Pabst Blue Ribbon in about three gulps and headed for the bathroom, which was just out of view in the next room. He apparently left the door open, because the sound of his pee hitting the water was quite loud.

"I really got to get going. I'll see you tomorrow, Jasmine," Ash said, putting his jacket on and leaving.

The motorcycle roared to life, then faded in the distance. As soon as there was silence Jasmine said, "Let's sit in the yard. It's gorgeous outside."

Jasmine turned off all the house lights except for one dim nightlight, grabbed a small flashlight, and led them outside to the backyard. There were four chaise lounge-style chairs all pointing in the same direction, away from the rear of the house. In the distance was nothing. Just darkness.

"It'll take a few minutes for your eyes to adjust," Jasmine said, adjusting the chair backs to the lowest positions and leading Paul and Kate to them. "Just relax here. While we're waiting, I'm going to cause a slight amount of light pollution while I light up a bowl."

Paul watched as a red glow illuminated Jasmine's face as she lit the bowl and inhaled. Without asking, she passed the pipe to Kate, who also took long deep breaths from it. Kate held it out for Paul.

"No thanks."

After a couple of exchanges between Kate and Jasmine the pipe went out and was placed on the table next to Jasmine's chair.

Nothing was said. For a while. And as the seconds and minutes passed, Paul, flat on his back, as were the others, noticed the stars becoming brighter. The sounds of bugs buzzing nearby become noticeable. And he began to become aware of the breathing and swallowing patters of his chair mates.

"There's one," Jasmine said, pointing east to west across the sky.

"I saw it," Kate added.

"What?"

Kate held up her hand, which was now visible to Paul because his eyes were used to the darkness. "A shooting star."

"It's a sign." Jasmine added.

Paul waited about a minute, then asked, "A sign of what?"

"I was asking for a sign. And then it appeared," Jasmine said softly. After another minute or so she added, "It's a sign from 67 P."

"What's 67 P?" Paul asked.

"Scientists are telling us that a comet called 67 P is approaching earth. But some say it's not a comet at all. It's an alien ship," Jasmine stated matter-of-factly. "It has been communicating, or should I say, attempting to communicate with earth. The European Space Agency landed on it a couple years ago and they're keeping their findings secret. Why would they pick that so-called comet to land on? One they already admitted was emitting strange signals that were like *singing*? Right where we are, right now, we sit on over 90 percent of the exact convergence of the earth energy force vortex that the Integratron sits on. Do you remember Heaven's Gate?"

"That big flop that ruined Michael Cimino's career?" Paul asked. He could hear Jasmine sigh deeply.

"No. Heaven's Gate, the commune that transitioned in San Diego to an extraterrestrial star ship that was using the comet Hale-Bopp as cover as it approached the earth. They were the first to understand the ancient astronaut hypothesis in terms of modern applications."

Paul waited about a half minute, wondering if Kate might jump in, or start laughing, but nothing but silence hung in the air. "Didn't they commit mass suicide?"

"That's what it appeared to outsiders. Hale-Bopp was close enough to earth that they could accept the human spirit forms. There goes another!"

"That one I think I saw!" Paul said excitedly. "Is that another sign?"

"Yes, signs of what is to come."

"Will 67 P be accepting passengers?" Paul asked and immediately got a poke in the arm from Kate.

"Absolutely," Jasmine said slowly.

"What's that?" Paul asked. "Over on the left. All the way. Brighter than everything else? It looks like it's…moving!"

All three rose from their reclining positions and sat up. It was clear as day; a bright round object, brighter than anything in the moonless night was traveling high across the sky.

"It could be a scout. Alien visitors send out scout craft from their motherships to survey earth. Those are the craft that…." Jasmines voice trailed off and there was silence for a minute or so. "Those are the craft that abduct specimens."

"Specimens?"

"Animal. And human," Jasmine said, noticeably upset. "I have to go in for a few minutes. I'll be right back."

Paul watched the flashlight lead her way, back to the kitchen door.

"What was that all about?" Paul whispered into Kate's ear.

"She gets that way when she's high."

"You mean psychotic?"

"She's not psychotic. She just…she believes she was abducted."

"You mean, like held for ransom by tweakers, right?" Paul said, referring to a slang term for a meth addict.

"No. You know what I mean. A victim of an alien abduction. It's not that unusual."

"Maybe here it's not unusual. Can we go inside? I need a drink."

Jasmine was in the darkened kitchen, and as soon as Paul and Kate entered she turned on the light. She had a pitcher on the counter with some reddish drink in it. She reached under the counter, retrieving a bottle of vodka, and began pouring it into the pitcher.

"Paul was wondering if he could have a drink," Kate asked.

"Oh, I'm making vodka Red Bulls."

Paul looked at the concoction and thought it looked too much like Kool Aid for him, in light of Jasmine's fascination with mass-suicide-committing alien-worshipping cult members.

"Actually, I drink my vodka straight up," Paul said, reaching for the bottle, removing the top, and taking a deep whiff. "I love the smell of vodka," he added, hoping he didn't arouse any embarrassing suspicions, with his checking out the purity of the spirits.

"Want some ice?" Asked Jasmine, as she got a tray of ice from the freezer and began dropping ice cubes in the pitcher.

"No, I'm good."

Jasmine and Kate sat on the sofa, and Paul sat across from them in the upholstered chair. The pipe was on the coffee table and Jasmine began preparing for another bowl. "You don't mind, do you? I usually don't smoke in the house, but…."

"No worries," Paul added, "You're the master of your domain."

"Shouldn't that be *mistress?*" Jasmine said, not smiling.

"Sure *mistress* works." Paul looked over to Kate, who gave him a wink, letting him know she was with him.

Jasmine was sucking on the pipe like an asthmatic sucking on an inhaler. Having been around druggies his whole life, whether on the job undercover, or just kicking back with friends, he knew she was smoking some strong stuff and was getting intensely wasted.

"That's some interesting-smelling weed," Paul said, at the risk of alerting Kate that his career instincts could be kicking in. "What is it?"

"Oh, are you familiar with marijuana strains?" Jasmine asked between drags.

"You could say that."

"This is Indica. You know, the one for a body buzz. Couch lock."

"Couch lock?" Paul giggled.

Jasmine gave him a wry smile. "Locked into the couch. You're not going anywhere."

"You got that right," Paul mumbled to himself. "Um, I love this place. Do you rent or own?" he said, trying to change the subject.

Jasmine put down her pipe in the oversized ashtray. "I would never have a mortgage. It's all part of the globalist banking, Vatican, Rothschild control of the world's economy."

"Well, it's nice to see the Jews and the Catholics agreeing on something," said Paul.

"What do you mean?" Jasmine asked stonily.

"Well the Rotchschilds, the Jews, are supposed to control world banking and the Federal Reserve, and the Vatican are Catholics. The Pope is still Catholic, isn't he?"

"Very funny, Paul," Kate said, trying to lighten up the atmosphere.

"Chem trails," Jasmine said, glaring at Paul.

"Chem trails?" Paul asked, clueless.

"You've probably been under too many chem trails. It's working. They're getting away with it."

"What are chem trails?"

"Those streaks of what look like cloud vapors across the sky. Those are chem trails. Chemical trails. The government is releasing them into the atmosphere to control the minds of the masses, and in some cases poison us outright."

"Aren't those just water vapor and condensation, trailing behind commercial airliners, forming in the atmosphere?" Paul asked, perplexed.

"Aha! That's what they want you to think!" Jasmine said, her index finger pointing to the sky.

Jasmine stood up, and patted Paul on the shoulder. "I think we should be going." She bent down and gave Jasmine a peck on the cheek. "I'll call you tomorrow." They left as Jasmine waved goodbye in slow motion.

Outside, Kate and Paul stood next to her car, and discussed whether or not it was all right to leave her in that condition. They both agreed it was.

"Let's get my car, then I'll follow you back to the main road that goes to the motel," Paul said, inching closer to Kate and wondering if it would lead to a kiss. It didn't.

Paul laid in his bed, staring at the ceiling, listening to the giggles and music from nearby rooms, and the crunch of people walking on the gravel through the parking lot. *I think it's time to get a place of my own,* he thought to himself as he went over in his mind what he would need to do to make this strange locale his home. But as eager as he was to start anew, he knew that subconsciously it could be his mind playing tricks on him. Maybe it was merely his need to be near his daughter. Or perhaps, this place was trying to tell him something.

Chapter Six

While having breakfast at an outside table at the Frontier Café, Paul listed pros and cons on his yellow legal pad. The pro column was leading: no winter, start new life, leave city living, be near Tracy. The con column only had one entry: fear. Paul looked around, surveying the clientele at the café: students doing homework, extreme elderly biscotti dunkers, bikers, artsy hipsters, immigrants, all either standing in line or sitting, all minding their own business peaceably. It reminded him of the coffee houses in the Village back home, back in the day. Written under TO DO: *Call Tracy. Find a place to live.*

He had driven past High Desert Realty every day since staying at the Joshua Tree Inn, as it was directly across the street. So he decided on the way back to his room to switch the order on his To Do list and visit them first. He opened the door and there were six desks in one large room. Two of the desks had phones, pamphlets, papers, and calendars on them. One had somebody's half-eaten burrito in a Styrofoam clamshell box. Paul stood there for about 30 seconds listening for a sign of life. Then he heard a toilet flush.

A man entered the room from a doorway in the corner. "Well, hello, friend! Excuse me, I was visiting the library for a moment. How can I help you on this delightful desert day? I'm Dwayne!"

Dwayne wore a cowboy-cut shirt with mother-of-pearl snaps and a bolo tie. He looked around 70 with his hair dyed too dark black, as were his mustache and eyebrows. He had a neat part on the side and it was slicked back with a slight pompadour touch in the front. He seemed quite fit and trim and his blue jeans had a sharp crease. He wore thick black glasses, and Paul thought this might have been what Buddy Holly would have looked like if he'd made it to seventy.

"Hello Dwayne," Paul said, reaching out to shake hands. Paul hated shaking hands with people after they had just come out of the bathroom. How could you be 100 percent certain their hands were moist from having just been washed? "I'm Paul. I'm just starting out in the process, but I'm looking for a place to live in Joshua Tree or Yucca Valley, and I'm not sure if I want to rent or buy. Can you help me out?"

Dwayne's nostrils and eyes opened a little bit wider. "Why absotively, posilutely! You have come to the right place! Let's go!"

"Go?"

"Let's go look at some properties!"

"You don't want to go over anything with me first, or go through some listings or something?"

"Why bother? You got to see something in person, don't you think? Why waste time?"

"Okay. Lead the way."

Paul wasn't in the passenger seat of the older, but well-kept, Jeep Cherokee five minutes when it began.

"Yes, I'm a recovering alcoholic. Been clean and sober for 18 years, and still go to meetings every day. I don't like to proselytize, and come off as holier than thou, but a greater power has turned my life around and it all began with the Twelve Steps of AA."

"Where do we go first?" Paul replied, totally ignoring the bait.

"Are you interested in renting, buying, looking at foreclosures?" Dwayne said, not at all phased by Paul's ignoring his born-again pitch.

Paul figured he was used to being ignored, and continued. "You know, I've been renting my whole life. Why don't we start with some foreclosures? I'm on a fixed income, but maybe I can swing it."

"You look too young to be retired!"

"I'll bet you say that to all the boys."

"No really. You do look young to be retired. Military?"

"No. Law enforcement." Paul never knew what to expect when he revealed that he was a cop. And of all things, a narc.

"My son's in the military. And up here, you know with the Marine base so close, we have a lot of military. In fact, when they do their artillery training in Twentynine Palms you can hear it all the way in Joshua Tree, nearly 50 miles away. And the jets, choppers, military convoys, guys in uniforms, it just gets to me after a while. Gives me the heebie-jeebies. I'm an old hippie. Peace and love. Make love not war. War is not the answer. Coexist...."

"You have some foreclosures in mind?"

"Now, you know foreclosures are like speed dating. You take a look and sometimes you know right away whether it's yes or no. You just walk away and move on to the next one. No hard feelings."

The Jeep made a sharp left by a FOR SALE sign with an arrow pointing onto a bumpy dirt road. Every few hundred feet there was a "house." Sometimes the house was just a cinder block square surrounded by junk. Other times the house was a spotless pre-fabricated mini estate with a chain-link fence topped by barbed wire. And sometimes the house was just a leaning box of lumber and boards that may have been a home many decades ago.

"There's one just up here a bit. Been on the market a few months. It's a little bit trashed, as some foreclosures are, but mostly cosmetic. It just takes a keen eye to see the potential,"

Dwayne said as he turned into what could be called a long dirt driveway. They went over a small hill and on the other side was a lot with a double-wide mobile home on it. "You know, double-wides can be very, very nice," Dwayne said earnestly.

"I've heard about them, but have never actually been in one."

"This one could be a thing of beauty."

Upon first glance, Paul seriously doubted it. And as they pulled up alongside it, he was certain. It wasn't level, the front steps were a foot away from the trailer, the skirt was missing around the home, exposing a haphazard and probably hazardous array of pipes, wires, and animal burrow-entry holes.

"Just be careful going up the steps...."

"If this is more than $500 I'm not interested."

"Well, not much more. It's $19,900 with five acres."

"Five acres? Really? $19,900?" Paul said, wheels spinning.

Dwayne liked to see that look, which usually gave him insight into the mind of a potential bottom-feeder buyer. "You could probably get it for half that! And you could spend a little more, and turn this into something to be proud of."

Paul got out of the Jeep and walked around the double wide.

"The property is fenced in. That alone is worth five grand. And you have electricity. You can always have water trucked in or spend a little and have city water."

"There's no water?"

"Nope. Not here."

"You're kidding me? How can you have a home with no running water?"

"People have had water trucked in for decades around here."

"Okay, I guess I need to set some guidelines. I want to look at houses that have walls, roofs, floors, electricity, and water. Can we just start there?"

"Absotively, posolutely! Let me ask you this: can you live well outside the town?"

"What do you mean?"

"If really want to get away from it all, I can show you some properties next to the BLM."

"BLM? What are you talking about?"

Dwayne laughed in a silly high-pitched way. "Near the Bureau of Land Management land. It's kind of like parkland, but not quite. It's federally owned."

"You mean like there are properties that are adjacent to the park?"

"Yes, but it's not exactly a park."

"How big is it?"

"Well the BLM I'm thinking of is around 60,000 acres."

"60,000? That sounds big."

"Almost 100 square miles," Dwayne said, smiling broadly, knowing he's got Paul hooked.

"Yes! That's what I'm talking about. Away. From. It. All."

They drove a good half hour on dirt roads, paved roads, no roads, and onto a two-lane blacktop highway. Paul thought this looked a lot like the pictures he remembered seeing from Mars. Red dirt, boulders, mountains of rubble. With the only difference being the preponderance of Joshua trees.

"Let me ask you something, Dwayne."

"That's why I'm here."

"Why are they called Joshua trees?"

"Legend goes that the first white settlers here, Mormons, who came through these parts to get away from the evils of the cities, saw these unusual trees and thought they looked like the Old Testament prophet, Joshua, with his arms outstretched leading them in prayer to the Promised Land."

"Interesting. What's with all the abandoned garages around here? We've been seeing them for miles," Paul asked, astounded by the scope, vastness, and emptiness of the landscape.

"Those aren't garages. They're homestead shacks. Starting in the Forties, they parceled out these lands and homesteaded them. All you had to do was build a shack, 200 square feet minimum, take a picture of it, and send it to the county. Then in five years send another picture of the shack in decent shape, and the property was yours, scot-free!"

"So some were developed over the years and some were just left to rot."

"Yup. Just like we humans," Dwayne said, not joking.

They made some turns, passed some decent double-wides, more dumpy shacks, some horse ranches, properties with big rigs on them, some cows in corrals, then went down a washboard dirt road several hundred feet and stopped in front of a gate that looked like it might have been from an apocalyptic cowboy movie. They saw two huge telephone pole-type posts at cockeyed angles with cables dangling from them and a sign swinging in the wind that read THE HOBNOBBIN RANCH.

"We're getting a little further out, but the lots are big, the wild life aplenty, and we're getting closer to the enormous expanse of the wide-open high desert," Dwayne said enthusiastically.

"But what's that over there?" Paul said, pointing to a next-door neighbor's property that looked like the aftermath of a tornado in a junkyard.

"Let's look at this first, and then we'll look at the adjacent community."

"All right," Paul said reluctantly.

They approached the front door, which had a screen door in front of it. "Stand back a little bit," Dwayne said as he pushed Paul a little farther away and leaned in to open the door. He pulled the screen door open, and a small snake scurried away. "Just a little garter snake. They're your best little friend out here! Keep the bugs and rodents under control!"

"Yeah, well, I'm not so crazy about new little friends. Or big ones."

Dwayne retrieved the key from the realty agent's box and opened the door. It hit Paul right away: something was dead in there. He smelled that odor many times when he was a cop, and he had hoped he'd seen the last of those stench-filled days. "I just hope that's a four-legged animal I smell and not a two-legged."

"You smell something?"

"You're kidding me, right?"

"Oh, yeah, I smell it now," Dwayne said looking around a corner.

The place looked like squatters had been living there: two filthy sleeping bags were in the middle of the floor, empty tuna and sardine tins were strewn about. And Paul noticed two spikes, aka needles, next to an empty bottle of grape soda.

"Let me just look around a bit," Dwayne said, nodding.

"Good luck."

"Oh yeah. A dead possum on the bathroom floor. Must have gotten in through an open window or door."

"Or maybe it was going to be somebody's dinner. Let's get out of there," Paul said, disgusted. He paused next to the Jeep. "Look, Dwayne, I know we're out here looking for bargains. But don't show me anything that requires a hazmat team and a bulldozer to begin my remodel, okay?"

"You are exactly right! We started at the bottom and we're working our way up! Don't you worry, it just takes some time. And seeing these, you'll know a peach when you see it!"

They spent the rest of the day going from dilapidation to disaster, with promises of finding that special property. But Paul was getting tired, hungry, and losing hope fast. "Dwayne, I've had enough for today. We've seen like a dozen locations from *Breaking Bad*, and I'm thinking more like *Little House on the Prairie*. You know what I mean?"

"I agree. Now that I know what you're looking for, I'll go through some listings and we'll get back at it first thing in the morning!"

"Really? You'll have more tomorrow morning?"

"You betcha!"

"Okay, let's call it day and try it again tomorrow."

Later that evening as Paul was returning to his room with some take-out Chinese food, he noticed Kate was at the front desk. "Delivery boy!" Paul said holding up his bags, just inside the door.

"Hi! Come on in! I just ate, but dig in. I just have some paperwork to do. I hope you weren't freaked out last night."

"Believe me. If you knew what it took to freak me out, you'd think I was from another planet. Like your friend."

"Funny you should say that."

"Is it funny or strange?"

"Strange."

After we left last night, Jasmine said she thinks she had a visitation."

"Visitation? That's the name of my Catholic grammar school back in my old Bronx neighborhood. Did a pack of nuns get out of a flying saucer and start hitting her with rulers across the knuckles?"

"Very funny. No, but she remembers seeing a figure in the house, and then she remembers nothing, but woke up with a strange felling in herself...down there."

"Yeah, well, I wouldn't be surprised if Ash came back with some roofies and visited her down there with his tinfoil hat on."

"Don't even say that! Did you get bad vibes from Ash?"

"Let's just say, if I was renting a house to him, I'd want more than a credit report from free credit report dot com."

"Jasmine says he's a good guy."

"Maybe just a good drug connection."

"Don't get all cop heavy on me. I'm worried about Jasmine. I don't give a darn about Ash."

"I'm sorry. I'd tell Jasmine to keep away from him. I'll just leave it at that."

"Would you go with me tonight? We're going to an event in Joshua Tree. Starts at eight. Meet me here at seven-thirty?"

"Sure. I'd love to. By the way, I'm looking at properties."

"Really? Going to flip a house and make some bread before heading back to New York?"

Paul walked to the door and held the doorknob. "Nope. I'm done with New York. When one door closes, another one opens," Paul said opening the door, smiling and heading back to his room.

Kate watched him walk down the path and wondered what the deal was with Paul. She never actually knew a cop. Her husband tried to keep as far from them as possible, since he was always either holding or with somebody who was. Cops in the high desert were usually just blurred faces whizzing past in an air-conditioned patrol car, or hiding behind a motorcycle helmet with dark aviator shades. Unless you were getting a ticket, or worse, as her husband experienced on more than one occasion when he was busted for holding. Then, cops were generally robotic and steely cold. But her husband told stories of guys who were roughed-up. These incidents happened decades ago under circumstances that Kate never heard described quite the same way twice, but her husband's cop-grudge was wound tighter than a Brazilian soccer player's man-bun. She still wasn't 100 percent sure about Paul. *It's hard for a zebra to change his stripes*, she figured, *and probably even harder for a NYPD lieutenant to change his.*

Paul was right on time. He was looking forward to going to an *event* and seeing what kind of cross-section of humanity was actually hiding in the washes, rocky hillsides, and remote homestead shacks he's constantly passing in the distance. "I forgot to ask, what kind of event are we going to?" Paul asked, as he opened the office door for Kate to leave her shift and get into his car.

Kate explained that the event would take place at Cap Rock, the spot in the center of Joshua Tree National Park famous for its UFO sightings and vast energy-vortex synergies, and infamous for being where they cremated Gram Parson's body. There would be music, stargazing, and – hopefully – UFO sightings. Paul nodded and listened. Being a cop he learned that no matter how outrageous a story, explanation, or alibi sounded, it was better to just hold off judgment until the suspect gave you everything they had. Sometimes what was laid on you was such an octopus ink swarm of obfuscation and bullshit that it was actually entertaining. And occasionally it was just the plain old truth.

"You know, it all sounds good to me," Paul said as they approached the entrance to the park, "but if they start anything to do with Satanism or ghosts or séances, that's where my deep-down altar boy fears start to kick in and I'm out of there. I've seen some terrible things on the job that would make most humans shit or go blind – sorry for the language – but the scariest thing I've ever seen was *The Exorcist.*"

"You witnessed an exorcism?" Kate asked while pointing where Paul should turn down a dirt road in the park.

"No. The movie."

"A movie was the scariest thing you ever saw, even as a cop?"

"It's all about fear. I've seen some horrible things in-person. I won't go into the gory details, but as you can imagine, cops see things that go beyond the norms of human behavior. Some things you see were perpetrated by subhumans. There's the sight, sounds, and smells of horrific crime scenes, but what really matters is the fear factor. Am I in danger? What can happen to me? Usually there's no danger in the aftermath of a crime scene. But then there's the active situation. You run into a chaotic, dangerous situation where your life is in imminent peril. But what's the worst that could happen? Death?"

"Are you asking me? By the way, you're kind of freaking me out," Kate said continuing to point her thumb where Paul should turn, with a sliver of the sun dipping below the distant rock piles.

"Death, to me, is not the worst fear. You can only die once. But damnation? Hell? That's a whole 'nother level of fear that goes deep into my being. *The Exorcist* tapped into something that I prefer not to think about or expose myself to in any way, shape, or form."

"This group is not into Satanism or any sort of dark arts. It's all about connectivity and harmony and energy."

"You ever go into a store to buy something because of a great sale? Then you find out they're sold out, and you come out with something you didn't really want but it cost twice as much? Bait and switch."

"You mean like taking a personality test, and next think you know you're emptying your bank account into a Scientology mutual fund? Been there, done that."

"You were into Scientology?"

"I dipped in my toes. That was enough. See those cars parked ahead, pull in behind the last one, we have to hike a little bit from here," Kate instructed him.

It was pitch-black in deep desert. In the distance there were drums beating and the flickering light of a fire was bouncing off the high piles of boulders and rocks. Kate lit the way down the dirt trail with a small flashlight. There was a scent in the air of burning wood, creosote bushes, and weed. Paul wondered what he was getting into. He thought the Integratron started out as a joke, but then turned into something real. He really did feel the vibrations of the singing crystal bowls reverberate through the space and through his body. It did make him aware of his physical self like never before. Sober at least. But this was something else. A gathering here, where a body was actually cremated. Not just any body, but Gram Parsons himself. It had all the makings of a primitive ritual: the drums, the fire, the pot.

"You're sure this isn't going to be some druggie-crazed satanic ritual?" Paul asked again, keeping a keen eye on his footing, hoping he didn't step on a snake or something else that gets startled and goes for him.

"No. I've been to several of these," Kate said, trying to reassure him. "It's more about the astronomy lecture and UFO gazing than anything else. The only drug is pot. There's a rule."

"There's a rule about drugs? And people follow it?"

"You'd be surprised how obedient some of these free-thinkers are," Kate said turning off the flashlight, since the small campfire was illuminating the path for them.

"Isn't that Jasmine?" Paul whispered to Kate.

Jasmine was in the middle of the drum circle, wearing an *I Dream of Jeannie* pants suit, which only Barbara Eden could get away with. She was shaking her belly baby fat in time with the rhythms of the four congas beating away. It seemed a little odd because no one was paying much attention to the drum circle or Jasmine dancing like a whirling dervish. "Yes, that's her. This is what keeps her going," Kate said, leading Paul to a guy sitting in a folding chair who she handed some money. She looked at Paul, "Somebody has to pay for the UFO expert. He drives all the way in from Parumph, by Area 51."

"Of course he does."

There were about 25 revelers, mostly women. Some looked like they might still be in high school. There was also an elderly man and woman using walkers. There was a circle of candles with the initials GP marking the actual location of the cremation. Paul looked up to the top of the rocks and there were several people up there with oversized binoculars scanning the skies.

The guy who took Kate's money stood up and took a position by the circle of candles. He raised his arms, the drums stopped and all became quiet.

"We will now extinguish the fires of earth, and give ourselves ten minutes to prepare. Thank you."

One of the drummers shoveled some dirt on the fire, then blew out the candles. There was a low murmur of conversations as people quietly rolled out yoga mats or sat in folding chairs.

"Prepare? How?" Paul asked Kate as she unrolled a yoga mat for them to sit on.

"Prepare your eyes so you can see. Your ears so you can hear."

Paul thought about Kate saying she dipped her toes into Scientology and wondered what he was stepping into. Conversations slowly stopped. And like at quiet moments during a play, coughs, throat clearings, and candy-wrapper rattling became the noticeable noises.

"We'll begin the program in two minutes," a reedy male voice said from atop the rock where the people with binoculars were stationed.

With the lack of light, flames, and flashlights, things gradually started to become more visible. And due to the absence of light pollution from the commercial strip malls of Yucca Valley or Palm Springs the sky was a deep swath of black velvet with sprinkles of stars, planets, and yes, the Milky Way itself becoming brighter and brighter to the human optic nerve system right on cue.

"Welcome one and all to the third annual meeting of the Foundation for UFO Believers Authenticators and Researchers: FUBAR," the reedy-voiced man said from atop the rock, as he began to come into focus in the darkness.

Paul was already trying to stifle his snickering. *FUBAR* was the name of the bar softball team back in the Bronx at The Buckeye. It was a common WWII term used by soldiers and officers alike, just as SNAFU was. *SNAFU* meant, *Situation normal. All fucked up.* And *FUBAR* meant, *Fucked up beyond all recognition.*

He thought about whispering this to Kate, but thought better of it after seeing the beguiled expression on her facing hanging on the speaker's every word.

"My name is Ken Nicholson. Just call me Klaatu."

Paul laughed out loud at that and got a look from Kate and a couple others. He whispered to Kate, "What? Klaatu barada nikto. *The Day the Earth Stood Still.* Everybody knows that."

Kate shushed him.

"The reason we gather here isn't just to raise money for FUBAR. It is to know that other like-minded people are out there," he said, opening his arms as if enveloping the crowd below. "And out there!" he added, now waving his arms to the heavens. The crowd applauded and yelled *woot woots* of approval. "We do have some exciting news to share, which we'll do now so we can get to the serious business of watching the skies. First, NASA's Venus Climate Orbiter has sent back images that have been verified as proof of a large structure across the planet's surface. This is of particular interest to us because, as you know, George Van Tassel, the builder of the Integratron, which so many of you are familiar with, received the plans for it from Venusians. Look for some startling revelations connecting many of the mysteries surrounding the Integratron, Venus, and the greys among us. The other thing I want to mention is that G.R.I.P. of London is again selling Alien Abduction Insurance policies. See me after the program. They have some very affordable policies."

Paul waited for the laughter from the crowd. There wasn't any.

With eyes finally adjusted to the darkness and only a sliver of the moon providing light, it was possible to surreptitiously watch people, which is exactly what Paul was doing. There were a few people in the crowd who looked like they would be right at home with a tinfoil hat and a divining rod, but the vast majority looked quite normal: dressed in hippie style, clean, and triple-digit IQs, but with expressions on their faces that told Paul they were going for this like swans on stale bread.

Binoculars were passed around, or you could venture up to the top of the boulders to look through two telescopes that were set up. No flashlights were allowed, so the climb up the rocks was only for the more adventurous of the bunch, which included Paul, Kate and Jasmine.

"Hold my hand," Paul said reaching out to Kate, who was already holding hands with Jasmine as they trekked up the rocky path that would lead them to the top of the boulder.

Three people were on line behind each of the telescopes when they got there. The telescope guides were explaining what they were looking at in hushed tones. Ken, the lecturer, was explaining where to look for comet 67 P. "See the bright spot in the upper-right hand? That's Saturn. Now go down 20 degrees, and over to the left approximately 45 degrees and you'll see what looks like a cluster of stars with a point at the top and two on the side almost like a Christmas tree...."

"Yes, yes, I see it," said a young man wearing a knit beanie cap, even though it was still about 80 degrees in the desert night.

Ken continued, "The star on the lower left of the Christmas tree is the comet and behind the cluster, using it as camouflage, may possibly be the star craft."

"I see it. Definitely. Amazing," the young man with the hot head said, then walked away offering the telescope to Kate.

Kate followed the instructions of Ken carefully, and did see the cluster of stars he was referring to. "I see it. But how can we be sure there's a star craft behind it? How is this any different than the Heaven's Gate theory?"

"I'll be lecturing on that next month. Are you on my email list?"

"Yes. Thanks. I'll look forward to that," Kate said to Ken as she gave way to Paul.

"I've got a lot of experience with binoculars from many years in the cheap seats at Shea Stadium, but this is my first through a telescope," Paul said, adjusting his right eye to the unexpected brightness of the image in the eyepiece.

"Owww!" There was a commotion below as someone obviously was hurt. Flashlights came on and one of the older people who had a walker was on the ground holding her ankle. Several people were on the case so Paul kept looking through the telescope.

"What the...?" Paul said to himself. "Did you see that?" Paul asked as he looked to whoever would be behind the other telescope, but no one was looking through it. Everyone was watching the injured woman being attended to. Paul looked back into the eyepiece, but it was gone. He didn't know if he was seeing things, but obviously nobody else saw it.

"Kate, Kate, come here," Paul whispered to Kate who was looking down on the action below. Kate slowly backed up towards him. "When you looked through the scope, did you see anything moving?"

"Moving? Like what?"

"Just anything at all?"

"No. Why? Did you? I know you're a skeptic. Are you getting ready to prank me?"

"I'm serious. Really. I saw something."

"Talk to Ken," Kate said pointing to him, now down below helping out with the injured lady. "Maybe it was a plane, or something else," she said unconvincingly.

Paul knew it wasn't a plane. Planes have navigation lights and move across the sky. This spherical object zigged, zagged, zigged straight up, fizzled in a cloud of tiny bright lights like the sparks from a sparkler, and then disappeared.

The event ended early because the lady seriously injured her ankle, and they had to get her medical attention. Kate, Jasmine, and Paul walked with the crowd back to the Escape, guided by the many flashlights now shining like so many beams of light cutting through the darkness.

"Tell Jasmine what you told me."

Paul thought about keeping it to himself. He knew that people going through a lot of stress, or illness, or changes in life sometimes see things. Like his buddy Mickey used to say on long drives from the Hamptons or the Cape, *It's time to pull over when you start seeing the gorillas hanging from the trees.* Because when you're overtired, staring at the white lines in the road, trying desperately not to nod off, sometimes you see things: a desk in the road or a pterodactyl swooping down on the car, or a gorilla hanging off a tree by the side of the road. He knew he was in a heightened state of stress ever since those Ivy League protesters messed with his late-night breakfast, which set off a nuclear domino effect culminating in retirement and the death of his ex, all of which placed him at a UFO hunting expedition above the spot where Gram Parsons was set on fire so his ashes would be sent to heaven like so many Catholic school kids dropping their letters to Jesus into a fire during the Mary Queen of the May procession.

"Yeah, I think I saw something. But maybe not. I don't know. I'm probably seeing things. I've been a little *fakakta* lately."

Jasmine and Kate both stopped in their tracks. *"Fakakta?"*

"Yeah, *fakakta*. Crazy. Mixed up. It's Yiddish. You never heard that?"

"Oh, I think it's in a Woody Allen movie," Kate said.

"Woody Allen's picture is next to *fakakta* in the Yiddish dictionary!" Paul added.

Once in the car, there was some small talk between Kate and Jasmine about how the event wasn't as good as others because of the mishap, and how Ken wasn't as well prepared, and the only musicians were drummers and they missed having the ukuleles. But after a good distance, when they were separated from the other vehicles leaving the event, and it was again pitch black all around, things became quiet except for the rumble of the tires on the uneven rural dirt road. The washboard road ended, and they were now on a long stretch of smooth blacktop but still in total darkness.

Jasmine came forward from the seat in the back. "Tell me what you saw."

Paul paused. He already thought Jasmine was kind of nutty, and now he was going to sound as nutty as she did. "It was short. Maybe five seconds. It moved fast. A spherical super bright light, almost like it had sparks around it. It went to the left, the right, the left, and then it went straight up, toward the heavens and was gone. I'm sure it was only visible through the telescope. And the other scope wasn't being used at the time. I guess I was the only one who saw it. No way could you see that with the naked eye."

"Shit!" Jasmine shouted loudly, startling Kate and Paul. "I want to see them! I want them to take me out of here! Off this insane planet!"

"Jasmine, calm down," Kate said, coaxing her back into her seat. "Just take it easy. Were you puffing with those drum circle dudes?"

"Yes, but only a little. I know what I'm saying. I do want to go on a UFO."

Paul thought perhaps he should be more selective about who he tells his desert weirdness sightings to. The majority of the people at the UFO lecture had a longing look on their faces, as though they all wanted a UFO to land and take them away. It was in their eyes. They were seeking something that would come from somewhere and take them away. Somewhere. Anywhere. Out of here. And maybe he has that same look on his face. Which is why he is thinking of getting a home in this God-forsaken land where crops won't grow, water is scarce, the winds strip the paint off walls, and the sun sucks the life out of your skin. Even the animals know better than to stay here. And those that do stay have thick skin and sharp teeth like the snakes and lizards. Or they're super paranoid and fast like the jackrabbits. The birds with common sense have headed down to the lush golf courses of the Coachella Valley. The ones that stay are the survivors. Kind of like the Bronx, if you really analyze who inhabits these parts. There are the ones who have a hard time getting away because of their shortcomings. And then there are those that just enjoy it the way it is, precisely because it's not easy to stay here. You have to want it. Tough it out. Something good might pop up out of nowhere. Only the strong survive.

They dropped off Jasmine at her place, and despite her begging them to come in to hang out for a bit, Paul could tell Kate wasn't up for it. He blamed it on himself to get Kate off the hook.

"Is Jasmine okay?" Paul asked Kate after a few minutes driving down the dark, dirt road.

"Yes. She's fine. She's going through one of those phases."

"What kind of phase is that?"

"She's getting high again. She was clean and sober for a while, and now she thinks just smoking weed and drinking is not that big a deal."

"How long was she clean and sober for?"

"A few weeks."

Paul just shrugged and didn't say anything.

Kate saw it on Paul's face, barely illuminated by the green glow of the instrument panel lighting. There he goes being a cop. What's more judgmental than being a cop? They have a license to kill, don't they? That's why so many in her circle of friends are out here. It's to get away from that judgmental Stepford Wives mentality that permeates the hippest and most politically correct enclaves of the American megalopolis. From the Upper East Side of Manhattan to Malibu, it didn't matter. You still had to conform to their rules. You must join their rat race.

"Some people struggle, you know," Kate said, with a defensive tone.

Paul flashed on some quick comeback lines, but continued driving in silence, onto the two-lane highway.

"Tell me where to turn to get back to your place," Paul said, sounding annoyed.

"Turn at the three reflectors on that pole up ahead. Do you want to hang out for a bit?"

Paul liked Kate. He found her very attractive. But he was afraid of the rebound romance. And it would be a double rebound. Both of their spouses had recently died, albeit his was an ex. But it still counts. He knew too well how the rebound romance often leads to disaster. As soon as Paul McCartney hooked up with Heather Mills after spending his whole life with Linda, McCartney with the sunny disposition suddenly started writing torturous songs about driving in the never-ending rain.

"Nah, I've got an early appointment with the realtor."

"Do you really want to live out here?"

"Growing up in New York, I spent time at beaches, mountains, lakes, streams, rivers, forests, even swamps. But this? This is new to me. I need it. I saw too much of the same for too long." He pulled into her driveway and put the car in park by her porch. "It's not that I need to get away from anything. I need something new."

Kate smiled and gave him a peck on the cheek. "Me too."

Paul watched as she unlocked her front door and went safely inside.

Abandoned meth labs, filthy squatter shacks, cinder block bunkers, roofless A-frames, double-wide dumps; these were a few of Paul's least favorite things. And after four days of foreclosure house hunting, Paul was about to give up hope finding something in his price range that wasn't a toxic waste site. Then he got a call from Jasmine, telling him that she knew someone in Flamingo Heights – the area next to the BLM that Paul liked – who told her about a house that was "sold," fell out of escrow, and was back on the market. Paul wasn't completely sure about the reliability of the tip, since Jasmine was a flake, but he did call Dwayne the realtor right away. Dwayne was happy to hear it fell out of escrow and, smelling a deal, suggested they meet there ASAP.

Paul was shocked upon arrival. There was a nice old-style ranch wood and wire gate to the property with several Joshua trees lining a gravel, not dirt, driveway. The house, although a plain ranch-style painted a drab beige, looked like it had straight lines, a new roof, and no broken windows. The huge front yard actually had a few trees, several large cacti, a huge grouping of amazing purple cacti, and a few ocotillo that were in bloom with bright red blossoms. And along the side of the fence at the far end of the fenced property there was…nothing. No houses, no sheds, no double-wides, no roads; just the full expanse of the California high desert in all its pristine glory. Joshua trees, nearby ginormous boulders balanced on top of one another, creosote bushes, tumbleweeds, rocky washes, cholla cactus, and in the distance beautiful mountains of mutlicolored rock.

Dwayne arrived and exited his car with the biggest toothy smile yet. "Well, I think you might have found a peach here! Let's take a gander at the inside!"

Paul tried not to tip the fact that he was elated with the property so far. "Okay, but I hope it's not another high desert disaster area."

Dwayne unlocked the door, and they stepped inside. It didn't stink. Everything was painted white, including the large timbers that went across the ceiling of the big front room. The carpeting was pure Eighties shag, but had lines from a recent vacuuming. The kitchen was clean, and the stove was a vintage Sixties model, but shined like it was just delivered by Montgomery Ward.

"I hope you have your check book, because the next person who drives up is gonna snatch this beauty up! Three bedrooms, two bathrooms, a den, central air and heat, and look at this, there's already cable TV outlets in all the rooms! See all those cards on the island?"

On the kitchen island there were at least 75 business cards strewn about, the ritual of real estate agents leaving their mark when they view a property with a client.

"Once they get wind of this place falling out of escrow, all 75 of them will be lined up down the road trying to get in on this beauty."

"Okay, okay, I get it. How much?" Paul said, still playing it cool, but inside now terrified he might lose this. After seeing what seemed like a hundred houses from a zombie apocalypse, he knew this was the place.

"They're asking $80,000. It's five acres."

Paul was shocked. Paul had friends who spent that much on a car; $80,000 was just a down payment back east, even in the Bronx.

"You think they'd take 75?"

"I don't know...."

"Cash."

"Probably, let's write it. Fast! Come on, let's go back to the office!"

"Give me few minutes to look around."

"Okay, but time's a-wasting."

Paul was more than pleasantly surprised at the condition of the home after the houses of horrors he had seen over that past several days. There were remnants from remodels in the Seventies, like a wood-paneled room, sparkly acoustic foam on the ceilings, and wall-to-wall carpeting like something out of pimp's pad on *Kojak*. But all those things were cosmetic. The walls seemed solid, the floors level, the light switches worked, and the toilets flushed. He began opening closets and drawers, and it was obvious that someone had gone over this place with a fine-toothed comb. He was curious as to what exactly was under the carpeting, so he walked to the corner of a bedroom and pulled up an edge, revealing a concrete slab. Not the worst news, as ceramic tile would go easily over it. He went to the corner of another bedroom and did the same thing. Only this time when he lifted up the corner of the carpet and the foam pad underneath he was shocked to see the top of a large underground "in-floor" safe. It wasn't the first time he had seen such hidden safes. They were sometimes discovered in drug dealer's homes. He knew that if it was locked, it would be quite an expense to have it opened by a locksmith. He reached down, and – lo and behold – the heavy safe top was unlocked and easily removed. Of course he had hoped to find a hidden stash of cash, but it was empty. Still, an "in-floor" safe like this one, embedded in a concrete slab, could cost many hundreds of dollars and would definitely come in handy. Just as he was getting ready to replace the safe top he noticed something up against the inside of the safe, barely visible from directly above. It was an envelope. He opened it and it was a Christmas card from probably the Sixties, judging by the artwork. It read, *Dear Dee, Merry Christmas, Love, Mary.* At first he thought it read *Love, Marcy,* his wife's name. But it was *Mary.*

Dwayne stuck his head in the doorway. "You can inspect all you want later today, but we've got to get that offer in quick. Believe me, this thing will be sold today!"

"I'll be right there," Paul said, sticking the envelope in his back pocket, putting the safe top in place, and patting down the carpet on top.

Back at Dwayne's office, Paul signed the necessary paperwork and was busy on the phone trying to figure out the quickest way to get a certified check for 75 grand into his hands. But after listening to a multitude of *new choices because our menus have changed,* endless

Kenny G solos, and getting disconnected four times, he juggled some savings and 401(k) money and had the funds in his checking account. All he needed today was a check for a ten percent deposit.

"Do you think I'll get this?" Paul said writing out a check for the largest amount he ever wrote. The only thing that came close was the security deposit for the Mets bus trip to see the Cubs at Wrigley, but he got some of that back after they charged him for fumigating, steam cleaning, and shampooing the floors and seats after a nearly 2,000-mile trip with four kegs of beer, three giant coolers of cold cuts and bread, and an on-board toilet that stopped working half way across Pennsylvania.

"It's bank-owned, so you never know. But I imagine there is an employee dying to get this property off the books with an all-cash, 14-day closing for nearly 95 percent of asking. But I'll make a call just in case. I've dealt with them before. If there's a hitch I'll call you."

"Okay, but I want it for 75."

"Shouldn't be a problem."

"Call me as soon as you know," said Paul halfway through the door. He knew he'd even go a little higher than the asking price if he had to, because he wanted this place. He was ready for it. He didn't know what the future would bring. He didn't really know why he was doing it. Maybe subconsciously it was because he wanted to finally be near Tracy. Twentynine Palms is only about a half-hour away. Close enough, but far enough. *Oh shit!* He thought to himself. *What if Tracy didn't want him that close? What if Tracy was moving out here to get away from the past, much like he was?* And now he was going to be ruining her new beginning. He thought that maybe after they drove cross-country together, and she began her new life, that her life didn't include him. He knew they had to talk.

Kate watched as Paul rushed by the office on the way to his room, and was taken aback that he didn't even look in the window or wave. Paul was rushing to call Tracy, which he did the moment he was in the room. He kept the conversation short, knowing that he wanted to talk to her about his move in person. They made arrangements to meet at her favorite vegetarian restaurant in Palm Springs.

Paul rushed by the office again, not even pausing to look in the window. Kate knew she had no right to think that Paul owed her anything. They were really just acquaintances. But it would have been nice if he thought enough to update her on the house she had told him about. And right on cue, there he was, rushing through the door.

"Kate! You're not going to believe this! I love that place. I put in a cash offer and the agent thinks it's a slam-dunk. And I couldn't have done it without you and Jasmine thinking of me! I owe you two! I'm going to meet my daughter in Palm Springs. I'll call you later!"

And just like that, he was gone. Kate just laughed as she watched him hurry to his car and drive off.

On the drive to Palm Springs, Paul went over everything that he was going to say to Tracy, and every possible comeback he would have if she came up with any objections to his big move. He knew it looked bad. Like he was forcing himself on her at this late stage of the game. But he really wasn't. At least he didn't think he was. He noticed the temperature rising as the descended the almost 4,000 feet down to the Coachella Valley. Once he was back on the interstate, with cars whizzing by him, some going close to 100 miles per hour, he realized that the slow pace of the high desert was beginning to be more his style.

Palm Springs, and the surrounding municipalities of Palm Desert, Rancho Mirage, and Cathedral City, were all products of the modern technology. Without air conditioning and irrigation they wouldn't be the booming golfer, LGBTQ, snowbird, retiree sanctuaries they have become, bristling with traffic, casinos, golf courses, and strip malls. Nine months out of the year, the weather was bearable. But in the summer, one had to be as serious about dealing with the outside temperature as one would have to be when dealing with a Fairbanks, Alaska winter. His GPS brought him in to the strip mall where Native Foods was located. After parking he went over in his head one more time how he was going to frame his moving to the high desert.

There she was. Tracy was sitting at a table drinking a glass of ice water. From outside the window, she looked so much like her mom to Paul. It still freaked him out a little. The last time he and her mom were in love, they were just about Tracy's age. And now, his love for Tracy was almost as overwhelming. Once Marcy started to take the downward spiral into self-destructive alcohol and drug abuse, Paul did everything he could to help her. Nothing worked. In fact, he felt the more he tried, the worse-off she became, perhaps as a weapon against the father of her child. But like the many traumas of his time as an undercover cop dealing with the life-and-death situations of the drug underground, he knew he had to just put all that behind him.

Tracy looked up and smiled when she saw Paul enter. That pleased him, but he knew he shouldn't take anything for granted.

"Hi, Tracy! How are you? You look fantastic!" Paul said leaning over and kissing her on the cheek.

"Oh my God. We have been working out like maniacs every day. Heidi has me on this program that is killer."

Paul immediately knew she was happy. Her eyes, her smile, the intonation in her voice; it all pointed to self-satisfaction. He wasn't sure if he would be giving off the same vibe.

"I've got to start working out. I think I'm getting soft." He settled into his chair and ordered coffee. "Tracy, I need to discuss something with you. I don't want to upset you…."

"Oh boy, here we go…."

"Please. Let me finish. After you hear me out you can pound away on me. I've been through a lot. We've been through a lot. I want you to be happy. In your new life, whatever that is. And I can tell you look happy and healthy."

"Here comes the big *but*."

"There's no *but*. I made a decision and I'm buying a house in Yucca Valley. I want to live there."

"That's it? That's what you thought would upset me?"

"Well, I was afraid…."

"Look…dad…."

They both looked at each other and could tell that word *dad* didn't come easily, but meant a lot to both of them.

"I'm glad you'll be close by. Yes, I wanted to get away but I didn't want to be entirely alone." A few awkward seconds passed as they both absorbed what was just said. She added, "What are you having?"

"Do they have burgers here?"

"Veggie burgers."

"Fries?"

"Yup."

"I'm good with that!"

Paul was so relieved that Tracy was glad he was relocating near her. If she said otherwise, he probably would drop out of the deal and go find somewhere else to begin his new life. But not back to New York. No way. Those days were gone. And except for his buddy, Mickey, and Tracy's grandma and Aunt Peggy, there was nothing east of the Rockies that had a hold on him. He couldn't wait to get back to the high desert and settle down.

Tracy had a good feeling about the future. Finally. She was glad to hear that her father's news was actually good news. Because she wasn't so certain that it would be good news he was about to lay on her. She was indeed happy that he would be nearby. When her mother died she thought that would provide closure. But there wasn't any. She still had an empty hole in her heart where her mom of so long ago held a special place. It was as if her mom died a hundred times. Every time she promised she wouldn't drink, or be wasted for days on end, or come home beat-up from somewhere, or got arrested, and on and on and on. Those were all the times she had died to her. But she kept coming back to life. There was always a small sliver of hope that maybe this would be the time that she didn't go out, or that she'd stay and help her with her homework, or go to parent's night at school, or tuck her in. Thankfully she had her grandma to do all those things and more. She knew her dad was somewhere out there. Grandma told her that her dad was a good man. He was helping her in ways that she would one day understand. And now, somehow, perhaps those days were here. And she was glad to finally feel like she had a family. But she was still working on getting the nerve up to tell her dad of her news; that she and Heidi were getting married. And like Heidi, she would also be joining the Marines.

Chapter Seven

The house was his. Once the bank heard *cash* they closed the deal immediately. Dwayne the realtor was solemn in his presentation of the keys, as if he was handing over the keys to the Ark of the Covenant.

"This is what I love about my job. If I'm just a small cog in the cosmic karma wheel helping to change people's lives, I'm happy," Dwayne said, tenderly placing the keys in Paul's palm.

"Now that you're happy and I'm seventy-five thousand poorer, I just hope *I'm* happy."

As he drove to his home for the first time as the owner, his cop senses were in overdrive. He turned onto the dirt road that in a couple of miles would lead to his front gate, slowed the Escape to just above a crawl, and noticed things he hadn't seen before. There was a house on a side street with three large pit bulls on the front porch with no fence around the property. Another home on the way had newspapers covering all the windows. And he noticed a small hand-lettered sign that read BIG HORN HORSE RESCUE 1 MILE. He took a turn down a road just before his street to check it out. There were two lots with decent-looking double-wides and pick-ups parked beside them, and then – up ahead – there was a beautiful group of towering pine trees. He slowed as he passed and gazed in awe at the oasis the owner created on his patch of desert dirt. At least a dozen pine trees surrounding an A-frame home that one might see on an Aspen hillside. The property had a brick and cast-iron gate in front, with a matching wall that must have stretched for a hundred yards in each direction. He could see through the trees that there were modernist sculptures in the yard and on the front porch. He surmised that an artist lived there, which was an excellent omen. He knew very well that when the artists started buying the crappy old lofts around Alphabet

167

City adjacent to the East Village it was a sure sign that prosperity and rising real estate values were sure to follow. And it looked like it could be happening here, too.

There it was: his new home. He stopped in front of his locked wood and wire gate and killed the engine. He stood outside the car and closed his eyes. He reveled in the pure silence. The loudest sound he could hear was a lifetime of city that was still humming inside his head. He wondered how long it would take to quiet those inner noises ringing in his ears, in his brain, from a lifetime of the subway's squealing wheels and of diesel engines idling in traffic. Horn-honking expletive-screaming-in-foreign-languages cabbies competing with mentally ill blood boilers shouting-to-no-one threats and pleas and prayers to be taken away from that corner that stairway that doorway that public restroom that bench. Jack hammers, wrecking balls, elevated trains, bad brake pads, Radio Shack loudspeakers blasting the owner's favorite music outside bodegas, bars, and bargain-basement junk stores. Barstool blowhards boasting how they'll fix it all. Bosses berating all those below. Babies, kids, drunks, and junkies in your face, drooling and spitting on the sidewalk and worse. Sirens and claxon bells warning everyone: Bad shit happening just around the corner, get the hell out of the way!

Opening his eyes, he turned slowly around, the gravel under his feet crunching as he shifted: the only noticeable noise. In the distance, maybe a few hundred yards away, rocky hills, with an inviting path of dirt, hardscrabble, Joshua trees, assorted cactus, and tiny vegetation. He wanted to know each by name. When he was a kid growing up in the Bronx, the best times were always seeking places where there was nothing. Not *nothing* nothing. But no people, no houses, no cops, no El's, no parent's spying eyes, no concrete, no bricks, no strange kids who wanted to rip you off or punch you in the face for no reason. And in that part of the North West Bronx there were places like that. There was Van Cortlandt Park. Over a thousand acres of everything most kids would give their throwing arm for: baseball fields, golf courses, playgrounds, football fields, ponds, woods, hiking trails, cricket fields, a lake, and even a swamp. But what Paul and his friends longed for were the quiet places away from the rest of the kids. They named the swamp the Okefenokees, which was actually the upper reaches of Van Cortlandt lake. It had rowboat rentals, picnickers, dog walkers, and sometimes lurking perverts. But who would venture into the stinky, mucky, swamp smelling of centuries of duck and turtle crap? Kids who longed for adventure. But it took some mischief to be able to explore such a forbidden place.

Long ago, when city kids spent more time outdoors than in their apartments staring at computer screens, Paul and Mickey would cobble together some fishing line, hooks, and a long, thin tree branch as a fishing pole – hoping to look like law-abiding young people – and rent a rowboat at the Vannie lake. They rowed around the lake a couple times and even fished in place for close to a half hour, in case anyone was suspicious of their motives. Then they rowed slowly to the far end of the lake where there was a railroad trestle, which was a gateway to the Okefenokees. There they were met by two other guys, on top of the railroad bridge, only about four feet over the surface of the water. Their partners in crime, Buddy and Mac, at great personal peril of falling into four feet of lake muck, climbed halfway down the chain-link fence and pulled up the bottom of the fence, allowing Paul and Jamey to duck down and go under the bridge into the forbidden swamplands. It wasn't *really* stealing because they would one day return the boat to the dock. But probably at the end of summer.

Or next summer. Many a hot afternoon, those pre-pubescent kids would have Huck Finn adventures in the swamps with the rowboat, which was concealed expertly by camouflage after each use. But never, ever, not once did they ever encounter any other kids or grownups in the muck and mire of the Van Cortlandt swamps. They were free to fish, chase frogs, smoke cigarettes, look at *Playboys*, shoot sling shots, or just sit on a fallen tree trunk. There were other places of refuge from civilization in Vannie: deep woods, the top of giant rocks, under bridges, and in secretly constructed forts. The best hideouts were places that had some inherent danger that kept the easily frightened away. And that's what Paul loved about his new home and the thousands upon thousands of untouched acres of rough desert that were now his backyard.

Paul heard something and whipped around, facing his gate. Could it be? Yup, there they were, a woman and a man on horseback coming up his driveway.

"Hello neighbor!" said the woman, long gray hair down her shoulders with a straw cowboy hat on top. "Are you the new owner?"

Paul was momentarily stunned at the sight of the visitors. "Yes. I'm just taking possession today, as a matter of fact."

"Congratulations! I told Mike here to buy it, but he who hesitates doesn't get the deal!" said the woman, laughing a loud laugh that made her horse jerk his head up.

"I'm Mabel, and this is Mike. I live about a mile down the road. It's the Big Horn Horse Rescue Ranch. You can probably see it from your roof. It's the red house with the red barn. I'm so glad somebody finally got this place. It was not the pride of the neighborhood for a while."

Mabel had high cheekbones, Asian eyes, and that leathery wrinkled skin that desert dwellers attain after decades of exposure to the sun and dust. From a distance, it was easy to see she was a beauty, but with each step closer, her age was revealed and put her close to seventy. Paul thought she might be an Indian. Mike was a young, clean-cut fellow, and Paul thought he could be in the military.

He took a few steps closer, and cautiously petted Mabel's horse. It was the first time he had done that when not paying 25 bucks an hour. "Glad to meet you Mabel. Mike. What was going on here?"

"Don't really know. But the nut-job who last lived here is gone and that's a good thing. Drove his pickup drunk, speeding past my place for beer runs, which was a huge problem because we have animals all over the place. And he was always crashing into something. Cops at his house. Gunshots fired. Ambulances. Swat teams."

"Stop, you're making me homesick!"

"You must be from L.A. We get a lot of ex-cops moving up here. The Hollywood crowd usually stays down in Joshua Tree."

"No. New York."

"New York City?" Mabel asked, shocked.

"Guilty as charged."

"How the hell did you wind up here?" asked Mike.

"Oh, my daughter is moving nearby, so here I am."

"Where's she living?" Mabel asked.

"Twentynine Palms."

"Is she in the military?" Mike asked with interest.

"No. Just…getting away from New York for a while."

"Can't get much farther without needing a boat," Mabel giggled. "We're going for a ride in the BLM. If you ever want to go for a ride, stop by!"

They turned and walked down the driveway, made a right, and were on a trail in the BLM. Paul watched them go up a small hill and disappear behind some boulders. *Just like the Wild West!* He thought to himself. And he hoped that didn't include *everything* about the Wild West.

Paul knew he had his work cut out for himself and wasted no time. Trips to the Super Walmart for paint, furniture, tools, and appliances, were the first steps to begin turning his house into a home. And shopping in a Super Walmart was also the best way to see the cross-section of humanity that inhabited these parts, including actual cowboys and Indians. Plus tweakers, hobos, huge Mexican families, blonde blue-eyed refugees from Hollywood, black, Asian, lesbian, gay, survivalists, hippies, active military, and ancient elderly barely able to steer their in-store motorized sit-on-top-and-drive mega shopping carts. He wondered how each of them would disperse when they exited the parking lot, and what kind of places they lived in.

He got a lot accomplished the next several days, cleaning, painting, fixing up, and he hung on the wall the only item he had taken from home: a framed team photo of the World Champion 1986 New York Mets. He was ready to start calling in some pros to get the difficult jobs done. First was a floor guy to take up the wall-to-wall shag carpeting and install tiles throughout the house. It would keep the house cooler in the summer, and in the winter you just scatter some area rugs. It only took a few calls and before he knew it, an early 1980s truck was in his driveway with a magnetic sign attached to the side reading FLOORS GALORE. After a few minutes of measuring, he gave Paul an estimate for laying ceramic tiles throughout the house, and the deal was done. He would back in a few hours with the materials to start the job.

Thomas the tile guy was a small man with dark, deep-set eyes. He could have been sixty if going by his face or forty if going by his wiry body. A soiled baseball cap was worn backwards as he unloaded heavy boxes of tiles from the back of his truck. He was all bone and sinew.

"That road up here has the steepest grade in the state. I didn't know if the truck was going to make it with this load. We've both got some mileage on us," he grunted as he piled boxes of tile onto a handcart.

Paul tried to stay out of Thomas' way, painting in the back bathroom. Every once in a while he would peek into a room to watch as Thomas pulled up carpeting, decrepit padding, and assorted layers of linoleum and tiles.

"You know some floor guys might stop a job to have these kitchen tiles pulled up and tested for asbestos. I just scrape 'em up! I've been smoking since I was twelve. What the hell difference would it make now anyway to breathe in some of that stuff? Maybe it'll fireproof my lungs!"

Thomas announced he was taking a lunch break and began eating what looked like a homemade burrito

"Mind if I join you?" Paul asked, as he grabbed some ham and cheese out of the refrigerator and made a sandwich.

"Be my ghost," Thomas chuckled. "Where did you move from?"

"New York City. You've heard of it?"

Thomas gagged a little. "New York? How did a New Yorker wind up here?"

"It's a long story. Let's just say family matters."

"Say no more. I've got ex-wives, kids, and a stable full of animals that keeps me working like a mule. You got here just in time, too."

Paul looked up from slopping some mustard on his bread. "How's that?"

"The cities. You gotta see what's coming. Riots, mayhem, race wars, terrorism, the breakdown of society."

"Oh, that." Paul said, taking the first bite of his sandwich. "What's going to happen here?"

"Our militia, we got it all mapped out. Ain't nobody coming up that highway that doesn't live here, once the you-know-what hits the fan. We got blockades planned at strategic points. You're lucky you're one of us now."

"One of who?"

"Us. Up here. We got enough food, water, and weaponry to keep them out for months."

"Who are you keeping out?"

"The coastal elites. They're gonna be the first ones to get it, and they're all gonna flee like stuck pigs to get away from rioters and head up here. We ain't letting 'em in."

"But I'm good?"

"You live here. You're good."

"I like that. You're right. I am lucky." Paul said, nodding in agreement. "By the way, how long is this job going to take you?"

"Three days, I reckon."

"Perfect."

"By the way, if you want to invest in gold, I've just the guy for you! Paper money won't be worth diddly once it all goes down. You get good discounts if you mention our militia group."

Paul had heard of these militias. He assumed they were just overgrown boy scouts. But he liked the concept of, *You're here, you're one of us.* He had been stereotyped throughout his life for many things: being dark-skinned, too light-skinned, being a jock, being a cop, and being a male. Now he was *in* just because he lived somewhere.

"I'll let you know about that gold thing. You'll take a personal check for payment for the flooring job?"

"Check, credit, cash, gold, whatever you got!"

He couldn't deny that Thomas knew his craft. He worked quickly, quietly, with amazing attention to detail, down to tiny pieces of hand-cut tiles for corners, doorways, and room transitions. He just hoped the militia didn't show up in the middle of the night and take him hostage. Who would pay the ransom?

With no furnishings in the house except for a beach chair and small refrigerator until the flooring was complete, Paul had to sleep in a sleeping bag in a corner of the house where the construction wasn't too disruptive. This would be the first night in his new home, such as it was. At least he had plumbing and electricity.

As dark as the desert night was outside, inside the house was a darkness Paul had never experienced. Total pitch-black nothingness. At first he thought it would lead to his best night of sleep ever. Then it began: the noises. First he thought it was a baby crying. But with no houses within several hundred yards, it couldn't be that, unless someone abandoned one just beyond his fence. Then it sounded like a yip from puppy. A lost puppy seemed almost as unlikely as a baby. But then, it hit! It sounded like somebody just threw a cat into the hyena cage at the zoo. There were yips and squeals. Screeches and growls and barks and gags. Fights and fits and gnashing of teeth, claws and flesh being torn into. It sounded like maybe ten or twenty wild, crazed, primal animals going at it for close to a minute. Then suddenly it stopped. He listened closely. Nothing. Just a silence as deep and dark as the night. The investigation for the source of this mayhem would have to wait until morning. There were other sounds that caused him to awaken, thinking another zombie apocalypse might be starting again outside his window. He attributed that to other animals or birds grabbing a quick snack, rather than feeding the entire pack.

With no window coverings, the early summer sun was in his face like a spotlight in an interrogation room. He put on some shoes and carefully avoided walking on the mess of flooring, tools, and old carpeting, and made his way to a coffee maker.

The red sun rising over the rocky hills created a scene rivaled only by his favorite John Ford westerns. And now he was part of the scene. Curious from last night's cacophony of carnage, he took a walk around his property, coffee mug in hand. It was impossible to tell where it might have come from, but then he saw amongst the brown desert dirt a scattering of small wispy material. He reached down a picked up a tiny clump of pure white fluff. It had to be the white cottontail of a bunny. But that was it. No skull, no bones, no rabbit's foot. He wondered what became of the little critter, but then again decided he'd rather not know. Some things are better left un-thought of.

Thomas the tiler showed up at eight and began to work. Only now he wasn't so quiet. As he scraped and cut tile and laid tile and smeared cement he went on non-stop about globalists getting ready to put Americans in concentration camps, black helicopters, the grid being neutralized, food becoming poisoned, Mexico re-taking California, and so many paranoid scenarios it caused Paul to put down his paint brush in exasperation.

"I'll be back in a while, Thomas. Do you need anything? Some lunch?"

"Could you pick me up a steak burrito from Santana's Mexican food? Extra spicy, please."

"No problem. I'll be back in couple hours," Paul said as he admired the beautiful work Thomas had already completed. He decided to cruise around the area.

The Big Horn Horse Rescue was only about a mile down a washboard road, so he thought he'd give a visit. It could be a good way to get back into horseback riding again like he did as a kid in Van Cortlandt Park. In the distance, he saw a few large animals in the road and wasn't quite sure what they were. He slowed down as he approached and decided to park the car along the side of the road so as not to frighten any of them. He was about 30 yards away walking slowly toward what must be the horse rescue ranch, and in the road there were two llamas, a camel, and a goat. While they were lumbering along, several large dogs crossed the road from one part of the ranch, apparently, to the other. At the entrance to the ranch he could see the gate was ajar, and that the animals must have slipped out. On the other side he could see a lady talking on the phone sitting under an umbrella next to a small, silver Airstream trailer. She seemed to be aware that her animals were in the road, but didn't seem to care. Paul just stood there by the gate and observed.

There were many horses everywhere. Some looked emaciated, some looked like they could win the Kentucky Derby tomorrow. The lady put down her phone and noticed Paul. It was Mabel.

He couldn't tell when she was sitting on the horse the other day, but she was tiny. She probably weighed 100 pounds, but her walk showed she still had the strength and agility of someone half her age as she paused to push a big pile of horse manure to the side with a shovel. She looked right at Paul and said, "Harry Truman said, 'Never kick a fresh turd on a hot day.' Glad you stopped by!"

"This place is great! I haven't seen this many animals in one place since I busted a kid selling pills at the Bronx Zoo." Paul said, as he took a position by her on the other side of the split-rail fence. "Do you rent horses?"

"Sure. Depending on my workload and if I have any volunteers around to guide you. Just check back. So, you were in law enforcement?"

"Yes. All my life, pretty much."

"We need more cops out here. You dial 911 and you're lucky if somebody shows up in an hour. Or at all. That's why everybody has an arsenal in the house."

"You too?"

"You betcha. Lots of wild animals out here. Some on two legs. Not to mention the kind that slink around without legs."

"I'll keep in touch. I'm still getting settled in," Paul said getting back into his SUV.

He took a detour to town to pick up a couple of burritos, and decided to pop in on Kate. He pulled into the motel lot, and on the other end he saw Kate talking to a guy standing next to a beat-up pick-up. It was Ash. Paul kept his distance until Ash touched her arm, and she pulled away. Then he approached them. As soon as Ash saw him, Paul could see Ash's hackles rise up, with chest and belly out in a subtle but defiant stance.

"Hi Kate, excuse me, am I interrupting something?"

Kate took two steps towards Paul. "No, nothing. Ash was just leaving."

Ash said nothing, got in his pick-up and sped off.

Kate and Paul walked through the empty lot towards the office. "He's pissed that Jasmine hasn't paid him for some stuff. I am so sick of this."

"You're sick of it? I think I'm going to hole myself up on those five acres and build a fortress complete with an underground bunker."

"I may join you."

They sat behind the counter in two folding chairs. This was the first time Paul sensed that maybe pursuing something with Kate was a bad idea. The last thing he wanted was to have a circle of friends that included the druggies and miscreants similar to the ones he chased from Alphabet City to the Bronx Zoo. That saddened Paul, because he really cared for Kate. Maybe now that her husband was gone, she could go on with her life and leave that baggage behind.

"I'm really glad you bought that place. It's a relief actually," Kate said, softly, confessing to him.

"Einstein said, *once you stop learning, you start dying.* I've got a lot to learn. You should come by soon. The place is in shambles now, but once the floor guy finishes I can get to work on making the place my own."

"Let me know when, and I'll be there."

"My burritos are getting cold. I should be heading back."

Driving back to his place, he thought a lot about Kate. Ash was probably part of the fun and games her deceased husband had been tied into. It's like being on one of those playground merry-go-rounds, where kids hang on to an iron pipe while others push it around at breakneck speed, and it goes so fast that kids just start flying off. Her husband was one of the first to go flying off. More are sure to follow. But he didn't want to be a hero. Nope. Not gonna happen.

"Here's your burrito. Great work! You should be finished tomorrow, don't you think?" Paul said, truly astonished at how beautiful the place was looking with wall-to-wall ceramic tiles.

"Yup. Tomorrow should about wrap it up. Came out better than I expected. Some of these homestead add-ons are way out of whack."

"You think this was an original homestead?"

"Definitely. This room here was the original cabin. The slab in this part of the house is heavy-duty perfection. Probably poured 60 or 70 years ago, and not a crack in it. Somebody knew what they were doing. I figure this here, with the kitchen on the wall, was just a one-room cabin. And they used the outhouse out back by the stable." Thomas walked a few feet through a doorway. "This bedroom and this bathroom were added on probably in the late Forties, early Fifties. Still a good concrete slab, but not as good as the front room. The rest is Seventies and Eighties add-ons. Not great, but above-average construction."

"You do other construction work? I might be looking."

"I do it all. But floors are my bread and butter. You have to do it all these days. If you don't, you're dead. I've got solar power, a greenhouse for my vegetables, and a 40 ft. self-sustaining fish tank."

"Fish tank? Like tropical fish?"

"No. I only eat what I grow. Catfish. I tried keeping a few head of cattle for food, but man, you ever see a cow get slaughtered?"

"Can't say that I have."

"Not pretty. Too much work. I keep one just for emergencies."

"Like having an extra freezer of steaks in the garage, only you don't need the freezer. I like how you think, Thomas. I'll be painting in the back bathroom."

It took about a week of cleaning, painting, assembling furniture, placing furniture, and assorted mind-numbing household duties for Paul to feel like the place was close to being ready. He worked hard, but it was the kind of hands-on work he longed for. For decades his police work was the stuff of books, movies, newspapers, documentaries, and reality shows. For others, that is. For him it was simply getting himself and his fellow officers home after every shift, no matter what the karmic wheel of the universe threw at him. It seemed whatever the zeitgeist was at that time, no matter what bizarre drug-inspired insanity was permeating the bottom-feeders of the city, he and his partners had to somehow go into the chaos and sort things out. Too many drug dealers? Put them in jail. Too many junkies breaking into apartments and stabbing people for their wallets? Find them and put them away too. But don't make a mistake! You could be arresting a senator's son. Or get caught on a video punching a criminal who just shot at your partner. Work was not mindless. Some say being a cop is worse than combat. Not because it's the same as being in a war, but because – like being a soldier in battle – there are times of just monotonous and mind-numbing boredom. But your subconscious better know that at any second all hell can break loose, resulting in the same heartbreak as in combat: death. But soldiers aren't in combat for 20 or more years, 40 hours a week plus overtime.

As he painted the inside of the house, sweating and uncomfortable from stooping, stretching, and raising his arms for hours on end, he could see that he was making something better.

181

His own house. The place where he wanted to live was going to look like he wanted it. Progress was being made with each finished room. Each Walmart bed that was assembled. Each thrift-store-bought antique dresser put against a newly painted wall. As he admired his new abode, he wondered if being a cop all those years was worth it. Who had he really helped? At what cost? Then he thought to himself, *Goodbye tension, hello pension!* Who cares? That was then. This is now.

He had only talked to his daughter, Tracy, a couple of times on the phone during this busy week of fixing up the place. She had already moved to Twentynine Palms with Heidi. Now Tracy would be starting her new life. He couldn't wait until he could invite them over, cook them dinner, and then sit outside to watch the shooting stars on a warm evening, with owls hooting and coyote pups yipping for their mom to bring back supper.

Maybe Tracy had an idea of where she was headed when they loaded up the Escape and headed west across the George Washington Bridge. But it was all like a crazy high-altitude hallucination to Paul. It seemed like everyone he met up here told you their life stories before they were even finished shaking hands with you. He had lived in a basement apartment for nearly 20 years, and he barely knew his upstairs landlord, never mind whoever the hell lived next door.

It only took a few days for Paul to discover his happy place at his new home: on the front porch just after sunrise. He had several bird feeders, a hummingbird feeder, and a birdbath he kept filled. The desert air was still cool early in the morning, no matter how hot the day would later become. He felt the soothing sounds of birds chirping, scratching, and humming by was doing more for his health than all the oatmeal he ate three days a week. To his right, the rocky hills of the nearly 50,000 acres of undeveloped desert were also coming alive as shards of sunshine spread across the hardscrabble and boulders. He no longer needed his morning fix of the *New York Times* and *New York Post*. A scan of his phone gave him sports news from the night before. But he realized he wasn't getting as deep into the trends and big data of baseball as he had been doing since freshman year of high school. Did he really need to know that the Mets bullpen was giving up .25 more runs than the same period last season? He didn't even know who the wild cards teams were or if the Mets still had a statistical chance.

But he knew that the sparrows in his yard looked just like the ones back in New York and were just as bold, coming up to him for a flick of toast or oatmeal. And that the gorgeous, graceful roadrunners were quite elusive. According to his bird guide that little bird that sat atop the tip of the Joshua tree was a cactus wren.

Paul noticed the telltale sign of what was probably a car on the road about a quarter mile to the left, which was a cloud of swirling dust. He stood to get a better look, and just over the brush and berms of his five acres he couldn't believe his eyes or his ears. It wasn't a car but a half-dozen horses clomping down the road full speed with no riders or saddles. He watched in amazement as they charged up the road and disappeared. Then just as the dust was settling, he saw Mabel from the horse rescue ranch in a mad pursuit after them. *This really is the Wild West*, Paul thought to himself.

He noticed another swirl of dust on the road. He didn't see a horse, but Kate's car approaching. The birds fluttered away as she pulled into the gravel driveway.

"So this is where you've been holed up?" Kate said, exiting the car and holding a large brown paper bag. "I brought some breakfast."

Paul was pleasantly surprised that Kate showed up unannounced. "What brings you up to these parts so early?"

"I was over at the Integratron. They had a sunrise yoga and sound bath special."

They sat at the table on the front porch, and Kate unwrapped the breakfast burritos.

"A morning sound bath sounds kind of like morning Mass," Paul said, noticing the sparrows were already running around his feet pecking for crumbs. "I used to be an altar boy for 6 A.M. mass. Sometimes there was only one person in the church."

"You were an altar boy? That must leave quite an impression on a young mind. All that sacred imagery."

Paul took a bite of his burrito and thought about that. It was absolutely true. There was something almost scary about those dark early-morning masses amidst the giant hyper-realistic statues of the mid-century Catholic Church, including Jesus on the crucifix with the red blood oozing from his open wounds. "Is that why you like the Integratron? Is it a church substitute?"

"I never thought of it that way. Maybe it is. But I never went to church. My parents weren't religious. But I always liked the imagery. Have you heard of Desert Christ Park?"

"No."

"What are you doing this morning?"

"Going to Desert Christ Park?" Paul asked, a broad grin across his face.

"Si. After the burritos."

They drove in Paul's Escape down the hill, past Flat Top Mesa, Yucca Mesa, descending a thousand feet or so and into the commercial district of Yucca Valley, which people just call *the town*. It's more a collection of strip malls on a blacktop highway separated by vacant lots, feed stores, and out-of-business car lots. Kate gave directions, which weren't many. Just a right turn here and a left there onto a winding dirt road that went up again towards the rocky foothills, and there it was: the gate to Desert Christ Park. They drove through the opened iron gates, and could see nestled into the hillside gigantic, white statues dotting the landscape in the distance. As they got closer the white figures and structures took shape; they were oversized depictions of Jesus Christ, the Apostles, and other New Testament figures and scenes from the Bible.

Paul stood at the entrance in awe of the spectacle of ten to twenty-foot-tall religious statues and tableaus spread throughout the rocky hillside. Without the statues, these few acres would be just another plot of hardscrabble and brittle brush a mile or so from the main highway. But it was transformed into a land of biblical giants. Not of typical roadside giants like Paul Bunyan or the *Pee Wee's Big Adventure* dinosaurs or Randy's ginormous donut or a mounted F-16 fighter jet. No, this was a veritable statuary forest of blindingly white, enormous depictions of The Last Supper, the Virgin Mary, angels, Christ preaching, praying, comforting children and animals, and even Jesus resurrecting from the dead in a custom-built cave.

"Wow. What is this place?" Paul asked as he stepped closer to the statues, noticing that many were in various stages of disrepair.

"A retired aircraft worker built these during the late Forties hoping to inspire world peace. If you get too close, the flaws really are noticeable. Like a lot of things, I guess."

They spent the next half hour or so walking among the giants of Christianity in the heat of the desert sun. Both were silent as they stood next to larger-than-life apostles and biblical characters and faced a giant Jesus with hands extending, as if spreading his seeds of wisdom across the rocks and dirt.

"When I first came up here years ago, I thought this whole thing was one giant joke," Kate said, putting her finger in a crack in the palm of one of Christ's outstretched hands. "But now, I don't find it a joke at all."

"You were a doubting Thomas."

"What's that?"

"Doubting Thomas. After Christ rose from the dead, one of his apostles, Thomas, said he wouldn't believe Jesus was alive until he put his fingers in Christ's wounds to prove it."

Kate immediately took her finger off the statue.

"And then when he saw Jesus risen from the dead, and Jesus told him to go ahead, 'put your hand in my wounds,' he asked 'But what about those who don't get to put their hands in my wounds to prove it to themselves. How will they believe?' " Paul asked, standing next to the giant Christ statue.

"It seems a lot of searching for meaning happens in the desert," Kate said, stepping over some rocks to stand in the shade that Christ cast.

Paul gazed upward in awe at the giant Christ before him. "Jesus spent forty days and forty nights in the desert before he was crucified. Then there was Saul's transformation by the blinding lights of the desert."

"Did you major in religion or something?"

186

"I was the last generation of Latin-speaking altar boys."

"Have you heard of Salvation Mountain?"

"No. What's that?"

"It's kind of a man-made mountain in the middle of nowhere with giant quotes from the Bible and prayers to Jesus, all built by a guy who died a few years ago."

"I'm realizing there's kind of a theme going on out here. I'd like to see it, but I still have a lot of work to do at the house. We should probably head back."

Kate always knew there was a theme of searching for something out here in the high desert. A sense of something larger, more powerful, and mysterious. She believed that one of the reasons her husband wasn't able to kick his booze or drug habits was because AA required a belief in a greater power, and being a stubborn atheist he refused to be part of it. And ever since he died, she held a grudge against this higher power. She once regarded Desert Christ Park as a ridiculous tribute to a fairy tale. Same as Salvation Mountain and every church billboard that lined the local highway and offered help to anyone in need. But as she watched Paul take in the scripture quotes on the giant religious icons she could see a different kind of reaction. It wasn't by any means ridicule.

"Let's go over to that little rock chapel," Paul said, leading her across the gravel path to a small cave-like structure constructed out of multicolored desert stones.

There was a white stone cross over the altar with a shard of sunlight illuminating it. The three small pews were also made of stone, as were the kneelers. Paul was silent as he walked ahead of Kate and knelt down on both knees, bowed his head, and clasped his hands in prayer. From the side, Kate could see his lips slightly move as he prayed in silence. She wondered if he was praying in Latin. Kate decided she would wait outside for him.

Paul hadn't really prayed in a while. During the past few stressful weeks he had recited a few Hail Marys and Our Fathers but he hadn't prayed to Jesus. The Jesus of the New Testament pictured in so many missals, catechisms, movies, and paintings as the bearded man dressed in white robes. He found it easier to talk to that Jesus. That version of the Trinity in human flesh who faced his fate with doubt and the felt pain of human flesh being torn and tortured, knowing it was his duty. Paul thanked Jesus for what he had. He survived the cop years. The crazy partying years. The being married to a drug addict years. The sad years separated from his daughter. He thanked Jesus for his now-beautiful, smart, healthy daughter. For Greta and Peggy who watched over her. And prayed for guidance from Jesus in his new life, out here, somewhere in the California high desert. Whatever that meant.

"You seemed like you were off in another world in there," Kate said as they crunched gravel on the way to the parking lot.

"I was very much in this world that whole time. I don't know. You ever look for signs? In little things. Even stupid things? Like when you're thinking some random thought, say *pizza*, and then a Domino's delivery car pulls up next to you?" Paul asked, staring at the huge concrete slab with the Ten Commandments carved into it.

"I'm always looking for signs."

"I don't know if it's just coincidence or significance."

"Isn't that what faith's all about? Not knowing."

Paul pondered that, pausing with his finger on the car remote for a few moments. He pushed the button, the loud chirp piercing the quiet and they got in the Escape.

Paul's new home was ready for his special guests. His daughter, Tracy, and her friend, Heidi, had already been sharing an apartment in nearby Twentynine Palms, but Paul didn't want them to come by until the house was together. And this was the night. He had hoped to cook them dinner, but not knowing tofu from toffee he enlisted Kate to assist in the meal. He did have second thoughts on having Kate over on the first night Tracy and her friend came by. They were sure to assume that Kate was his significant other, which was not the case. Then of course he thought, *what the hell is the difference? She's a friend, right?* Who cares if it's not clear who he is romantically involved with? Yeah, he's her father and her mom just passed away, but he's been out of the picture for a long, long time. They're all grownups, right? Should he tell Tracy in advance? Nah. No biggie.

Tracy was terrified. This was the moment she had been dreading since the first time she realized that she was different from other girls on the softball team. And that some teammates were just like her. Times had changed, and she didn't have to live in secret as a lesbian after high school. Nearby Utica and Syracuse had a pretty good LGBT scene, and New York City was an Amtrak ride away. But this would be the first time she told a family member. She never even bothered telling her mother, because she was so deeply troubled in her own ball of confusion, she didn't want to throw another unknown into her poor mom's shrinking capacity to handle any of life's complications. She didn't tell Grandma or Aunt Peggy, but she actually had a feeling that Aunt Peggy may actually be a lesbian, even if she didn't realize it. Yet. But telling her father would be a big moment for her and Heidi. She knew how most of the people in the old Bronx neighborhood thought about progressive social issues. She even heard Grandma slip and use the N-word or the F-word or some of the other capital-letter words not used in polite society anymore. But Grandma was from that old generation where those words were part of family gatherings and jokes were told about ethnicities and sexuality. Even in mainstream entertainment.

She had no idea where her father fit into that old-versus-new world. He was a cop for Christ's sake! Being judgmental was in his DNA. But she knew she couldn't live her life as a lie, no matter the consequences. She checked with friends, and reactions were about split fifty-fifty as to how parents reacted to the news. But even among the ones that supported their children upon coming out, whether gay or lesbian, there was a common theme of disappointment. But so what? She could certainly handle disappointment. What kid doesn't disappoint their parents? Unless you're a brain surgeon, president of something, or have a spouse who adores their in-laws, all parents are disappointed about something. And if her father couldn't handle it, so be it. Certainly it would be nice if he was cool about it, but the truth of the matter was, she's only known him for five minutes out of her life, and if she needs to know about any hereditary diseases or conditions he might pass down, she'd probably know about it by now. But as she looked in the full-length bathroom mirror upon getting out of the shower, she could see her mother and her father: in her eyes, her lips, the shape of her legs, her hairline. She is the daughter of her parents and she does sense that deep connection of blood, bones, and soul now more than ever. She did hope he wouldn't freak out.

Kate knew her way around a vegan, gluten-free, organic, paleo diet cookbook. Paul was in awe of the things she was chopping, mixing, and measuring.

190

Paul picked up the cook book. "What's a paleo diet?"

"That's food that appears naturally. Made by nature."

"Oh, you mean like pork chops?"

"I guess…."

"You remember Jack LaLane?"

"Vaguely. Didn't he have an infomercial for a juicer?" Kate asked, chopping away at veggies.

"That's him! That's when he was in his 90s, I think. But going back to the 1940s he was out there saying, 'If man made it, don't eat it.' "

"Same thing."

It was really the first time Paul felt at home in his new house. The aroma of the food cooking, the neatness of everything in its place, the sight of a woman busy helping make the evening a success, awaiting special guests. He couldn't help but think of how he had dreams of a day like this when Tracy was born, and he and Marcy were making their home together in the early days of their marriage. He would always flash ahead to the future, wondering what it would be like when Tracy came of age and he and Marcy welcomed her back into their home as an adult. Those dreams disappeared quickly, as if Marcy was bitten one night by a werewolf or a vampire, or as if her body was commandeered by a body snatcher, causing her to become a destructive creature he no longer recognized. And he had just resigned himself to accept the fact that not only did he lose Marcy, but his only daughter was lost as well.

Being there, in that house, soft jazz playing in the background, Kate in a flower-print apron floating around the kitchen like a butterfly, and Tracy coming by to visit had him feeling at peace. Finally. He didn't think it would ever happen. That domestic bliss he had seen on *Leave it to Beaver*, and had glimpses of at friend's houses, seemed a universe away. Or at least another galaxy away. And now, somehow, here he was.

The table was set, the food just about ready, and Paul was like a kid waiting for company to show up on his birthday. Then he heard the unmistakable sound of tires slowly crunching gravel in a driveway.

"They're here. How do I look?" Paul asked Kate, smoothing his Who t-shirt.

"You look great. Just relax and enjoy."

Paul walked out to the driveway as Tracy and Heidi were exiting a large Ford F-150 pickup.

"Welcome to the ranch, podners," Paul said, approaching Tracy, and sharing a warm hug.

"You remember Heidi," Tracy said as Paul and Heidi hugged.

"Pleasure to meet you again, sir," Heidi said formally.

"Call me Paul. Let's go inside. My friend Kate has a vegan feast set up for us."

Tracy and Heidi watched each other carefully for telltale signs of just when Tracy would ease into "the talk." Heidi was probably more nervous than Tracy. She had been a Marine for a couple years, and her first year in was before they announced that gays and lesbians could serve openly in the corps, which was a great relief to her. But she knew that once Tracy got through this hurdle of telling her father that she was a lesbian, the wheels would be set in motion that would include their wedding, and her also joining the Marines, which may or may not cause seen or unforeseen issues.

Kate had placed all the food on the dinner table and all were helping themselves. Paul sampled all the vegan fare, but he was the only one with a large NY strip steak on his plate and a can of Guinness. Small talk ensued and all caught up on the whirlwind of activities over the past few weeks. But Paul sensed that Tracy was nervous about something. He kept the conversation lively with funny cop stories and new high-desert adventures, but he had a sixth sense that Tracy was going to wait for a long pause and drop something on him. And there it was.

"Dad, I'm really glad we're all here. Friends, I mean. The four of us. Because I have something to say. An announcement, I guess you would call it."

Paul's mind raced. An announcement? He didn't expect that. He expected maybe some kind of a confession. Or a request for money. Or some kind of kid-versus-bad-parent lecture. But not an announcement. "Shoot," Paul said, with a nod and a wink.

Suddenly, there was that familiar sound again: tires crunching gravel. But these tires were going a little too fast, and skidded to a stop.

"Who the hell is that?" Paul said as he rose. A troubled look on Kate's face told him she might have an idea.

"I did tell Jasmine I would be here this evening," she said. "But I didn't exactly invite her over."

"Well," Paul said looking out the front window, "she didn't exactly show up alone, either. That guy Ash is with her."

Tracy sighed deeply and Heidi held her hand under the table in support.

The front screen door swung open. "I hope we're not disturbing anything. I didn't realize you were having guests, or I never would have imposed," Jasmine said, leading Ash into the house.

"We were just getting ready for dessert. Sit down. Would you like something to drink?" Paul said, mustering up as much politeness as he was capable of, which even surprised him a little.

193

"I'll have a beer," Ash croaked, as he sat on a stool next to the kitchen island.

"Wine for me," Jasmine said, sitting at an empty chair at the dinner table. "I'll just pick," and began sampling the foods on the table, using her fingers. "You should try this, Ash."

Ash walked over to the table as Kate, Paul, Tracy and Heidi made their way over to the counter to get coffee and homemade brownies.

"Tracy and Heidi, come with me, let's look at that gorgeous night sky and see if we can find any UFO's," Paul said, leading them out to the front yard.

The sky was as clear as it could be: black velvet with spots of sparkling light, some twinkling like stars do, and the planets hiding among them, just beaming away with their steady light. And down the middle was the magic carpet of solar systems, glistening in all its glory, the Milky Way. Paul arranged the chairs in the dark so they could look up at the sky. They settled in their seats and quietly watched more and more stars appear as they're eyes became accustomed to the darkness.

"If you think about it, why would we be the only planet with life?" Paul asked. "If there are billions of galaxies and billions of stars in every galaxy why would we be the only ones in all that?"

"Dad, I'm glad we're out here. I mean the three of us here, right now, under the stars."

"Yeah. Me, too. It's a nice night."

"No, I mean, the *three* of us. Dad, Heidi and I are...." Tracy's word got stuck in here throat and she paused. Heidi held her hand in the darkness.

"Go ahead, Tracy," Heidi said, squeezing her hand.

"Dad, I'll just say it. I'm a lesbian. Heidi and I are getting married. And then, I'm going to join the Marines. Heidi is a sergeant and...

Suddenly screams were heard inside the house. Paul spun around and through the window he could see water gushing from the kitchen sink and shooting up to the ceiling.

"Holy jumpin' shit! Tracy, this will have wait," Paul said as he rushed to get back into the kitchen. "But I don't approve! We'll talk later," he shouted, running into the house and letting the screen door slam behind him.

"Dad! What? I knew it! Heidi let's go! This is bullshit!"

"No doubt," Heidi said, now holding Tracy's hand. "My father did the exact same thing when I came out! That's their problem, not ours."

Tracy and Heidi walked towards their truck.

Paul rushed into the kitchen, with water spraying everywhere from the broken faucet. "Damn! And I just fixed that! I'll shut off the main water valve in the front yard!" He said, grabbing a flashlight as he ran outside. He paused when he saw Heidi's truck in the distance as they drove off. He weakly waved the flashlight towards their red taillights in the distance.

"Shit. I screwed that up. Big league. Tracy in the Marines? No way...." He said, whispering into the night.

After turning off the main water valve, Paul returned to the kitchen. Kate was drying everything with some towels, as Jasmine and Ash sat on stools around the island. There were two empty wine bottles and a half empty bottle of tequila on the counter. Ash's eyes turned towards Paul like a chipmunk keeping an eye out for a predator.

"I think we better be going, Jasmine. It's getting late," Ash said, picking up his weed pipe.

"You can hang if you want," Paul said, as if he was really telling them to get the hell out by the tone of his voice. "Did I have a can of Guinness?"

"I think Jasmine put it in the fridge," Kate added.

"No I didn't. Ash and I need to go," Jasmine said. Ash looked surprised by her remark. The two of them gathered their things, said goodbye, and were soon kicking up gravel up the driveway.

Paul got his Guinness out of the fridge and took a gulp.

"I'll help you clean up," Kate said, gathering things off the counter.

Paul took another swig from his can of Guinness and put it back in the fridge. "No need to. It's just a few things. I'll take care of it."

"Are you sure?"

"Yeah, I'm sure."

"What happened out there?" Kate asked, understating her concern. "And where's Tracy and Heidi?"

"They had to go. That's all," Paul said, containing his anger, but making it clear he was shutting down any further discussion.

"I have an early day. Call me tomorrow and we'll talk. I want to hear all about it."

"All about what?"

"Tracy and Heidi."

"Nothing to discuss," Paul said, flatly.

Kate shook her in disgust. "Yup. Nothing. Just shut it down. Goodnight."

He watched her red taillights disappear up the driveway and down the road from the front window. Paul looked at the mess and decided he would just finish the cleanup in the morning. He didn't feel right; his stomach felt funky and he was a little light-headed. *That happens when one's upset,* he thought to himself. He went to the bathroom sink, threw some cold water on his face, and studied it in the mirror. Did he really look like this? Maybe it was his wet skin, or the bad lighting or something he ate, but he didn't like what he saw. He changed t-shirts, put on some pajama bottoms, and went to bed.

It wasn't the first time in his life that Paul felt as though the room was spinning. Usually it lasted a few minutes until he fell back to sleep. If he was lucky, he wouldn't throw up in bed. He knew how dangerous that could be. He sat up on the side of the bed. His bare feet touched the tiles and he was surprised that the floor didn't feel cold. It actually felt warm, and seemed to be getting hotter. The room stopped spinning, but now the floor was so warm, he reached down with his hand and *Ouch!* It was hot to the touch. He put on his Indian moccasins that were next to the bed, and noticed there was an unusual light coming though the venetian blinds on the other side of the room, through the window facing the 50,000 acres of federally owned land. He shuffled over to the window, and was reluctant to open the blinds to see what might be on the other side. His mind raced. A fire? Headlights? A spotlight? He steeled himself, grasped the venetian blind cord tightly and tugged it. *What the hell?* He shouted to no one.

A blinding light, or laser, or light beam came down from the above his house, went across the patio and appeared to be going under the house. Is that what's making the floor so hot? But what was it? He heard a very low humming vibration that felt as though it was penetrating his bones. *Like the Integratron sound bath?* He asked himself.

He raced through the house, grabbing his car keys and phone, and went to the rear patio. And there, hovering just above roof level was a light so blindingly bright he could hardly make out what it was. Was it a plane of some kind? A drone maybe? An experimental military chopper or something? No. Can it be? Then it came into focus. A UFO! It had to be! The Integratron was only a couple of miles away. If it truly was the vortex of universal energies, those same energy centers would most likely be under his house as well, right? And attracting UFO's is exactly why the Intergraton was initially built.

The craft glowed and hummed. Pulsated. It flashed. Signaled? It began to move over the house. Paul ran to the front yard and got in the SUV. The craft was laying down a beam of light on the dirt road. Was he supposed to follow it? Of course. It picked up speed and he followed it.

Sweat was pouring down his face, into his eyes. His hands were like rubber. It took all his strength to grip the wheel as he turned off the dirt road and into the open expanse of the desert on a trail. It was a full moon, so he could see where the trail was leading in the distance. He thought it might be easier to see if he turned off his headlights, which he did. He was amazed at how bright the moonlight was. There were shadows cast across the road from boulders, yuccas, and Joshua trees. He could see desert critters' eyes hiding off to the side as he whizzed by. They were watching him.

The craft was leading him somewhere down this trail. It came into focus. Is it Morse code they're flashing? Then strange lettering appeared on its side. Arabic? Greek? Hebrew? Latin! It's in Latin! Think. Think. Paul struggled with the words: *Confiteor. Deo. Omnipotenti. What? Jesus Christ, this can't be. It's the Confiteor! From Latin mass!*

Suddenly out of nowhere, a creature darted across his path. What is it? A beast? *The* beast? Paul pulled the wheel to the left sharply onto the rocky hardscrabble and *THUD*, the Escape SUV went down a wash and *WHAM*, came to a violent stop in a culvert. The engine stalled. Silence. Darkness.

The beast. It's coming. I knew it. God, Jesus, help me. Help. Me. Help....

During a full moon, Mabel sometimes led a group from the horse rescue ranch, but tonight she was solo. You could actually read a newspaper, it was so bright out, she noted. But thinking she heard something in the distance, she decided she would take a detour off the marked trail and see if there was something unusual out in the hardscrabble and brush. Jerks were always dumping trash out there because they were getting $75 to clean out a garage or a yard, and didn't want to pay the $25 dump yard fee. She wasn't frightened venturing out on her own. She had her cell phone and her 9mm Glock just in case anybody was going to mess with her. The moonlight seemed to be glinting off something in the distance and she headed for it.

What the hell is that thing doing in the middle of nowhere? She asked herself, seeing Paul's Escape stuck in a culvert.

Christ, there's got to be somebody in there! She galloped the rest of the way, took out a flashlight and shined it inside the SUV. *Damn! That's that new neighbor guy, Paul!*

Mabel tied up her horse to a nearby Joshua tree and rushed to the SUV door. It was unlocked but jammed. She managed to pull it open a couple of inches but it wouldn't budge any further. She went to her saddlebag, and pulled out a multi-use tool that was a combination hammer, axe, and crowbar. She shoved it in the opening and with all her strength was able to get the door open enough so she could get inside. She immediately went for his neck to check for a pulse.

"Thank God!"

Paul was unconscious but breathing. She pushed him back in his seat, clearing away the debris from the exploded air bag. He wasn't bleeding externally as far as she could tell. She shined the flashlight in his ears, mouth and nose and didn't see any blood there either. But she was puzzled. Why the hell was he in his pajama bottoms? She removed the keys from ignition and as she was leaning over inside the car, she noticed a phone on the floor sticking out slightly from under the passenger seat. She quickly dialed the most recent number on there. A female voice answered.

"Hello?"

"Hi, who is this?"

"Tracy, who's this?"

"Tracy, are you related to or friends with Paul?"

"He's my dad. What's going on here?"

"Tracy, there's been an accident, and Paul is hurt. I'll call 911, but it will take them forever to get here. We're about two miles from your dad's house."

"We can be there in five minutes. We just stopped for coffee down the road. My friend's an EMT."

Tracy got the directions, and she and Heidi sped to the location. Heidi was ready for anything. Her Ford F150 was a 4x4 and she had a medical-grade first aid kit on board. They went a little airborne when they turned off the washboard dirt road and went over a berm. A left turn at an old shed, and there they were. Mabel had turned on the four-way flashers on Paul's Escape just ahead.

"I called 911, but they won't be here for 20 minutes at the least," Mabel said, waving them over as Heidi grabbed her heavy-duty tricked-out Sears Craftsman multileveled and drawered tool kit. "I got here a little while ago. He's still out, but breathing."

"Hurry," Tracy said quietly but firmly to Heidi. She was not going to lose her cool. She was not going to lose her father. Not now. Not after all she's just been through. Not even after the big blowout they just had. Not after just getting him back into her life. Could God be that cruel?

Heidi was as calm as she was swift. She went through every protocol to ensure survival. She thought he was definitely going to make it. No broken bones. Neck, face, air passages all good. She doubted there was internal bleeding. The vehicle was not badly damaged. She surmised it came to an abrupt stop against the soft sand berm, rather than in a high-speed crash. He missed a large boulder by about three feet. She inspected his eyes.

"This is weird," Heidi said calmly.

"What? Is he okay?" Tracy said trying to contain herself.

"He seems all right. He's unconscious, but I think he might be...."

"What?" Tracy said, staring to lose her cool.

"He may have drugs in his system. The eyes. The respiration. The pulse. The skin. I don't know."

They all heard a siren at the same time and saw the flashing red light in the distance.

Heidi ran to her truck, turned it around with a move worthy of Danica Patrick, and positioned it on a high boulder facing the road, with her roof-top searchlights illuminating half the desert. She flashed them on and off.

The ambulance arrived and swiftly went into action. Everyone helped get Paul onto a stretcher, then a gurney, and into the ambulance. Heidi identified herself as a Marine

Sergeant/EMT/medic. Tracy went in the ambulance with Paul and they sped away.

"How did you ever find him?" Heidi asked Mabel, both gazing at the accident aftermath. "Are you like the Lone Ranger or something?"

"I don't know why I was even out this way. I haven't done a moonlight ride solo in while."

"Thank God."

"Oh boy, did I!" Mabel said, tending to her horse. "Wait! What's that? Oh no. Poor thing!"

Off to the side of the trail hunkered against a boulder was a large injured dog, licking its back paw with a gash on its head.

"Maybe that's what Paul saw and he had to swerve to avoid hitting it," Heidi said, shining her flashlight on it. "What can we do?"

"If you can wait here a few minutes, I'll go back to the ranch, get my truck and a doggie crate, and I'll take care of him. I've already got about thirty animals on the mend. And he'll be the smallest of the lot. I run the horse-rescue ranch."

"I'll be here," Heidi said, comforting the dog, who seemed to be quite appreciative of her concern. She petted his head, and the large pit bull mix, which must have weighed over 100 pounds, made whimpering noises like a puppy who wanted a treat. She remembered she had some beef jerky in her truck. The dog watched her as she went to the truck and returned with something in hand. He was thrilled to have something to eat. He didn't have a collar. *Typical for the desert*, she thought to herself. It was a veritable dumping ground for unwanted animals, from rabbits bought at Easter, to sick, old, or just plain unwanted dogs and cats, to even lizards and tortoises. Usually just the larger dogs survive in this hostile environment. There are many predators looking for easy prey in the harsh dog-eat-dog desert.

Mabel arrived quickly with her truck and parked a few yards away. The dog only growled one time as Heidi and Mabel coaxed him into the dog crate with some dog food. It took both of them to load it into the back of her pickup and secure it. He was quiet and nuzzled up against a plush dog toy.

"He's on the mend already. I'll get him to the vet in the morning," Mabel said hopping into her truck.

"Who pays for that?"

"I do. Like the dozens of other critters that find me somehow. I'm a 501c non-profit, so I do fundraisers, but I haven't been in the black since day one. I'm not complaining or soliciting. The good Lord provides."

Heidi reached into her pocket. "Here's forty bucks. It's all I've got."

"Twenty would be fine," Mabel said, stuffing a bill in her pants pocket. "Call me at the ranch if you want to help out in person."

"We will. I'll give you an update on Paul. I'm going to the hospital now."

Heidi knew the High Desert Medical Center well. There was a hospital on the Marine base, but she made many runs to and from the medical center, with patients and sometimes with a body bag.

Paul was in a private room, which she thought was unusual until she poked her head in further, and saw a sheriff sitting on the other side of the bed from Tracy. She recognized him as a former Marine from the base.

Paul was groggy. Incoherent. And babbling.

"I've got to...chase. What in the? Where?" Paul said, barely understandable.

"What did the doctor say?" Heidi asked Tracy quietly.

"They said he could be under the influence of something. But his injuries, thank goodness, seem to be minor."

"That's why the sheriff is here?"

"Yes. He could be under arrest."

Heidi crossed over to the sheriff. "Hello sir, I'm Sergeant Heidi Orloff, active duty. Aren't you McQuade?"

"Yes, ma'am. Are you related to Mr. Santo?"

"My friend's father. He's retired NYPD. Is he under arrest?"

"Not exactly. Just waiting for the alcohol results. If that's okay, then we wait for toxicology, which takes a few days."

A nurse popped her head in. "Officer, may I see you?"

"Excuse me."

He stepped outside for about ten seconds and was back inside the room. "He had a trace of alcohol, but below the limit. I'm done here. Good luck!"

Heidi and Tracy stood next to Paul as Tracy stroked his forehead. Suddenly he turned towards her.

His eyes opened but he struggled to get words out. "Where am I? I saw something. In the sky. Lights. Followed. Latin. Ashes...."

"You're okay. You were in an accident. You're fine. They're trying to figure out what happened," Tracy said, calming him. "There aren't any ashes. There's no fire."

"Ashes.... Beast."

"There's no beast," Tracy said calmly.

"It was a dog, Paul. A dog. He's okay." Heidi added.

"There was a dog?" Tracy asked, puzzled.

"We found an injured dog there. Mabel the horse-rescue lady is taking care of him. Paul must have swerved or something to avoid hitting him."

"Ashes...." Paul continued weakly.

"What about the ashes?" Tracy asked slowly.

"UFO...."

"UFO? Tracy asked. "Too weird. Let's wait and see exactly what's in that toxicology report. Maybe he was hallucinating. He called me recently after he thought he was slipped some pot brownies."

Paul was released later that evening, which would have been about 24 hours after he perhaps unknowingly ingested something. They did an MRI to see if there was any head trauma, and that was negative. And after examining Paul thoroughly, the doctor didn't think he had any kind of a psychotic episode. Everything was pointing in the direction of being slipped a mickey, and Paul thought the person doing the sneaky deed was Ash. And the mere thought of that had Paul escalating in way that was beginning to scare him. What if Paul had driven home Kate or Heidi and Tracy when the drugs took effect? He could have killed them. And maybe wiped out a vanload of innocent people in the process. What kind of sick mind would do such a thing? It was like a fire burning in his belly that he hoped would not trigger an inferno that he wouldn't be able to control. He always used that rage to survive throughout his life as a cop. Rage must translate into action in order to do things that most humans would run away from in horror. But a cop has to run towards the danger, despite the imminent confrontation with injury, death, or worse.

Only one time in his cop years did he have to channel his most primal instinct to use deadly force. If he didn't, it would have been certain death for a woman, her child, and himself. But the squeeze of a trigger stopped evil with a single bullet. It was hard to see the entry point of the 9mm missile, but it went into the perp's open mouth. There was no mistaking the exit wound. The wall behind him had a giant Rorschach splotch in deep red. Three people were alive, a mother and child and himself, because he controlled and focused and turned chaos into order with one shot. But he still had regrets. Could he have avoided killing him if he tried something else? If he had waited for backup, or tried talking to him, or who knows? Yes, he had to live with the fact that he killed another human being. It was his job. He just hoped he wouldn't have to get to that point ever again. But now he needed to find Ash. And whatever happens, happens.

Chapter Eight

Three weeks had passed, and Paul was still embarrassed about the entire episode. Tracy called two, three, four times a day to check on him. Since nothing was definitive in the toxicology report, he could tell that she was asking things to see if he possibly had a stroke or something else brewing in his head, like early onset dementia or Alzheimer's. It was a well-known fact that Alzheimer's could begin in one's forties and Paul was closer to sixty than forty.

But now that the bumps and bruises of his crash were wearing off, he was having flashes of what happened that night. And he sure as hell wasn't going to tell anyone about it. Then they'd think he really popped his gourd.

The nights were getting cooler in the high desert and the night skies were spectacularly clear. He hadn't returned any of Kate's calls or voice mails. He figured he'd just let that be for now. He was actually enjoying the pestering phone calls from Tracy. It really was the first time in his life he had a family member concerned about his well-being. All those years he spent flirting with death on a daily basis, he knew that if he bought the farm one night in a junkie shooting-gallery basement, there'd be an article in the *New York Post*, and a funeral with hundreds of cops saluting at attention, phony platitudes from politicians, and some teary-eyed toasts at The Buckeye for maybe a night or two. But he also knew back then that there wouldn't be a first pew in the church filled with a grieving widow, sobbing kids, and family members. The last time he felt like he had a real family was that first week when Marcy came home with Tracy from the hospital. So it was a strange, new feeling that someone actually cared enough for him to call several times a day. And he liked it.

Paul enjoyed lying in his yard at night on the chaise lounge, gazing at the dazzling dome of stellar spectacles while sipping vodka on ice. But it was during these solitary nighttime sessions that images began to emerge from that night.

Shooting stars were commonplace. It was a disappointment if you didn't see one after an hour or so of sky-gazing. But when there was a double dose of cosmic debris shooting in opposite directions, Paul remembered. There had been something in the sky that night. It wasn't just a shooting star. It had to be a UFO. And he did follow it.

Was he losing his mind? Did he see a UFO? They told him he was wearing his pajama bottoms and didn't have his wallet. He knew he wasn't drunk. Could it be dementia?

He remembered when his mother was in the nursing home at the very end, she was convinced that her roommate, a practically comatose 101-year-old, was a vampire. She was so convinced and made such a stink, that she had to be moved to another room with a new roommate.

No. He wasn't losing his mind. But did he lose his mind that night? The toxicology report showed no signs of opioids, uppers, downers, heroin, pot, or pharmaceuticals. But did they test for everything? Did they test for that old hippie favorite, LSD? He remembered Tracy asking him when he got back home about "ashes." That he kept mumbling "ashes." And how they thought he was referring possibly to the accident and if there was a fire.

"Ash is!" he said out loud, scaring a few birds that apparently were sleeping in a nearby tree and flitted away. "Ash is responsible," he whispered to himself.

The hospital confirmed it. They do not check for LSD as part of the routine toxicology report. And it's too late to do another test now. So it could have been LSD that caused his hallucinations. Of course! Ash easily could have slipped it into his drink.

Paul was driving too fast and he knew it. He had his wallet on the top of the dash so he would be at the ready to present it to a cop in case he got pulled over, just like he did back in New York when he was on the job. He reached down to pat his Beretta semi-automatic .22 that was tucked in his ankle holster, which was another nervous habit he had whenever he drove in the squad car. His .38 was under the seat. He needed to talk to Kate. She would have the skinny on Ash. And if she didn't, Jasmine certainly would. He was going to take care of this himself. No need to get the local authorities involved. Plus, what proof did he have? Zilch. Just the thought of presenting his case to a detective made him laugh. Who would believe such a preposterous story?

As he drove down the dark dirt road in his fully repaired Escape, he began to imagine the look on the detective's face as he laid out the details of that strange night. And as he began to go over the scenario, little bits and pieces from that evening of insanity and drama began to come back to him. The strange sounds out his window. The beams of white light shining through the blinds. His panic when he ran through the door and saw it. There it was in front of him. A freaking UFO hovering just in front of his house. Beckoning him to follow. Which he did. In a panic.

"Am I nuts? Did this happen? Was it a hallucination? Am I having a PTSD flashback?" He asked himself, watching for the turnoff to the highway.

Kate was surprised when Paul walked into the office. She was still behind the counter because her replacement was late. She could still see the bruising on Paul's face from the accident and he didn't seem himself.

"Well look what the cat dragged in," she said, trying to lighten the moment. "How's your recuperation going?"

It was easy for Paul to hide his innermost feelings. Or so he thought. He played these games for decades while trying to get what he needed from a witness or rookie assistant D.A.

"Great. Everything's great. I've been laying low. You know, just taking it easy for a few weeks. Enjoying life. Living the dream."

Living with an alcoholic druggie for all those years, Kate was no newbie when it came to obfuscation and lies. "Yeah, I know what that's like. Me too. Living the dream."

Fake smiles and laughter were exchanged.

"So to what do I owe this surprise visit? I tried calling you. Several times. Many times."

"Yeah, like I said, just getting myself back on track. Do you, by any chance, have an address or phone number for Ash?"

"Ash? What do you want with that ass? Oh no. Don't tell me. You're going to be some kind of hero now? Rescue us damsels in distress from the bad man who sells nickel bags of a legalized substance. You know it's totally legal now?"

"I don't care about that. I need to talk to him. There's something very important I must know and he's the only one who can tell me."

"And if he doesn't? Then the Lone Ranger pulls out his silver revolver and saves the day? Well don't expect me to be Tonto in this episode."

"You're not being very cooperative."

Kate rolled her eyes. "Your honor, I'd like to deem Kate now as a hostile witness. Come on, Paul what are you playing at?" Kate even surprised herself that she was shouting so loud.

"Kate. Calm down. Whose side are you on?"

"I'm on nobody's side. I don't want to be the one who causes some narc to go busting people for nothing and stirring up a hornet's nest of animosity and vitriol where there was none."

"He could have killed me that night."

"Okay, I'll bite," Kate said, exasperated.

"He slipped me LSD. I'm sure of it. They don't test for it with the toxicology report. I had no drugs in me that they found. It must have been LSD. You know he doesn't like me. He thought it would be some kind of a joke. Slip the narc some acid. Well, I ain't laughing. I could have killed somebody. My daughter. You."

Kate walked around the counter, grabbed Paul by the hand, and pulled him to the office sofa for a sit down. "It's a dead end. I can't believe he would do something like that to you. To anybody. He's not that way."

"I need to talk to him. I won't go Rambo on him."

Kate knew that this could be the end of whatever chance they had for a relationship at this point. If she refused to give the information, it was over. And if she did, and Paul got Ash busted, it was over.

"I'll get it from Jasmine and I'll call you with it."

"Thanks. It can be a lonely journey for somebody who's looking for answers. Believe me, I know," Paul said, forlornly as he exited the office.

The cool evening's temperatures were stretching longer into the morning and the afternoons had a hint of the desert fall. Kate had been good about calling and checking on him, but he dared not let her know what his true intentions were regarding Ash. He didn't even want to admit it to himself. Yeah, he had anger issues, but they were under control, weren't they? The truth was, he hadn't been really tested in a while. Those "anger issues" were part of a cop's survival instincts. Act fast. React with force. Deadly force if needed. Survival of the quickest.

His new desert home was perfect for the solitude he needed. If he turned off his phone there was no connection to the outside world. His mailbox was close to a half mile away. His closest neighbor was a few hundred yards away. Living in the Bronx in the shadow of an elevated train, several bus lines, an interstate highway, and hustling, bustling Broadway – yes, that legendary Broadway on which George Washington rode upon his horse and George M. Cohan staged his shows (although the two men were a couple of centuries and about a dozen miles removed) – one's senses become dulled by the all the clatter and clutter, noises, and distractions of the city. If one doesn't ignore the constant assault on the senses insanity would surely follow.

Now hours and sometimes days would pass before Paul heard other humans. Maybe a chain saw in the distance, or a pick-up truck clanking down a distant road would catch his attention. Usually, his solitude wasn't interrupted by humans. It was enhanced by the coo-coo-cooing of the mourning doves. Or the varied howls and hoots of the quail herding their chicks to and fro. Or the nighttime calls of owls, coyotes, and mysterious creatures hiding and surviving in the harsh unforgiving terrain.

No more bars. No more bus trips. No more concerts, baseball games, Italian street festivals, stifling subway rides, jammed elevators, or long lines at Jewish delis. Finally he could hear himself. The inner voice that he hadn't been able to hear began to become audible. But what was it telling him? Or rather, asking him?

He decided to turn on his phone and saw that there were several messages, including the one he had been waiting for from Kate: *Hi, Paul. It's Kate. Ash is in Landers. I have an address but GPS won't get you there. You'll need a map. I can go over it with you. Let me know if you want to stop by here at the office or I can come to your place.* There was long pause, then *Bye.*

Paul needed a couple of things from the store, so he decided to go down the hill and see Kate as well. He found it interesting that there were still places in Southern California, one of the most populous locales in the country, that even Google Maps hadn't bothered with yet.

He opened the door to Kate's motel office and the bell tinkled. He approached the counter and there was a map with some red lines drawn upon it.

"Howdy stranger," Kate said appearing in the doorway. "How are you?"

"I'm great. Been doing some woolgathering."

"What's that?"

"Thinking. You've got a lot of red on that map. Doesn't that usually mean *danger?*"

"Sometimes. Sometimes it's just to make something stand out."

"Did you ever think of why we use red to signify danger?" Paul asked, picking up the red-tipped pencil and examining closely.

"It's just a color that stands out, I guess."

"Why does it stand out? You know, more than yellow or bright blue?"

Kate shook her head.

"Blood. It's the color of blood."

"Well, I'm glad your woolgathering has put you in your happy place. Let's get to the map. Next time I'll use the yellow highlighter. Now, these friends of Ash's, I have a feeling they're not from a church group. Ash is like a worker ant. He leaves the colony to do his work, but always goes back to the nest to deliver the fruits of his labor."

"Is there a queen?"

"Presumably a king. Are you sure you want to do this? Can you tell me what exactly is going on? I need to know, before I give you this. If I'm setting up some kind of drug bust, I'll first have to move to New Zealand."

"I need to talk, just talk to Ash. I need to know if he slipped me something that night of my accident."

"Like what? Pot brownies? St. John's wort tea?"

Paul saw where she was going.

"I'm not paranoid. I need to know. If he slipped me LSD, then at least I'll know."

"Know what?"

"If I was hallucinating. Or…."

"Or what?"

"Losing my mind."

Kate understood. She pursed her lips and touched Paul's hand with affection. Before her husband died, she knew he was losing it. But she always thought that it was a phase; being forgetful, moody, obtuse, distant, and yes, paranoid. Drugs and alcohol could do that, but perhaps it was self-medication to treat something more serious that he subconsciously was aware of. Like the onset of dementia or Alzheimer's. "Be careful. These guys aren't boy scouts."

"Believe me, I've dealt with worse."

"That's what worries me."

Landers was a sprawling desert wasteland several miles from where Paul lived. Its claims to fame were the Integratron, Giant Rock, and a motel consisting of 1950's Airstream campers owned by a 1980's rock star. There was no town in Landers to speak of. Just hundreds of square miles of desert with the occasional homestead shed, double-wide, and abandoned shotgun shack. Paul waited until evening to make his journey in search of Ash. In the flatland area he would be going, they'd see his dust cloud approaching from miles away.

Under the cover of the desert darkness, he turned off his headlights when he made a left onto a dirt road indicated on the map. There was a dangling street sign hanging off a tilted pole that had been run into more than once. In the distance he could see a single-wide trailer with some lights shining. He slowed to a crawl and now could make out several vehicles and maybe four motorcycles in the yard, parked close to the front door. He knew that meant Ash wasn't alone. About a hundred yards away he killed his engine. He took his .38 from under his seat and stuck it in a holster that was in the small of his back. He tapped his .22 in his ankle holster and started walking.

Shit he thought to himself. He might as well be walking on bubble wrap, because the damn desert dirt and gravel made so much noise under his feet. He remembered reading about how George Washington had his men wrap the wheels of their wagons with blankets, clothing, and rags to deaden the noise when they were on a covert mission. He bent down to take his boots off.... *What am I, crazy? I'm busting into a meth gang in my socks? What an intimidating sight that would make. Nah. I'll risk it.*

Paul walked right up to the three steps that led to the shoddy aluminum screen door and knocked.

"Who's there?" A gravelly voiced male said from inside.

"A friend of Ash's. Paul. Jasmine and Kate's friend."

An inside door was unlocked, then the screen door. It was Ash.

"What do you want?" Ash said, the door only open enough for his head to fit through.

"Can we talk?"

"About what?"

"Can you step outside?"

"Hold on a minute," Ash said closing the door. Thirty seconds later, the door opened wide. "Come inside."

The room smelled like Willie Nelson's clothes hamper. A mix of weed and man stink. Ash was probably about Paul's age, and looked like any middle-aged hippie you'd find working in a motorcycle shop or feed store. But sitting around the small living room of the trailer at a card table, on a couch, and at a kitchen counter were seven bald-headed, scraggly bearded, tattooed twentysomethings. Hanging off the tile support of the ceiling was a "Don't Tread On Me" flag.

Ash pointed to the fattest one on the sofa. "That's my son, Douglas."

Paul nodded. Nobody was smiling. "Can I talk to you alone?"

"No. We'll talk here. What's the issue?"

"Remember a few weeks ago, when you came over to my place with Jasmine?"

"What about it?"

"I wound up in the hospital that night."

"What of it?"

"Ash, I need you to be truthful...."

"Who the hell are you?" barked Douglas, pounding his empty beer bottle on the plywood coffee table.

"Ash, can you please answer me?"

"You're a cop, right?" Ash asked.

"Retired."

"You have no jurisdiction here."

"I'm not here to bust anyone?"

Douglas yelled, "You sure as hell ain't!" Causing all to laugh hysterically.

"Ash. I'm serious. Did you slip me something? Put something in my drink?"

"Hell no! Are you kidding me? Get out my house!"

"Wait. No. Seriously. Just tell me. I don't care. I need to know what made me...sick."

Douglas stood up. You're gonna be worse than sick, if you ain't outta here in five seconds!"

"Look. You can kill me if you want. I'm done with my killing. No more. I just need to know, did you slip me a hallucinogenic like LSD?"

Ash, waved at Douglas. "Back off, son! Dude, we don't mess with that shit. Weed and beer. That's all we do. Straight up."

Paul stuck his hand straight out to shake hands with Ash. "Straight up?"

"Straight up."

"Gentlemen, I bid you farewell," Paul said, turning and exiting.

He was about ten yards from the door, when it opened. "Hey Paul, if you want to know who messes around with that LSD shit, ask that little fairy princess Jasmine."

"Thanks."

Paul believed Ash. Maybe he shouldn't, but he did. Could it have been Jasmine? She does seem like her distributor ain't wired right. But is that another Pandora's Box he should be opening? He didn't want to involve Kate anymore. She's definitely going to think he's losing it if he goes back to her and implicates her best friend, Jasmine. Doesn't she realize that Jasmine is on a razor's edge between nuttiness and downright drug-fueled insanity?

Paul didn't have a choice. He would consult with Kate first. It was just a matter of how to do it without everything blowing up in his face. If he let on to Kate that he suspected Jasmine of such a serious misdeed, she was sure to tip her off, and of course probably never talk to him again. He pulled into his driveway and locked the gate behind him. He knew he should sleep on it before doing anything rash.

Several more days of sleeping on it did not have the desired effect Paul had hoped for. Yard work, changing the oil in the Escape, and scrubbing the bathrooms until they sparkled didn't calm him. Instead of cooling off, his anger intensified as he saw his window of opportunity closing on him. Ash might have already tipped her off. He called Kate and asked to see her that night at the Mexican restaurant by the motel.

He couldn't see his knuckles in the dark, but knew they were white as he gripped his steering wheel. He also sensed his nostril flaring and his jaw clenching. He couldn't understand it. He knew he had to control himself and not lose his cool with Kate. But his anger was escalating into the kind of rage that saved his life on more than one occasion while he was on the job, but it had also ruined relationships and friendships in his personal life. The skills he needed to survive as a cop didn't do much for that.

He parked the car far from the others, and as he walked around the corner of the restaurant he saw Kate wasn't alone. Surprise! She was with Jasmine. He stopped, thought about leaving and saying he got sick. Then went in.

"What a pleasant surprise," Paul said.

"I hope you don't mind that I tagged along," Jasmine said sweetly. "I really did force myself onto Kate so don't blame her if you're mad."

"No worries."

Paul tried his best to listen to their polite talk about a new antique store that opened, rude French tourists at the motel, and guys who grunted and sweated too much at the gym, but his mind was trying to figure out the best way to see if Jasmine would admit to putting a tab of acid in his beer.

"Jasmine," Paul blurted, interrupting her in mid-sentence.

Kate and Jasmine just looked at each other in stunned silence for a moment.

"Jasmine, I'm going to ask you something that might make you uncomfortable in front of Kate."

"Paul, are you sure you should be doing this?" Kate asked mystified.

"Jasmine. I need to know. My mind…my life…I need to know something important."

Paul knew he was blowing it. His anger was bubbling up like the bubbles in a newly poured glass of Guinness. "I need to know!" Paul shouted, causing nearby diners to stop and stare at him briefly.

"Come on Jasmine, let's get out of here," Kate said, putting her napkin on her half-eaten plate of nachos.

"No. Wait. I'll quiet down. Really," Paul said apologetically.

219

"Paul, are you okay?" Kate asked.

"Jasmine, did you or did you not slip me a tab of acid that night?"

"What? Are you kidding me?" Jasmine said, mortified and about ready to melt under the table in embarrassment.

Paul, now red with rage, snarled through his teeth, "Did you? Ash told me you did."

"Ash!" Kate said, dumbfounded. "Are you sure you were a New York cop all those years? You believed that fool? What kind of sucker are you?"

Paul sat back in the booth and put both hands up, covering his face. Was he losing his mind for real? He pushed hard on his face his neck his chest so that the air was pressed out of his lungs. He looked at Jasmine, who was being consoled by Kate. He flashed on those awful weeks in his marriage after Tracy was born, and he laid down the law on Marcy as she began to fall off the wagon. No more smoking weed! No more drinking! His way or the highway! Little did he know that Marcy and Tracy would take the highway and not allow him back in their lives again. Didn't he learn anything?

"I'm...sorry. I think I'm just stressed. I'm really, really sorry."

"You went to see Ash at the compound?" Kate asked.

"Yeah. He blamed Jasmine for dropping the acid on me. That coward."

"I would never...." Jasmine was softly trying to control her weeping. "Why did you think I would do such a thing?"

"I have no idea. I guess, I just assume that deep down inside, certain people want to harm me because of what I did for a living."

"This is unacceptable!" Kate said forcefully, grabbing Jasmine and leading her from the table and out the door. Just before she exited she shouted, "You need help!"

Paul was alone again. He didn't know where to turn. All he could come up with was Tracy. Probably the last person on this planet who loved him unconditionally. He called and asked if he could stop by, just to chat. Tracy declined. They were busy. That was that.

He didn't know where he was going at such a high rate of speed down the main two-lane highway back towards his house about 25 miles away. He did know that he was in that danger zone of anger. It always surprised him that even when he knew very well that he was out of control, he couldn't just pull himself back to rationality. It was almost as if he nurtured this primal rage to see where it would take him. Shut down emotions. His years as a cop did teach him that those instincts could save his life. They did. That's why he needed them. That's what would protect him. That's what would keep him alive. And sane.

He passed the turnoff that would take him to his house, and kept going straight. His mind was focused. Screw them. Screw them all. Ash and Jasmine and Kate and Heidi and Tracy. They don't know shit. He's the one who knows. Don't mess with him!

The dark highway was calling him. Suddenly he yanked the wheel hard to the right, with reckless abandon. He didn't care what was up this road. He was going to speed up it like a lunatic in the dark. It wasn't until he reached the top of the hill that the dark iron gate seemed to jump at him and he jammed on his brakes, skidding on the dirt to within a few inches of crashing into it. And there was the sign – DESERT CHRIST PARK – right in front of him.

Paul rushed to the gate and tried to force it open, but it was locked up tight. He turned off his lights and his engine and stood on the hood of his car. He grasped the top of the gate with two hands and hoisted himself up and over. He could feel the blood pumping fast through his body. Too fast. Heart pounding, feet kicking up dirt and gravel, he bolted up the path in the dark night. In front of him, slightly illuminated by the incidental light coming from the street lights on the main highway almost a mile away, the gigantic, white tableau of the Last Supper was in front of him. He threw his arms into the air like an Italian soccer player after being issued a red card and began ranting to each of the Twelve Apostles, running back and forth, left to right, right to left, and back again.

"Why? What's going on here? Why me? I'm a survivor! The streets didn't get me. The job didn't kill me. Why so much on me? Why me? You took my wife. My job. My friends. Now my daughter hates me. My freakin' mind is going, going, gone. So what! So I made some mistakes? Yeah! I killed a man. Yeah, I had to. It was him or me and his girlfriend and his kid. Is this all payback?"

He stopped. He listened to his breathing. He heard his heart beating and put his hand on his neck to check his pulse. It's fast. Too fast. He walked slowly to the center where Jesus was sitting. "I was doing my job. Living my life. Surviving. I didn't want my wife to commit suicide. I didn't want my daughter to grow up without a father. I didn't want to kill a man."

He turned slowly and just across the path were two huge tablets. He pulled out his phone, and used its light to see them better. The first thing he focused on the tablet was THOU SHALT NOT KILL.

He shook his head in defeat. Turned around and went back to Jesus.

"I tried. I really tried. I thought I was doing the right thing. And now. I might as well just…I've got nothing. Please help me, Lord. Please…."

Suddenly there was a hand on his shoulder.

"Alright, buddy. Just put your hands behind your back and there won't be any problems."

"Oh, Christ! No worries, officer. You'll get no issues with me. I'm 100 percent compliant."

Paul put his hands behind him and heard that unmistakable sound of zip handcuffs being tightened around his wrists.

"Is that too tight?"

"No. Fine. Can you give me a hand to get up? My knees aren't what they used to be."

"That's your SUV by the front gate?"

"Yes, sir."

"A tow truck will come and get it," the cop said as he led Paul to his patrol car. "Do you have ID on you?"

"Yes, sir. In my left rear pocket is my wallet."

The officer took out the wallet just before he sat him in the back seat of this car. "NYPD? Retired? Damn. Sorry, bud. But I've got to take you in."

"I totally understand."

Paul sat in the back as another patrol car showed up, and the officer handed the other cop Paul's wallet. "He's gonna run your info."

"Okay."

Paul didn't know what was going to happen. He was sure he'd be booked on trespassing, but figured that would be it. Probably a summons to appear in court, plead guilty, and pay the fine. Served him right.

"You're under arrest for...."

Paul listened intently to the cop's arrest pitch, and noted there were just a few slight differences from the speech he gave, oh, several hundred times. They started driving out of Desert Christ Park, and he noticed the tow truck hitching up his vehicle.

"Where's your precinct?" Paul asked, as he watched his Escape being winched onto a flatbed.

"We call it a station. Yucca Valley, in the town center by the post office. But you're not going there."

"I'm not?" Paul asked, perplexed.

"No, sir."

"Where am I going?"

"You're going down to the Medical Center in Palm Springs. You're getting a psych evaluation down there. They're the only ones staffed for that at this time."

"Psych evaluation? Why?"

"Weren't you involved in an accident not too long ago in the BLM?"

"Oh that."

"Captain says, you need a psych evaluation. Sorry, bud."

"No worries."

Paul started thinking about the big picture. His recent accident. The story he told the doctors about chasing a UFO. His having a clean toxicology result. *Of course*, he thought, *they think I'm out of my ever-loving mind. Am I?*

Paul sat on an uncomfortable steel chair in a small, brightly lit, spic-and-span room at the hospital with the arresting officer at his side. At least his cuffs were off. His attempts at small talk were rebuffed by the young sheriff deputy, Jesse Ramirez, who was staring at his smartphone, just as Paul himself used to do, so he wouldn't get involved with perps after an arrest. The room was in stark contrast to the roach-infested waiting-room holding pens he had been stuck in at assorted New York courthouses, precincts, stadiums, subways, bus terminals, and public hospitals.

The door opened and a fortyish female wearing black slacks and a gray blazer entered with a single file folder. Only her ID tag gave a clue that she was a doctor.

"I'm Doctor Slater, Mr. Santo. I'm a psychiatrist. Officer Ramirez will remain in the room as I conduct a preliminary interview," she said, sitting across from Paul at a small table.

"Interview? Am I up for a job?"

"This is not a laughing matter, Mr. Santo."

"Sorry. You're right."

"You were arrested this evening for reckless driving, leaving the scene of an accident, destruction of property and trespass. Do you understand that?"

"Yes, I do."

"You were involved in an accident several weeks ago and admitted to a hospital?"

"Yes."

"Do you remember the circumstances of that accident?"

"Well, I kind of blacked out after crashing. But yes, I remember what I told the police and the doctors."

"Go on."

"I was, I thought I was chasing a UFO, is what I told them at the time."

Officer Ramirez looked up from his smartphone for the first time.

"And tonight, what were you doing when you were arrested?"

"I was talking to the statues of Jesus and his Apostles in the park."

"Have you ever taken drugs?"

"Doc, I don't know what you have in your file there, but I was an NYPD narc."

"I know that. Please answer the question."

"I've never knowingly taken any illicit drugs."

"And why do you say *knowingly*?"

"I think maybe I could have been slipped something on the night of the accident."

"And what about tonight?"

"No. Not tonight."

"Have you been under any strain lately, Mr. Santo?"

Paul looked at young Officer Ramirez and wondered what he had witnessed on the job as a cop up here in the high desert during his short career. Paul had seen a dead body cut in half on the railroad tracks, a friend killed on a high tension wire, witnessed a gunfight in the street, and smelled a rotting human body in his own apartment building hallway. And that was all before he was thirteen years old, just growing up on the streets of the Bronx.

"Officer Ramirez, you can step outside and observe from the door window," the doctor said to the deputy. He gave a weak smile to Paul and exited the room.

Dr. Slater took notes as Paul gave her *just the facts ma'am* about ending his law enforcement career in a rage, his wife's drug-addled life and suicide, moving to the desert with his estranged daughter, and experiencing things that he could not explain very well, including chasing a UFO. As the words left his lips, he realized he could be nuts. Textbook case of losing it.

"In your years of being a police officer, did you experience trauma?"

Paul laughed. Like an old soldier, he didn't like to look back at the horrors of his sworn duties, swimming in the filth mixed with blood and despair as he trolled the abandoned tenements of New York's Lower East Side, in the very same apartments and cellars haunted by the ghosts of so many immigrants who died from the disease of poverty over a hundred years ago. But while giving his highlight reel of death and desperation of innocents, he realized where she was going with all this.

"Mr. Santo. Have you heard of Post-Traumatic Stress Disorder?"

"Of course."

"I'd like you to see a specialist. If you agree, I might be able to have the charges against you dropped."

"Is there a catch?"

"I could put you on a 72-hour hold, which according to state law puts in place a series of protocols to determine if you are a danger to yourself or others."

"Yea, I'm aware of the protocols. I've arrested some real psychos in my day."

The doctor shot him a dirty look.

"Sorry. Mentally ill arrestees. Is there another option? I mean, as far as the hold. That sounds serious."

"It is, Mr. Santo. Or you could do a voluntary admission. That way, you could be evaluated without having to go through court proceedings. You've had some...unusual episodes. There could be something going on that needs professional help. You'll get the medical attention you need. With a Marine Base right in the neighborhood, we're fully enabled to assist PTSD patients. It's what I would recommend."

"You think I'll avoid the charges? The last thing I want is any kind of criminal record. I mean I was a decorated cop. I retired a lieutenant with all kinds of honors. You know how many times I could have gone dirty? I never, ever took a dime. Not even a cup of coffee! I was clean!" Paul's heart was racing. He was on the verge of breaking down, but he didn't let himself. He stiffened himself. Sat up straight. Shook his head. Took a sip of water from a bottle on the table.

"I'd be shocked if they charged you, if you go for help," the doctor said, smiling.

Paul paused and took another sip of water. He thought about his options, and knew he didn't have many. "I'll do it. Is there any kind of…alcohol treatment? Not that I'm an alcoholic."

"Yes. All of that will be addressed. It will be good for you."

Paul was ready. He had a feeling this day would come eventually. Why wouldn't it? He had been pushing aside or bottling up or drowning with Guinness or vodka or partying or gambling or raging away those deep-down-in-his-gut emotions that try to bubble to the top. Those things that you busy yourself with, swatting away the annoying mosquitoes, thinking that the charging rhinos coming right at you won't be a problem. He remembered counting down the months to when he was old enough to take the cop test. One minute he was waiting for life to begin, and now it looked like life as he knew it was over. He had more behind him than ahead. Maybe it wasn't worth the doctor's time. Maybe he was a lost cause. He was exhausted and glad he didn't have to ride in an ambulance to the Mental Health Clinic. He was in an unmarked sheriff's car. But sitting in that back seat, with the cage in front of him, and no buttons or levers for the windows, made him realize *he* was now, after all those arrests he made, on the other side.

The hospital wasn't really a hospital. It was a two-story clapboard building that looked more like a barracks. He was checked in, searched, given some scrubs and a robe, and sent to a secure room, not unlike the cells he saw in Bellevue where they kept the psycho prisoners. He was able to call his daughter to water the plants in the yard, and keep an eye on his place. Despite the bright florescent light coming through the door window, and the nightlight next to his bed, he was fast asleep as soon as his head hit the pillow. Seventy-one hours to go.

Paul's first day was packed with doctors, nurses, blood tests, and of course several interviews with psychiatric nurses, therapists, and psychiatrists. He answered all the questions to the best of his ability. Every one of the mental health care providers was cordial, respectful, and professional. But he had a feeling they were filling their notebooks, charts, laptops and computers with enough information to justify their recommendations for additional treatment if he needed it. The more he revealed about the decades of battling bad guys in the worst of what New York could throw at him, the more concerned his team of evaluators appeared. He was beginning to understand that although he didn't have the physical scars like the Marines coming in here with limbs blown off, Seeing Eye dogs, and heads still bandaged, he was nevertheless just as damaged.

Paul knew Dr. Slater would probably be the person making the final decision on whether he would be locked up for even longer in a psych unit. "And you saw your friend get electrocuted on the high-tension tower?" Dr. Slater asked.

"Yeah, I wasn't the only one there."

"What did you do?"

"I ran to a candy store and told the guy behind the counter to call the police. Then I ran home and cried."

"You didn't try to help?"

"If you saw what happened, you'd know there was nothing anybody could do except scrape a smoking crispy critter off some steel."

"How old were you when you witnessed this?"

"Around twelve or thirteen."

Paul went on and told of the other grisly things he saw before his sixteenth birthday: a wild-west-like running-down-the-street gunfight, a bum who got cut in half on the railroad tracks, and a small kid hit and killed by a bus. Stuff that most cops from small towns wouldn't see right up until they received a plaque and a nice pension as a parting gift.

Paul mostly kept his cop memories locked up tight. He never shared them with family members, and rarely with non-cop friends unless it was to prove a point in an argument, say like maybe if somebody thought all drugs should be legal. Cop friends were another matter. Sharing details could mean the difference between life and death the next time a similar circumstance came up. Kind of like when research scientists share their results from experiments at conferences in fancy hotel ballrooms. Except his conferences were usually held in dive bars, like The Buckeye, and his fellow research scientists were cops who patrolled all over New York City. Some were housing cops, trying to keep the vast majority of New York's poorest families safe in the projects from the scumbags who prey on them. Then there were the subway cops, who literally deal with the scummiest underbelly of New York. Then there's correction officers, bridge and tunnel guys, school cops, parole officers, court officers, even sanitation and department of health guys. All of them have stories about how a tip, a witness, dumb luck, or a hunch meant the difference between going home to their family or becoming an organ donor at the end of their shift.

But he liked Dr. Slater. She was young, attractive, and had on a honking big wedding ring. She had a no-nonsense way about asking questions, and a poker face when reacting to his stories as she made notes on her laptop.

"How often do you think about the trauma you've experienced in your life?"

"Frankly, never."

"Never?"

"Oh, I think about the friends who have died. Just like you do. But I'm not beating myself up about my job. It was a job."

"Would you say you repress the trauma you've experienced in your life?"

"If by *repressed* you mean block it out of my mind, then yes."

"Do you think you have anger issues?"

Paul paused longer than he had after any of her other questions. Did somebody rat him out? Who would know out here? Tracy? Maybe. He knew they must have talked to her about him. But she's really only known him for like a couple page-turns on a calendar. But then again, she grew up listening to her mother bad-mouth him like Rachel Maddow on Trump.

"I can lose my cool. I'm not a robot. I hate to think somebody's getting over on me when I know I'm right."

"We all have those decisions to make every day in our lives. When to fight and when to compromise."

"Sometimes compromise can have deadly consequences."

"With friends and family?"

"You got to my daughter, Tracy, didn't you?"

"Mr. Santo, your daughter is a lovely person. And she loves you unconditionally. She thinks the world of you and wants nothing more than for you to be well."

Paul felt like an ass. Ashamed that he was about to go off on his daughter. Probably the one person who actually did love him right now.

"I'm a mess. I'm a fool. I'm embarrassed."

"Mr. Santo, have you ever been to an AA meeting?"

"No. I don't consider myself an alcoholic. A binge drinker, yeah. A social drinker, yeah. An everyday drinker, yeah. That doesn't sound too good, does it?"

"A lot of people get help at AA and AlAnon meetings. They have a lot to offer. Some people need…reminders. Some need more. Think about it."

"Does that mean I'm not being held any longer?"

"No, I'm recommending your release. You're more sane than most of the people I work with. Just take this next day or so as a chance to reflect on things. Good luck, Mr. Santo," the doctor said, holding out her hand to shake. "Be well."

Paul thought that was it. But it wasn't over. He had a clean bill of health, more or less mentally, but physically was another matter. After his lab results came back, his blood pressure, cholesterol, and liver functions were in the red. They prescribed diet, exercise, and abstaining from alcohol. And if in six months his numbers didn't improve, he'd have to go on meds. Maybe for the rest of his life. Paul contemplated all this over the next day and a half while he was still technically on hold. He could do it. Why not? He could have an entirely new start. Not just a geographic one of changing your scenery to temporarily trick yourself into thinking you've changed, but really changing. Eat right. Exercise. Stop drinking. Calm down. Simple enough.

First thing Paul did after being released from the hospital was call a cab and head right for a pizza joint, where he ordered a pepperoni pizza and a pitcher of beer. He only ate half the pizza and drank two glasses of beer, so figured he was on the right track.

He was determined to make things right. That is, once he got things straightened out with Ash, Jasmine, Kate and his daughter, Tracy. He knew he wasn't crazy. And now that he felt that Jasmine wasn't responsible for slipping him the acid, he was convinced that it had to be Ash. Doing nothing wasn't an option. But the timing had to be right, so first things first.

Tracy was nervous. She thought she was doing the right thing by being honest with Dr. Slater. She thought he'd get help with his issues. She didn't realize that he could just be released and be back where he left off. And now he was hurrying over to talk to her in the middle of the day, when Heidi was on duty at the base. She knew part of the reason she could do what she was doing with her life at this point was due to the strength of Heidi – both emotionally and physically. Just looking at Heidi – with her Marine posture, steadfast composure, and straight talk – reminded her that she had the strength to survive and thrive. Meeting her dad under these conditions would be a good test for her. She placed the official portrait of Heidi in her Marine uniform right next to where Paul would be sitting on the sofa so he would be sure to see it. She knew it was the picture that would be in the papers if Heidi were to die while she was in the service. Just as she knew that if Paul died, even after retirement, his official NYPD photo would be next to his coffin. And she wanted her official photo to be in a uniform as well. She placed Paul's framed picture on the other side of the room.

Paul took ten deep breaths after he turned off his engine, as one of his therapists suggested he do when he felt anger rising up in his bones. He looked at his firm grasp on the wheel and stretched out his fingers, hoping to dissipate the tension. He needed to know who was on his side once and for all.

He stepped out of his SUV and walked across the gravel, thinking about clearing the air with Tracy, then Jasmine, then Kate, and then Ash. One by one he'd know where he stood. Who was with him and who was against him.

He looked through the screen and saw Tracy at the sink washing something. He knocked softly on the metal part of the door.

"Delivery," Paul said holding up a brown bag with some left-over pizza. "That pizza place on Old Woman Spring road up by me isn't that bad. It's not Bronx good, but it's California good."

"It's open. Come in," Tracy said, turning off the water and wiping her hands thoroughly. "Sit here. I'll be right with you," she said going in to the bedroom.

Paul immediately noticed Heidi's photo. He saw in her so many of his fellow cops who had that look of pride, strength and youth. Not like the pictures on their retirement ID's, taken at the end of their careers, when their faces had the effects of decades of "on-the-job" written all over them.

Tracy took a seat in a chair across from Paul. She expected him to look different after his hospital stay. He didn't.

"I'll get right to the point, Tracy," Paul said leaning forward, jutting out his jaw, and already creating tension. "Did you bad mouth me to Dr. Slater?"

"What? All I did was answer questions. They called me in and I answered the questions. I didn't recommend anything, nor was I asked to. And I don't really appreciate the tone this has already taken."

"Where's Heidi?"

"She's on duty. Listen, I need to tell you something," Tracy said, getting up from her chair and standing next to where she put the picture of Paul. "I'm signing up."

"Signing up what?"

"The Marines."

Paul rose and stood behind the sofa. "Are you crazy? You know we're still at war, don't you? You think you'll be doing duty on a golf course in Palm Springs? You'll be driving ambulances over IED's in Afghanistan. No, you're not!"

"Why do you think I came out here at all? It was to be with Heidi and join the Marines. I've always wanted to…be part of something bigger. Something that mattered."

"You're a big girl. You can do what you want. But don't count on me for support!" Paul said, raising his voice, on the verge of yelling.

"Are you kidding me? Why would I expect that after all these years?"

Paul knew he was done. He was angry. He had no control over Tracy. He was back where he started. Not before today, but before everything. Back when he lost his daughter and wife. Back when he realized that he was alone, and all he had was his cop friends in the same boat as him: without a paddle and up the same shit creek. He dealt with it then and he'd deal with it now. "Okay. You do this and you're on your own."

"I'm not on my own. I have Heidi."

Paul rushed towards Tracy, and she braced herself for whatever might follow. He grabbed his picture off the table and stormed out. "I'm outta here."

Chapter Nine

The nights were much cooler now that autumn had arrived, especially at the 4,000 ft. altitude where Paul lived. But as he drove in the flatlands of the desert east of the Coachella Valley just before sunrise, the temperature was in the 70s and rising fast. He had spent too many nights looking to the sky, waiting for a sign. Maybe if he hadn't been drinking, he might have stayed up later and seen something. But since that night of the accident he'd seen zilch. Everything just seemed dull to him. Maybe he was just becoming duller.

Paul decided to seek something that wouldn't be an obscure, hidden sign requiring concentration and all sensory powers fine-tuned to his environment. He was on the way to something that some say can be seen from space: Salvation Mountain.

Salvation Mountain is actually a man made, five-story-tall, multicolored, pile of hay bales, stucco and paint. Gazillions of gallons of every shade of paint put together in the middle of the desert by a man named Leonard Knight, a Korean War veteran and mechanic who toiled over three decades to create this monument to Jesus with biblical verses and giant hearts, GOD IS LOVE signs, all topped off by a cross. Some call it a fever dream hallucination, but thousands of visitors say they have been changed by experiencing it. Knight died in 2014 at the age of 82 but his legacy lives on thanks to a dedicated group who have kept the bulldozers at bay.

He parked about a half mile away on a side dirt road, the sun just starting to illuminate the panoramic desert landscape that stretched as far as the eye could see. Knowing that tourists come by the busload to witness this mountain of rainbow love, he wanted to beat the crowds. He was tired and wired at the same time, having slogged down cup after cup of lukewarm coffee from his thermos. Of course he wanted a drink, but his days of drinking and driving were over. One more time being pulled over for even a tick on the breathalyzer would surely lead him to the dreaded 5270 hold, which was a minimum of 30 days locked in a psych ward or even jail time.

Paul hadn't heard from Tracy since he stormed out. And hadn't bothered to confront Kate or Jasmine or even Ash. What was the point? He was alone now in his desert world, which was slowly becoming a dystopia. It was easy to isolate one's self on his five-acre fenced desert lot. He went to the 24-hour Super WalMart to shop, only in the wee hours of the morning when it was mostly just him and the workers stocking shelves. He was starting to relish his loneliness, although he never thought of it as such. He was merely living life on his terms, or doing the things he wanted to do, or not answering to what others expected from him. It was much easier to do this when you were behind your wall and the few people who knew you existed didn't even want anything to do with you. He had finally cut the cord and no longer even had satellite TV. His phone would suffice if he needed to know a Mets score or the definition of *dystopia*. There was a developing routine to his lack of having a routine. But he still needed to know the things that gnaw at one's soul when everything else is stripped away or walled off. And he hoped that maybe a visit to Salvation Mountain would be that thing.

By time he walked the half-mile, the sun was well over the distant horizon, causing a long shadow of the cross atop the mountain of praise to create a path for him. The low light of the bright desert sun caused the bold colors of the wildly painted mountain to jump out at him. A mishmash of primary colors made it look like the game board from Candy Land. Of course, like most remote desert experiences, the only time there was pure silence was when one stopped to observe and not crunch gravel as you walked. The air was still slightly cool, but the sunshine was getting hot quickly. The giant GOD IS LOVE letters in pink and red were reminiscent of the flying words in the Beatles' *Yellow Submarine* animated film. Multi-colored flowers, trees, waterfalls, hearts, and giant LOVE signs were not unlike the psychedelic depictions in "Lucy in the Sky with Diamonds." He stepped slowly forward to actually touch the surface of the mountain itself, and it felt like the papier-mache props they used to make when he was with the Cub scouts. This monument to God was about as permanent as a humming bird's nest. It amazed him that it stood here for over 30 years.

Paul heard an approaching vehicle coming from behind. It was a 1960's Chevy station wagon painted with similar colors and a psychedelic motif. It pulled up next to a wooden booth off to the side, and an old hippie, stooped over with curvature of the spine and scraggly long gray hair, got out and began putting literature on the plywood tabletop.

Then another vehicle crunched its way towards them. This second vehicle looked like something out of the *Jetsons* and once it was upon them Paul could see it was the latest jet-black Tesla SUV. Its gull wing doors powered open and four twentysomething hipsters stepped out. The two males had shaved heads and bushy beards, and the two females had straight hair, Smoky Bear hats, and dresses that looked like a bunch of connected crocheted potholders that kids make in summer camp. Each of them had selfie sticks and started spinning around in circles heading for the mountain giggling and laughing hysterically.

Paul meandered over to the information booth where the old hippie was setting up shop. "Are these the usual seekers of truth who come out here?"

He smiled a big toothless hockey-player grin. "That's why Baskin Robins has 31 flavors. Different strokes for different folks. As long as they drop something in the donation jar and we can keep this going, we welcome all kinds. God bless you!" He said holding out a large mason jar with DONATIONS written on it.

Paul pulled out a five and put it in. "Do you think people come here because it's an unusual roadside attraction? Or they're looking for some kind of religious experience?"

"Jesus did miracles to attract a crowd. Some folks just went for the show. Some heard what he was saying and were saved."

The four hipsters fell onto the ground and were hugging each in the dirt like a mud-wrestling match.

"I'm not sure if they're the saving type," Paul said watching the foursome. "Then again, Mary Magdalene was one of his closest followers."

"Oh, you know your Bible!"

"Just an old altar boy."

"You're a Catholic?"

"I guess. I stopped going to church after I found out that the priests in high school who were prowling the locker rooms and showers were looking for more than just rowdy kids."

"Take a flyer. It's about salvation. Non-denominational. Some good local churches are on there, too. You never know where you'll find salvation." the hippie said, clear eyes beaming warmth.

"Thanks," Paul said, taking the single-paged flyer, folding it, and sticking it in his back pocket. "I'll check it out," he said with a wave as he got in his car and drove off, in the opposite direction of the Priuses and Teslas looking for their versions of salvation.

Being an alcoholic within walking distance of a bar had its advantages. You got a little exercise on the way there, you talked to people, and you could pick up some food to go. But there were no such benefits in the remote area of the desert where Paul lived. He didn't realize how much he had been drinking until he would take an empty Guinness can or vodka bottle to the recycle bin he kept in the garage. It was so full the lid wouldn't close. His garbage bin was filled with empty frozen food boxes and cans. Once a connoisseur of New York diners and ethnic eateries, he was now content with Aunt Jemima frozen scrambled eggs, sausage, and hash browns for breakfast. He convinced himself that the small pile of peas in his frozen Hungry Man dinner satisfied the veggie portion of his food pyramid. And why bother showering and shaving every day? Since he didn't have a bookie nearby, even his interest in sports was waning. He started going to bed earlier and earlier. And sleeping later. And later.

His phone rang occasionally, but if he didn't recognize the number, he didn't answer. In fact, lately, even when he recognized the call he let it go to voice mail. And those messages were Tracy saying "Hi. Just checking in. Nothing up. Take care." Other voice mails were offers on refinancing, getting rid of unwanted timeshares, discounts on solar panels, and other assorted phone scams. Sometimes he'd answer his phone when he knew it was a telemarketing call just so he could lead them on, making them think he was interested, then yell and curse at them in a rage until they hung up on him.

There was an ease to going native in the high desert. During late-night visits to a gas station or convenience store or the Super Walmart one would see many others who had decided to abandon all norms regarding dress and hygiene. An overweight woman's Depends are sticking up out of her sweatpants while on line? So what? A toothless tweaker has a cart filled with candy and cold medications? Big deal. A hobo pays for his booze with loose change, mostly pennies? Be patient and just wait your turn. Having a few days growth on your face and wearing jeans and t-shirts well after the smell of Tide and Bounce faded away didn't cause stares or dirty looks. Nobody cared. Sure, there were also hipsters in line with $500 hats, real estate agents in Wall Street-worthy business suits, and well-to-do retirees stocking up on supplies and loading them into their Cadillac SUVs. As long as you didn't cut the line or hassle anyone, you were part of the community that cherished the freedom and live-and-let live attitude that most desert dwellers cherished, whether in a fenced-in security-alarmed compound or living under a blue tarp lean-to next to a dry wash. There was also an understanding that a dusty hobo might be an eccentric expat rock star or Beverly Hills refugee needing time and space to find the person they were before they became what they are. Which is also why there are giant statues of Christ, man-made mountains to Jesus, and standing room only AA meeting halls and ramshackle chapels filled to the rafters.

Paul enjoyed the late-night trip to the Super Walmart. He planned his trips a day in advance to make sure he was sober for the half-hour drive. He finally was beginning to get the feel of the massive mega store. A wrong turn down an aisle could send you on a half-hour detour. Which is why he found himself in a part of the store he had never been, where there were actual bales of hay for sale. There was a tap on his shoulder. "Paul, is that you?" It took Paul a second to realize that it was Mabel, the horse-rescue lady who was instrumental in his rescue at the scene of his accident. "Are you doing okay?"

"Mabel! Hi! Sure, I'm doing fine."

"Are you sure? You don't look so well. Did you recover okay from the accident?"

"Yeah, everything is great. Look, I'm kind of in a hurry. Do you know where the drug aisle is from here?"

"Front of the store. Do me a favor, Paul. Stop by the ranch soon, okay?"

"Sure, yeah, thanks. Bye."

Paul hurried away and as he pushed his cart through housewares he caught a glimpse of himself in a full-length mirror. *I do look like hell!* he thought. *It's probably just the awful lighting in here.*

As he drove back home on the winding two-lane highway he tried to keep an eye on the black velvet sky. He had seen so many odd things up there when he first moved to the high desert that he thought the sightings would become routine. But there was nothing. And that was just fine with him. Whatever all that was, he was content now to just stock up on his stout, vodka, and frozen foods and live his life far from the entanglements in the lowlands.

When he was ready, he'd call Tracy and Kate. He just needed some time to readjust. Everybody needs that, right?

His readjustment was becoming a gradual tolerance for abandoning the normal activities of daily living. Garbage cans stayed full longer and sometimes overflowed. Dirty dishes piled higher in the sink and onto the counter. Dust bunnies went from wispy to resembling Tribbles. It became easier to sleep in a sleeping bag than in a properly made bed. And his ever-expanding Afro and beard were similar to the hipsters that he saw more and more even in his own nearby gas station. He discovered that if you stopped dusting entirely, after a while you didn't notice. The joy of listening to birds and mysterious creatures in the distant desert landscape disappeared as he found solace on the sofa facing his television, which he hooked up to a DVD player to watch compilations of long-forgotten cowboy and Indian movies that were long forgotten. Adventurous hikes seemed a waste of time. And why gaze at the night sky? It never changes. He even stopped unlocking his front gate, which had allowed people to just pop in. His gate had been locked for days.

Tracy was concerned about her father. He answered the phone one time for every five she called. And then she got the bum's rush to get off the phone with a *Everything's fine, gotta go, bye.* But after all she went through with her own mother in those awful final years, she wasn't exactly anxious to get involved. Now she had Heidi.

It became obvious to Heidi what was up with Paul. She had seen it too many times with friends who returned from combat and then left the military. The isolation, the fits of rage, the depression. Interventions were tricky business. Not only for the person suffering from addictions or PTSD, but for their loved ones who were also in a state of denial. Heidi knew the time was fast approaching when she would have to convince Tracy that an intervention on her father might be the only way to save her from losing both her parents to essentially the same disease and fate.

Paul knew someone was trying to call him overnight. He always put his phone on vibrate and stuck it in the end-table drawer before going to bed. But he slept so softly, even his vibrating phone would wake him up. He thought he was dreaming when he heard some loud banging, until he awakened and recognized it as someone actually banging on his door, which was extremely unusual since he knew his front gate was locked. An unannounced visitor at 6:30 A.M. can never mean good news. He opened the drawer, picked up the phone, and stuck a large folding knife in his sweatpants pocket.

The pounding on his door was furious. He peeked through a side window and saw it was Kate. Her car was parked outside his gate with the driver's side door open.

He opened the door to find Kate in a state of obvious panic.

"Paul, let me in, please!"

"What's wrong?"

She rushed past him and took a position next to his kitchen island.

"You've got to help us! I don't know what to do! It's Ash!"

"Go on! What?"

"Jasmine called me, totally hysterical. She wouldn't even tell me where she was. She said Ash called her and said they were all busted, and that you ratted them out. And that one of the guys in their gang or whatever said they were going to kill Jasmine and me unless you turned yourself in to them. And we can't got to the police."

"I thought you said they were all busted?"

"Not all of them. Not yet. They're looking for them. They didn't find Ash yet."

"Okay, calm down. Do you want something to drink?"

"Did you?"

"Did I what?"

"Did you rat them out?"

"No. I didn't."

245

"Tell me the truth!"

"I swear on my mother's grave, I did not. Do you think they'll look for you here? Ash has been here."

"Jasmine and I need somewhere to go."

"Hold on. Let me make a call. Go get your car and pull it around back. Here's the key to the lock. How did you get in here?"

"I climbed the fence. I cut my hand," Kate said, holding up a bloody palm. The wound looked reminiscent of something to Paul. Like he had seen it before. What was it called? A *stigmata*. She took the key and went out to move her car.

Paul decided to call Tracy, but had no idea how she would react. She had every reason to shut him out as he had done her. "Tracy, please call me back. It's urgent," he said to her voice mail.

A moment later his phone rang.

"What is it? What's wrong?" Tracy asked, her voice fraught with concern.

Paul went on to explain the dire circumstances, and asked if Jasmine and Kate could stay at their place for a day or two until things got straightened out.

"Yes, no problem," Tracy said without hesitation.

"Do you have to check with Heidi?"

"She's right here next to me. She agrees. Tell them to hurry over."

"Thank you sweetheart. And…." Paul couldn't finish.

"Hurry," Tracy said, urgently.

Kate called Jasmine, arranged a pick-up, and headed to Tracy and Heidi's to hide out until Paul could figure out what to do next. But now the panic was spreading. Paul sat on a stool in his kitchen watching his coffee maker dripping into the pot like the sands of an hourglass. He had to get to Ash. And do what?

As he coffee'ed up, his brain was spinning, churning, digging for solutions. But instead of logic and reason, he was losing his mind to rage and retribution. He began his plan, laying out the weapons he thought he would need to eliminate the threat from Ash and his gang and whoever else he may have to deal with to protect Kate and Jasmine, as well as Tracy and Heidi, who will be hiding them. If he had a drink or two now, just to calm his nerves, and cut himself off in the afternoon, he was sure he'd be sober by nightfall when he would make his move.

Fueled by Guinness, vodka, and Starbucks home-brewed coffee he plotted everything out, like he was back on the job planning an elaborate undercover operation against a major drug dealer. Those perps back in New York weren't just some hicks cooking cold medicine in abandoned shacks. The guys he went after in the heyday of drugs in the city were like CEO's of corporations, complete with a corporate pyramid structure with one or two at the top that lived "clean" lives in the affluent suburbs of New York right next to Wall Street titans, high-powered lawyers, brain surgeons, and the other one-percenters. They sent their kids to the same elite private schools, used the same Lear Jet leasing companies, belonged to the same country clubs, and hid their money offshore in the same banana republics. They were far removed from the war raging on the streets of New York, destroying the lives of kids in Harlem, the South Bronx, and on Manhattan's Lower East Side. Their hired apprentice thugs, who did the necessary street-fighting – killing the competition for their turf, terrorizing innocent families, and hooking a generation on heroin – believing that one day they too would have a shot at the top. Sure.

Paul risked his life in undercover operations doing the dirty work to get at those kingpins. And now he was back at it again. He was going take on Ash and his gang, or militia, or cub-scout pack, whatever the hell they were.

He was thinking all of this while he stumbled through several drawers trying to remember where he kept the keys to his gun vault. *Why did he have so damn many keys loose in all these drawers?* Drawers in the bathroom, bedrooms, kitchen, garage, were all rummaged through and through. Would he have to break into the armored cabinet to retrieve the guns he felt he needed for the operation? Or maybe he just needed knives. Go stealth. Blackout on his face like a Seal Six assassin. He shoved his hand into a kitchen drawer and pricked his palm right in the center with an ice pick and stared at his hand as it bleed. He held it up, and watched the blood drip down, onto his wrist, and down his bare arm. It looked similar to Kate's cut palm, and something else. His phone rang somewhere. But where? He followed the sound and found it under a pile of dirty laundry on his bed. He looked at the number. A New York number. Mickey? His old pal from the Bronx?

"Hello."

"Paul, how the hell are you? Keeping out of trouble?" Mickey asked, excitedly.

"Uh, yeah. Mickey, how are you? Anything up? I'm kind of in the middle of something."

"I'll make it fast. I'm coming out."

"You mean, like you're coming out? Like out of the closet?"

"Very funny. I'm coming to visit, you knucklehead! Me and some guys are going to Vegas, and I'm going to rent a car there and drive to see you. Maybe tomorrow or the next day. Can you believe it?"

"Oh, yeah, that's nice. Okay, call me when you get here. Bye."

Paul turned off his phone, and went into the bathroom to clean off the blood and stop the bleeding. He stood in front of the mirror and looked at the blood trickling from his palm as he held it up. "Mickey coming here? Now? Jesus!" He said to his reflection in the mirror.

The hours passed slowly as he waited for the sun to set. He finally found the key to his gun vault and laid out his arsenal on the kitchen floor. A shotgun, two handguns, a Bowie knife, and zip-tie handcuffs. He had stopped drinking alcohol three hours ago, and according to his calculations he should be below the legal limit for driving in two more hours. What he didn't calculate was how his brain was already way over the limit. He was consumed with rage, revenge, anger, and confusion from the decades of his chosen livelihood and lifestyle. He was locked-in to attack mode purely from muscle memory. And now he was taking action. This would be his way to solve this problem. No need for meetings with supervisors and lawyers and his fellow officers to coordinate a systematic takedown with minimum chance for failure and maximum possibility for a slam-dunk prosecution in a court of law. He would be dealing his own instant karma.

If it wasn't for a coyote's howl Paul probably would have slept through the night. His elaborate plan gave way to a good old-fashioned alcohol-induced power nap. It was just after 11 P.M., and his raving mad rage had been lost in a fuzzy-headed fog. He went to take a leak and upon passing the bedroom, saw his arsenal laid out on the bed. It was time. He loaded everything into the Escape and was on his way.

As he drove up the highway, his rage began boiling from below. And with each passing white line in the road, coming faster and faster, his anger, angst, fury, ferocity, and focus would be the weapon that would drive him. Propel him. Primal, cave man, red-zone passion would be his guiding light. Isn't that what kept him alive all those years on the job? He didn't even have a weapon on him in his most dangerous undercover situations. He didn't even have on a wire. He relied on himself. His smarts. His intuition. His guts. That's what makes him what he is. He knows how to do this. Nobody else could tell him. That's why he is where he is. Alive.

He jerked the steering wheel to the right and went down the dark dirt road that would take him to Ash's. Ash and his gang of inbred hillbillies were nothing. Paul took down some of the worst thugs in the hellholes of New York during the worst period of crime in history. These *Breaking Bad* wannabes were just a bunch of small-time punks.

Paul turned off his headlights as he sped down the washboard road. It was almost impossible to see anything, but he was on autopilot anyway. Led by guts and guile. He was ready once and for all to have it out. Maybe this would be his final blaze of glory, but he didn't care. He was going to win. He was going to put an end to Ash and whoever else thought they could get over on him. In his head, he took one last inventory of the tools of his trade: A shotgun, two handguns, a large knife, and enough ammo loaded to take down a Taliban platoon. If nobody got out alive, so be it. He is the one who put Jasmine and Kate in jeopardy. And he would get them out of it.

Suddenly, there was a blinding flash of light for a nanosecond and everything on his car went dead. It rolled to a stop, the thumps of the hard washboard dirt road slowing until the SUV was at a total standstill. He turned the ignition key and there was nothing. Not even the slight click when there's a tiny sip of juice still in the battery. He opened the door and stepped out. No lights anywhere. Just a slight glow of light above the horizon many, many miles in the distance, probably from Twentynine Palms. He tapped his pocket, feeling for his .22. He felt a little safer now. He took out his phone. Dead. Nothing. Weird. He went back into the car and grabbed a flashlight from the glove box. Also dead. He pushed the side illumination button on his cheap Casio watch. Nothing. *Okay, what is going on? Oww!* A sudden burst of blazing heat was burning his leg through his pants pocket where he kept his gun. He frantically reached in his jeans pocket and struggled to get the gun out. He jerked it out, and in doing so the gun went flying in the air, landing somewhere in the dark hardscrabble brush and dirt. Paul closed his eyes and covered his eyes with both hands. *Wake up! Wake up! This is not happening! Wake up!*

Paul lowered his hands and ever so slightly opened his eyes, unsure if he would be seeing the inside of his home with him safe in bed, or if he was still in the middle of the deep, dark, desert. He started to see some light through his partially opened eyelids. *Thank, God. It is a dream.*

But when he widened his eyes, what he saw was not a lamp in his living room, but some kind of circular doorway, with an illuminated ramp lined with soft dots of light, like the emergency LED markers on an airplane floor. He was frozen with fear. Here it was again. Is it his mind playing tricks on him, like the night of his accident? Is this some kind of flying saucer? But there was no *saucer*. It was merely an opening into something without any shape or form. He took a step forward, and the crunch of gravel underfoot was evidence that he wasn't dreaming. This was real. He knew he had to go up the ramp.

He stood with both tips of his shoes inches from the ramp. He lifted his right foot and held it above the ramp for what felt like an eternity, but was probably only about 30 seconds. He ever so slowly lowered his foot and planted it on the ramp. A slight vibration, like a hum, traveled from his foot throughout his entire body. It made him feel different. No rage. No anger. No fear. He began his slow ascent towards the opening. Five steps later, he was in...something.

The ramp disappeared behind him, and he was again in total darkness. He closed his eyes for three or so seconds and when he opened them, there she was.

"What the? Tracy? Is that you, Tracy? What is this?" Paul asked, staring in disbelief.

Sitting before him, in what looked like a folding beach chair, complete with a red cup in a drink holder, there she was. "Hi, Paulie. I'm not Tracy. If you want to see Tracy, just turn around," the strangely familiar voice said calmly.

"I don't want to turn around, but I will," Paul said as he did a 180. "Great God almighty. What in the...?"

With jaw dropped, Paul stared at the vivid scene in front of him. In crystal clear, better than 4K HD was a twentysomething Paul, on the beach helping a toddler dig and build a sand castle on a sparkling summer day, with soft waves lapping ashore just behind them. "That's me and...Tracy. On Ponquoge Beach. I remember that day. It was the Fourth of July. And...."

Paul turned back around and did all he could to speak aloud and not collapse in a quivering mess of emotion. "Marcy? That's you, Marcy? Am I...dead?"

It was Paul's deceased wife, Marcy, appearing to be around the age where she gave birth to their daughter, Tracy. Her face glowed as if the bright July beach sand was reflecting upwards. Her raven hair shined like it was still damp from a dip in the ocean. She was wearing a blue Mets tank top and orange shorts. Her skin glistened as though she had just applied baby oil. "You're not dead. You're very much alive," Marcy said, calmly.

"Is this some kind of cosmic hallucination? Is it all just in my head?"

"No, Paulie, this is real. I'm real. What you see behind you, on Ponquogue beach, that's a scene I keep on the interior walls of this vehicle. It's one of my fondest memories of life. On earth."

"You are real? I'm not dead? I almost forgot how beautiful you were. Are. How can you be real?"

"Come here," Marcy said, picking up the red cup form its holder. "Taste this."

Paul inched towards her. *Maybe this is hell? Maybe she's the devil?* He thought to himself.

"I'm not the devil. Taste this!"

He reached out, took the cup, and drank a sip from it. "I better watch what I'm thinking, huh? This tastes like…V8."

"It is. It's like drinking vegetables. Taste this," Marcy said, picking up a white cup with a plastic spoon in it from the cup holder on the other arm rest.

Paul took a small spoonful of the creamy white substance. "Yogurt?"

"Greek yogurt. That's all we really need to survive. These two substances."

"You're alive? I don't.…"

"I know it's a lot to comprehend. Yes, I'm alive. I have a physical body. This is a vehicle. A machine. I'm here to help you."

"Where did you come from?"

"I'm going to tell you where. It's not exact, but it's a way you can understand."

Paul was only a couple feet away from her. He could smell the baby oil, her sweat, her yogurt breath. "I doubt it, but I'll bite."

"Purgatory."

"Purgatory? That's where you came from? Like in the Catechism purgatory? I thought they said there was no purgatory a few years ago."

"Like they did away with Saint Christopher and Latin Mass? Those are things of the earth. Do you think an all-loving God would let good but troubled people just go to hell? Or just allow them into heaven without having earned it? There is judgment in the end. Purgatory is real. It is a real, physical place. I came from there."

"And that's where UFO's come from? Purgatory? What about the UFO I saw the night of my accident?" Paul asked, with a touch of earthly skepticism in his voice.

"Do you remember Frankie Doherty?"

"He was my best friend all through grammar school, until eighth-grade graduation! We were altar boys together. I haven't seen him since."

"Well, he passed away a few months ago. That was his first trip back to earth, the night of your accident. We still have free will. He won't be traveling for a while. He has more to learn. He was not supposed to do that. He was messing with you."

"Damn. Passed away. I always meant to look him up. And he got caught just messing with me? That explains the altar boy Latin on the side of the UFO. That knucklehead."

"He didn't just get caught. You don't get away with anything where we are. You do remember God is all-knowing?"

"I was good at Catechism." Paul closed his eyes to concentrate. "I got it. God is eternal, all-good, all-knowing, all-present, almighty."

"Don't forget, all-wise, all-holy, all-merciful, and all-just."

"You don't mean to tell me that the Catechism from third grade is all literally true?"

"No. Not at all. But it was what we had to go by, and close enough."

"Why is this happening? I'm sure it's not to give me a pop Catechism quiz."

"Sit down, Paulie."

Paul sat on the floor of the vehicle, and as he did the area around him became warm, fine, white sand. Like the sand on the Ponquogue beach on the eastern end of Long Island. He put his hand in the sand, and let it run through his fingers. Marcy got up from her beach chair and the surface below her feet became sand. She sat just across from Paul. Their knees were just inches apart. He looked around the circular vehicle, and like a 360-degree surround video, the scene of that day on the beach was playing out before him in real time. He felt the cool spray of ocean water on his neck and the warm sun on his face.

Marcy was perfect in her youthful beauty. Her eyes were a clear sparkling blue, her raven hair so shiny it looked like it had streaks of silver in it. Her skin had no blemishes or redness. Just the pure white skin of what they called the "black Irish" in the old neighborhood.

"Paulie, we in purgatory must earn our way to heaven. By making a difference on earth. I am doing this to save you."

"So, you know where I was going and had to stop me?"

"I didn't have to stop you."

"I was going to get killed when I busted in on Ash's house and you saved my life? How could I ever thank you...?"

"No, Paulie. I wasn't trying to save you from getting killed. I was saving you from killing. I was saving your soul. You were

255

blind with rage and confusion. As you have been for so long. You had weapons and you were going to kill. And your soul would be lost for all eternity and damned to hell."

"Yeah, but I'm already lost. I already killed. I know my Catechism. The sixth commandment: thou shalt not kill. I have killed."

"That's not the sixth commandment. The sixth commandment is thou shalt not murder. A police officer, a soldier, a good Samaritan who takes a life to save lives is not murdering."

"I wanted to make a difference when I became a cop. I didn't want to lose my soul."

"You didn't."

"You are flesh and blood? Like a real human? How can that be? Where do you…live?"

"You've heard of Andromeda?"

"Sure, *The Andromeda Strain.* Good movie, based on Michael Crichton's book."

"We're on a planet in the Andromeda Galaxy, 2.5 million light years away. Humans will never be able to travel that distance. All human-type advanced life forms are separated by hundreds of millions of light years, so they can't contaminate each other."

"Like keeping petri dishes separated in a lab."

"Exactly."

"Only we have the technology to travel light years. It's designed that way."

"How come I couldn't see the vehicle? Was it really invisible?"

"Yes it was. *Cloaked* I think is the correct term. The responsible travelers always are."

"So if you have a human body, you eat, drink. What about... sex?"

"Kiss me."

"Really?"

"Really."

Paul leaned in, closed his eyes, and ever so gently placed his lips on Marcy's. But he felt nothing. No hint of the blissful sensations he had when they were young and in love. He pulled away.

Marcy smiled. "Sexuality really is a glimpse of heavenly bliss that human beings experience. We in purgatory are denied that sensation. Until we attain full blissful purity in heaven."

Paul stood up, and when he did so, the sand disappeared and he was back on the hard surface of the vehicle floor. "I don't know. Maybe I am dreaming. Maybe this isn't happening. Maybe I have gone mad. Maybe I'm in a mental ward right now."

Marcy returned to her beach chair and took a sip from her cup. "Do you have a piece of paper?"

Paul searched through his pockets, and pulled out the flyer from Salvation Mountain that he had folded and stuck in the back pocket of his jeans.

"Tear off a little piece."

He tore off a small corner and handed it to Marcy, refolded the flyer, and placed it in his back pocket. She picked up a pen from a pouch on the chair and wrote something. "Fold this, and stick it in your pocket. The little side pocket in your jeans."

Paul did just that and stood there staring at Marcy. He felt ashamed that perhaps he was the cause of her pain on earth. Her downward spiral into addiction and despair and self-destruction.

"No, Paulie. You weren't the cause of my problems. You gave me the two most important things in my life: true love and Tracy."

"Can I ask you something? About UFO's? Are they real?"

"UFO's come from where I came from. That's all. Sometimes UFO's are seen on earth when they are piloted by deceased humans from purgatory who haven't learned their lessons yet."

"Like Frankie."

"Like Frankie. But not from other places in the universe. It will never happen. It's against the laws of physics. That's how it was designed."

"Now what? Will I remember all this or will it be like *Men in Black* and you just erase my memory with that pen?"

"Do you remember being born?"

"Of course not."

"But you were born. And deep in your subconscious you remember the love of your mother as she held you for the first time. And that love of your mother never will leave you. That is where these memories will be stored. The place where dreams come from. You'll remember two things: first, Ash is not going to hurt anybody; and second, when shooting stars go up, not down, that's when we earn our wings, and go to heaven. But before you go, I want to tell you an old joke."

"A joke? Shoot."

"A pompous pastor was warned about an imminent flood. As the waters rose above his front step, a rescuer in a 4X4 jeep offered his escape. The pastor said, 'No need to. The Good Lord will take care of me.' Then the waters rose to his second-floor window. A rescuer in a motorboat came by his window to rescue him. 'No need to,' the pastor said again. 'The Good Lord will take care of me.' Then the waters rose to where they were above his roof line. A helicopter flew overhead and dropped a rope ladder down to rescue him. 'No need to. The Good Lord will take care of me.' The pastor drowned. When he arrived at the Pearly Gates he confronted Saint Peter: 'Why didn't the Good Lord take care of me?' Saint Peter looked through his notebook pages. 'Aha! It says here, we sent a 4x4, a motorboat, *and* a helicopter!'"

Paul chuckled. "I guess some signs aren't so subtle if you're paying attention."

Suddenly in one forceful jerk, a rush of desert air poured into the vehicle as the opening reappeared behind him. He looked at Marcy, wondering what was next.

"I love you, Paulie. And I'm watching out for Tracy, too. See you in your dreams," Marcy said, putting both hands over her heart.

The vehicle jerked forward and Paul fell backwards out of the ship into the desert dirt.

He lay there unconscious. Marcy's space vehicle was gone without a sound or spark of light.

Paul had no idea what happened when he started to come to. His first reflex was to check his pocket for his gun, which put him in panic mode, since it wasn't there. His phone began to vibrate, so he took that out of his pocket, and noticed it was powering on, which was strange because he didn't remember turning it off. His SUV was barely visible in the darkness. He opened the door, put his hand by the ignition and the key was already inserted. He turned the key, and it started right up. He turned on his headlights, grabbed a flashlight, which popped right on, and started to search for his gun. He didn't even begin to wonder what the hell had happened to him. First things first. He looked around the car for his gun, under some tumbleweeds, and began expanding his search circle, and there it was, in some dirt. He had no idea why it was partially embedded in the soil, as if it had been tossed high in the air. He dusted it off and put it back in his front left pocket.

He sat in his car with the engine running, trying to remember how he even got here, when it came back to him. He recalled that he turned off the car to hike the rest of the way to Ash's house to confront him about his death threats to Kate and Jasmine. He remembered that he was furious, mad with rage, intent on confronting Ash and his cohorts, come what may. What was he thinking? What good would that do now? He put the Escape in drive and headed for Ash's with his headlights on.

As he thump-thumped over the washboard ridges in the road, he tried to piece together what had transpired over the last little while. Why was he on the ground, unconscious? Maybe he was having seizures or fits or some kind of alcohol or schizophrenic blackouts. But his head didn't hurt. In fact, he felt a peaceful calm that he hadn't felt in a while.

He went over a hill and stopped at the top. Just down the road, less than a hundred yards was Ash's house. Lights were on, and there were two vehicles parked outside and Ash's motorcycle. Paul reached into his pocket and took out his gun. He got out of the SUV, went to the rear door and opened it. He lifted a hatch where the spare was and retrieved a metal box. "Oh, sheesh," Paul said upon seeing the box that contained Marcy's ashes. He had forgotten they were there. He opened the firearm box, put in his guns, and secured them in the trunk. He closed the hatch and the rear door and got back in the driver's seat. He was on his way to Ash's.

260

The house was quiet. Paul knocked on the locked steel security screen door and waited. He could see that someone was looking at him though the wooden door's peep-hole because it darkened. He could hear whispers. The wooden door behind the security door opened, revealing Ash. He was wearing a leather cowboy hat, and a camo vest over a black t-shirt. Paul could see that the pockets of the vest were loaded with heavy objects by the way they sagged.

"It's you," Ash said calmly. "Come inside."

Across the room, sitting on a stool by a counter was his floor guy, Thomas. He was also wearing a camo vest over a black t-shirt. "Hi, Ash. Hi, Thomas."

Paul stepped inside. He knew the smell of gunpowder well and the room was thick with it. "I think you've been wanting to talk to me about something. So here I am," Paul said in a friendly voice.

"Shoot, I don't know what to say," Ash said, apologetically. "You talked to Kate and Jasmine, right?"

"No. Have things changed?"

"I'll say. I know you didn't rat us out. I said things to them I never should have said. I was losing it. I didn't know what to do."

Paul sat down, relieved. "What happened?"

"There was an informant in our…group. He had been with us for months. Turns out, one of our members was dealing heroin and meth. Mostly to kids. School kids. He was even selling lollipops laced with meth, that sumbitch. I got two kids in school. My ex has custody."

"What about you? Were you busted?"

"Just a minor infraction for weed. My lawyer says I'll get off easy. We're gonna testify for the state. Screw that asshole. I want to shake your hand, sir."

Paul was taken aback, but held out his hand. "For what?"

"I thought you were nothing but a professional squealer. But now I understand what you guys do. You risk your lives."

"So Kate and Jasmine have calmed down? You went off on them pretty bad, didn't you?"

"I couldn't control myself. Sorry. I'll make it up to them. And you."

"Don't worry about me. I'm a big boy. By the way, Thomas, I decided to re-do the tile on my kitchen counters. Interested?"

"Yes, sir! Can I use Ash as my helper?"

"Why not? I'll call you."

As he drove home, Paul shuddered at the thought of what might have happened if he hadn't calmed down and secured his arsenal in the trunk. And as far as waking up in the dirt? He thought it was best to just forget about that. Maybe he had a brain tumor. Or maybe just an alcoholic blackout. Either way, it would be his little secret.

He turned down the dirt road that led to his driveway and there was a car waiting at the gate with the lights on and the engine running. It was Kate's car.

She jumped out and looked frantic in the harsh lights of the Escape's headlights.

"Paul! I need to talk to you! Why didn't you answer your phone?" She said, running to him, and then hugging him tightly. They held each other for a little while in silence.

"I just didn't have the phone with me for a little while. Calm down. Are you okay?"

"I was terrified you were going to do something to Ash or he'd do something to you."

"I just came from there. He's going to help re-do my kitchen tile."

"Don't joke."

"I'm not. He told me everything. About the informant, and the scumbag selling smack and meth to middle-schoolers."

"Really? Everything is okay?"

"Yeah. Fine. Let's go inside and have a cup of tea."

They sat at the kitchen island, mugs of tea and Oreos at the ready. Kate smiled and her eyes glistened as the steam from her tea rose towards the ceiling. Paul thought about having a double of vodka. He even went over to the freezer and opened it to look at the bottle he kept there.

"The tea is nice," Kate said.

Paul closed the freezer without taking out the vodka. He picked up his mug of tea and sat across from Kate. It had been a while since he noticed how beautiful she was, as she carefully sipped the hot brew.

"I forgot to mention, I called Tracy. She was super concerned. I guess I was kind of still panicked when I called her."

"I better call her now," Paul said picking up his phone. He stopped dialing when he heard tires crunching the gravel out front. "That's her!"

"Daddy!" Tracy shouted, bursting into the room.

"What's going on? Everything's okay."

Heidi also entered the room and exchanged smiles with Kate. "Is that tea?"

"Yes. Herbal."

"Can I have a cup?"

Kate nodded and watched as Paul and Tracy whispered to each other. Kate knew that deep down love that a parent has for a child. It struck her that this was the first time she saw Paul displaying it. "Let's sit in the living room," Kate said, pouring the hot water into two more cups.

Tracy sat next to Paul on the sofa and noticed his pants had patches of dirt on them. "Why are your pants so dirty? You look like you've been crawling under the car."

"Oh, I dropped my phone and it's a long story. I think I'll change into some shorts."

Paul went into his bedroom and took off his jeans. He removed items from his pockets and placed them in the drawer on his side dresser; keys, phone, some papers, some change. As an afterthought, he checked the small pocket on the right front of Levi's jeans. He pulled out a little slip of paper, shaped like a triangle. He had no recollection of sticking it there. He was ready to toss it into the trash when he noticed writing on it: *Serenity Prayer.* He was stumped. How did it get there? Maybe he put it there during one of his drunken escapades. But it didn't look like his writing, which was always a mess. Maybe Tracy had written this and secretly put it in there, planting some kind of seed? And what exactly *is* the Serenity Prayer?

He put on some gym shorts and a clean Mets t-shirt and returned to the living room with the small, triangular piece of paper in his hand.

He sat back down next to Tracy and took a sip of tea.

"Do you know what this is?" He asked Tracy holding out the slip of paper.

"The Serenity Prayer?" Tracy said aloud, causing a chuckle from Kate. "Yes, I know what it is. And I think Kate does, too."

"Yup. Do you want to hear it?"

Tracy and Kate recited in unison, *God, grant me the serenity to accept the things I cannot change, courage to change the things I can, and wisdom to know the difference.*

"How do you both know that?"

Tracy and Kate looked at each other, smiled, and again said in unison, *Al-Anon.*

"It's kind of like the mantra of all the twelve-step programs, especially Alcoholics Anonymous, and Al-Anon," Kate said.

"But who wrote it?" Paul asked.

"I know this from bible study!" Heidi chimed in. "Reinhold Niebuhr, an American theologian from last century."

"No," Paul said. "I mean, who wrote this here, on this piece of paper. Tracy is this your handwriting?"

Tracy examined the scrap, intensely. She looked baffled. "It's not my handwriting. But it…," she stopped, unable to speak, obviously looking like she was searching her brain for something that would compute.

"It what?" Paul asked.

"It looks like…mom's handwriting."

"Well that isn't the answer I was looking for," Paul said, taking back the paper and studying it again. "I would say it's a female's penmanship."

"*Penmanship!*" Heidi exclaimed. "I haven't heard that term used in ages! That's what my mom called it. She said the nuns would spend hours trying to make every student's handwriting look the same according to some chart above the blackboard. Or else! *Smack!* Did your mom go to Catholic School?"

"I think so," Tracy said, softly.

"Yup. For all twelve years. So did I. And she had excellent penmanship," Paul said. "But my penmanship is terrible. The nuns couldn't whip me into shape, like they did Tracy's mom. Tracy, would you do me a favor? Would you write out the serenity prayer on a piece of paper for me? Let me get a pen."

Paul went to his bedroom and grabbed a pen and piece of paper from his nightstand drawer. He handed Tracy the pen and paper, and she took a seat at the kitchen table. She began writing out the Serenity Prayer carefully. When she was finished, she checked it over and thought it looked good.

"I wrote it out for you," Tracy said. Paul took it and stuck it in his pocket. "I'll memorize this."

"It's been a long day," Kate said, walking over to Paul and giving him a neck rub. "I think I'm going to head home."

Paul walked them to their cars and kissed each on the cheek without much being said. There was an air of comfort and relief as hugs were exchanged and they drove off, waving. Paul watched as their red taillights disappeared in the distance, leaving nothing but darkness behind. He stood there in the cool desert night and looked to the sky. He could see the Milky Way clearly on this night, as he had on so many nights since he had moved to the land of heavenly wonders. But as he gazed upwards, he felt a sense of peace and calm he hadn't felt since...he didn't know when, actually. He attributed it to working things out with Ash. After all, sometimes it takes a messy confrontation for things to be worked out, once the wreckage is cleared. Walking back to the front door, he stuck his hand in his pocket and felt the piece of paper there. He made a mental note to memorize it before bed. Maybe even do some praying. It had been a long time since he said his bedtime prayers.

Without his usual nightcap of vodka or Guinness, he went through the normal ritual of washing up, brushing and flossing, and turning out lights. He emptied his pocket and placed the piece of paper with the Serenity Prayer right next to his bedside. Finally comfortably propped up in his bed, he picked up the paper to read the prayer so he could make sure the words sunk in. He didn't know why, but felt this was important on this night at this moment. He read the prayer a few times, a few times more, and more and more. *God, grant me the serenity to accept the things I cannot change, the courage to change the things I can, and the wisdom to know the difference* over and over and over until he began committing it to memory, and the words on his lips slipped silently down into his subconscious sleep soul of deep inner knowledge and understanding.

Chapter Ten

Tracy woke up and looked at the clock in the darkness. The red glow read 4:30 A.M. An hour before it was supposed to buzz her and Heidi awake. She hadn't dreamt about her mom in a while. Usually they were nightmares. She sat up, trying to remember the dream she'd just had.

"Are you okay?" Heidi asked, concerned about Tracy.

"Yea. Fine. I just had a strange dream. It seemed so real. My mom was in it. I think."

Heidi sat up. "You think?"

"Let's get up. I know it's early, but I can't sleep anymore."

Tracy thought about calling her father and telling him about the dream. But not at this ungodly hour.

A phone was ringing in the bedroom. Tracy knew it was her phone because of the ring tone, so she rushed in to get it. Calls this early are rarely good news. It was Paul.

"Tracy! I'm sorry to call so early."

"I was already up."

"Listen. We didn't get to talk last night about, you know, abou...stuff. I just want to say. I'll always be there for you. Always."

"This is so strange. I had this dream. Mom was in it," Tracy stopped, her mind spinning with emotion. "Mom said, she'd always be there for me."

"We will be. I just know it."

"Let me know when you can stop by."

"I will. I love you."

Paul didn't want to tell Tracy on the phone that he also had a dream and that her mom was in it. It was too weird. It was all a jumbled dreamy mess, but it had something to do with a flying saucer. Why waste time trying to make sense out of something so ridiculous. He walked over to his bedside table and saw the Serenity Prayer she had written out. He picked it up, stuck it in his pocket, grabbed a cup of coffee, sat on the sofa, looked out the window where the sun was beginning to rise, and recited it over and over and over and over.

After breakfast and a shower, Paul felt good. He had a plan for the day. First thing he did was write out on a dozen slips of paper the Serenity Prayer. He was going to make sure he thought of it no matter which room he was in or what he was doing. And as he was cleaning the dishes, he said aloud, "Mabel!" He started to think that he hadn't thanked her fully for saving his life the night of the accident. He went and got his checkbook, wrote out a check for a hundred dollars, and drove over to the ranch.

Mabel was busy emptying giant bags of food into bowls for her menagerie of goats, llamas, donkeys, horses, cats, chickens, and dogs. Paul followed her around, mumbling about being grateful, trying to hand her the check.

"You know who this is?" Mabel said pointing to a large pit bull mix wagging his tail as he munched on kibble in a stainless steel bowl. "This is Beast! He's the dog who was on the scene after your accident!"

"Really?" Paul said kneeling down to pet him. As soon as Beast saw him, he jumped up, almost knocking Paul over, and started licking him to death. "Hey, big fella! What's the deal with him?"

"You want him? He's yours. I'm trying to get him placed."

"Um, well. Yeah! I do! And I have a donation for you," he said, trying to get the check out of his pocket as he struggled with dog slurps.

"That's great! How'd you like to really help me out?"

"Sure!"

"You were a cop, right?"

"Yeah. You got trouble?"

"We all got trouble. I'm trying to get a program going with "at-risk" teens. Get kids from the inner city out here, and teach 'em something about the outdoors, animals, and maybe a few other life lessons outside of the street life they grow up in. A guy with some experience like yours, combined with a heart, could do wonders."

"You know what? I'm in. What do I do?"

"You already did it. You said yes. I'll be in touch."

Beast sat in the passenger seat of the Escape, looking out the window like anyone who enjoyed the desert landscape passing by. His ears perked up, and he straightened up in his seat when he saw a jackrabbit dart back and forth. He gave out a single bark, just to let him know that he saw him.

"Good job, Beast. You can keep an eye out for anything out of the ordinary!"

Beast looked at him and, essentially, smiled.

Paul stopped at the store and picked up a giant bag of dog food, bowls, dog toys, treats, and a large dog bed. Beast waited patiently in the car, and was doggie-excited when Paul emerged from the store with his cart full of his new stuff. Beast watched, turned around in the front seat as Paul loaded all of his new items in the back.

"Now how do you know all this stuff is for you? Maybe I'm giving it to Mabel for her dogs. I'm just kidding; it's all for you! Let's go to your new home!"

Beast was even more excited than when he saw the jackrabbit a little while ago, and kept turning around to look at the stuff in the cargo area.

"You're a very smart boy! You know that, Beast?"

Beast smiled again.

"What is this, now?" Paul said to Beast as he turned onto the dirt road that lead to his front gate. There was a small sedan sitting there with Nevada plates. "Holy jumpin'…."

The door swung open, and Mickey hopped out wearing a Rolling Stones t-shirt, Yankees hat, and cargo shorts.

"I can't believe it! You made it!" Paul said getting out of the SUV and rushing to greet him, with Beast right behind him.

"Paulie! What the hell is this place? It looked like I was driving across Mars to get here!"

"Welcome to the California high desert! Is this a trip or what?"

"You own this place?" Mickey said, gazing up on the five fenced acres and the rocky foothills just a stone's throw away.

"A far cry from 238th Street, huh? Let's go in and get settled. By the way, this is Beast. My new best friend."

Beast plopped into his dog bed as soon as Paul placed it next to his favorite chair in the living room, as if he had done it for the thousandth time.

"What kind of beer you got out here?" Mickey asked opening the refrigerator. "Guinness in a can. Not bad. You want one?"

"Nah. I'm on the wagon."

"I'm good at going on the wagon. I've done it hundreds of times," Mickey said.

"Yeah, doctor's orders."

"Let's sit out front," Paul said, grabbing a bottle of water and leading the way for Mickey and Beast.

They sat down, facing the rock piles in the distance with acres of cactus, Joshua trees, tumbleweeds, and assorted spiky shrubbery in between.

"This is where it starts to happen," Paul said, holding up his water bottle and pointing to the landscape. "This is where all that you knew from the time you were screaming when you were born, to the crib by the window, the school by the el train, the honking horns, the busses churning out black smoke, the cabs cursing you, the shots fired, the funeral dirges, everything becomes just a memory. Just a slowly disappearing racket of humans and machines in a big old bucket being shaken and stirred by somebody, all the time. And you look out here and see rocks, and dirt and Joshua trees reaching up toward heaven. And hear the birds, the coyotes, the silence, and it all starts to change."

"I was going to ask you if you're following the Jets, but I guess you got other things on your mind."

"I didn't know what was happening to me. All those years of being in the bull's-eye of it all," Paul said, watching a hummingbird go from red blossom to red blossom on the ocotillo tree. "You see that?"

"See what?"

"On the ocotillo. That spiny thing with the long green branches and the red flowers on top. See the hummingbird?"

"Holy shit. I've never seen a hummingbird before. That's amazing."

"You know there are hummingbirds in New York. We just never saw them. Or were able to see them. I'm seeing a lot of things, now that my nervous system has been dialed back to factory settings."

"Are you sure you're not getting peyote from the cactus?"

"Oh, I'm getting high. Higher and higher and higher. But I don't know why. Not yet. But I'm trying. And how *are* the Jets doing? I just haven't been following sports lately. I don't know. Maybe I'm losing it."

"You know, I've been here for less than a half hour," Mickey said between gulps of his stout, "and I think I learned more about you than I have since eighth grade. What is going on?"

Paul looked at Mickey, who was partially backlit by the bright sunshine off in the distance, making it difficult to see his face. He couldn't see the wrinkles, red blotches, or the scars from chasing bad guys for the past 20-something years, and chasing good times for the 20-something years before that. He could see those blue eyes, and the gap-toothed smile, the very same ones from their grammar school graduation class pictures, wild Hunter Mountain and Hamptons Polaroids, staged wedding photos, and proud Police Academy clips from newspapers. Mickey was the first real link with his own personal history. Even Paul himself wasn't so sure about the past, given what had been happening to him the last few months, and how he felt now. Here.

"I don't know Mickey. There's been some weirdness going on, ever since we landed here."

"Landed? I thought you drove?"

"We did. But I feel like we landed here."

"Like what kind of weirdness? I mean come on, we faced weirdness for a living."

"Guts, blood, CPR on unconscious strangers, that's of *this* world. I'm talking about another level of weirdness. Out of this world."

"You're going all Rod Serling on me, Paulie. I think you need to step back, take out your police report pad, and just give an eyewitness account of what the PR saw."

"Yeah, the PR. Person reporting. That's me. I think I'll just write this up later, just before the end of my shift. For now, let's just relax. I'll show you around."

Paul was very interested in Mickey's reaction to the topography, sights, sounds, smells, and vibes of the high desert. The sky was a shade of dark blue like the photos from those Space X flights when they are at the edge of the earth's atmosphere. And not a cloud or wisp of moisture in the air. They drove in Paul's SUV up Kickapoo Road next to Paul's property. On the right were a few mobile homes, horse ranches, decrepit sheds, and modest houses. On the left side of the road was nothing but the BLM; rocky foothills, Joshua trees, cacti, tumbleweeds, and hardscrabble. Mickey was eyeing everything with sheer wonder and amazement.

Mickey seemed overwhelmed with the scenery as they bounced on the rough dirt road. "When I thought of the desert before. I thought of *Lawrence of Arabia*, you know, endless sand dunes. Now I'm thinking of those John Ford movies with John Wayne, like *The Searchers*. There must have been Indians here."

"Oh yeah!" Paul said, sharply turning the wheel towards the rocky road that went deep into the BLM. The same road he chased a UFO and crashed on that fateful night. This was no well-traveled washboard road maintained by the county. This was more likely an ancient trail with much of the loose sand and dirt blown and washed away, leaving sharp stones, volcanic rock, and the edges of subterranean boulders just above the surface. "We take this road a couple miles, and then up those boulders over to the left."

"You're kidding, right?"

"No, I've done it before."

"Please don't pull that famous line on me: *What's a redneck's last words: Hey, y'all. Hold my beer and watch this!*"

"Nah. But hang on."

Paul skillfully directed his all-wheel drive Escape up a ten-foot rocky incline, and onto a path that led to some rock formations in the distance. It was hard for one to get a feel for the rock piles from a distance, but once they were about 50 yards away, it was evident that the rocks were gigantic boulders precariously balanced on one another in an impossible Alexander Calder-ish rock sculpture.

"How the hell does something like this happen?" Mickey asked, dumbfounded.

"Well, they say these are leftovers from a glacier that passed through here millions of years ago. Maybe part of the Lilliput Glacier that still exists a few hundred miles from here. I want to show you something."

They were up on the boulders, now in the shadow of the biggest one just in front of them.

"Wilmaaaaa!" Mickey yelled in his best Fred Flintstone voice, as he got out of the vehicle.

"Over here, Fred." Paul said, leading Mickey around the side of the largest boulder and up around the back side of it. They climbed the steep side of another boulder, and then up a smaller one. At the top of that, there was a large flat area, about the size of a basketball court. "Stand here in the middle with me."

Mickey stood next to Paul, and from that vantage point could probably see five miles in each direction.

"See that just in front of your feet in the top of the rock? What does that look like?"

"Oh yeah, it's like a bowl has been carved out of the rock."

"Yup, that's where they built their fires. Now look over here, and here, and here," Paul continued, pointing to small, circular holes about the size of a silver dollar going around in a circle every few feet. "These were where they put their poles for the teepees."

"You yanking my chain or what?" Mickey asked, scoffing at him.

"This very spot is where they lived and died. Look around, you'll see the same set-up for around six other teepees. Now come with me over here," Paul said, leading Mickey over to a large boulder at the edge of the flat area. "Look in here," he said pointing into a crevice. "Shade your eyes, and look on the right side here."

"What is that? Graffiti?"

"Those are petroglyphs. Ancient writings. They survived only because of where they are located. I wish I knew what they said."

"Wasn't there some TV show about the ancient petroglyphs and UFO's and all that crazy stuff? How do you know all this Indian lore?"

"A friend of mine who runs a horse rescue ranch up the road is Native American. Her people have lived in these parts forever. A lot of this area is holy, even sacred to them."

"Kind of like Visitation was to us," Mickey said referring to the grammar school and Catholic Church parish that was the center of their lives.

"What do you mean *was?*"

"You didn't hear? The Cardinal closed the church and the school. It looks like it's going to be a Walmart or something."

"Are you kidding me? And the people of the parish just let it happen?"

"Now you're really kidding. Go up against the Cardinal and the Archdiocese of New York? That's as bad as the Indians going up against the U.S. Government."

"At least the Indians went out with a fight."

Mickey and Paul were back in the SUV, driving through the dirt trails of the BLM. Mickey was enthralled with the landscape, soaking in the vistas, mentioning every rustle in the brush from a jackrabbit or chipmunk. But it was Paul who was in another world. Visitation was closing? The school he graduated from. The church where his parents and so many friends and relatives, young and old, had their earliest get-together at First Holy Communion, and final get-together at their funeral mass. Where he laughed as an altar boy and wept as pallbearer. He even thought that if he died out here at the other end of the continent, he would still have his funeral at Visitation.

"Where are we headed now?" Mickey asked, with enthusiasm, snapping Paul out of his funk.

"Oh, just a little side trip to the energy vortex of planet earth housed in a structure built with plans designed by aliens from Venus to attract UFO's."

"You're not kidding, and that's what scares me."

The gate to the Integratron parking lot was open, so Paul pulled inside. They looked at the Integraton's blazing white walls against the deep blue desert high-noon sky in silence. And suddenly a huge tan and black-spotted snake whipped past them and slithered into the nearby brush.

"Holy shit! What was that?" Mickey yelled.

"No matter how otherworldly things seem sometimes, nature has a way of keeping you involved with planet earth. That was a gopher snake. Beautiful wasn't it?"

"Is it poisonous?"

"No."

"Then it's beautiful. Do they have rattlesnakes around here?"

"All over the place"

"What kind of place is this? I'm in front of a freaking UFO magnet built by Venusians and I gotta worry about a freakin' rattlesnake biting my ass! Klaatu barada nikto!" Mickey shouted with both hands held high in the air.

"That's what I said when I got here and everybody thought I was nuts!"

"Well they got that right. Can we go in?"

"Let's find out."

They walked around the building, with its UFO-esque lines, protruding poles and wires, and ordinary Home Depot-esque doors and windows.

They both turned when they heard another car pull into the gravel driveway. It was a 1960's era VW bus driven by a skinny hippie.

"I know this guy. His name is Ranger."

"You are way deeper into this lifestyle than I thought."

Ranger shuffled through the gravel towards them, with his recyclable grocery bags in each hand. "I'm sorry, we're closed right now. I left the gate open accidentally."

"Hi, Ranger. I don't know if you remember me. I'm friends with Kate and Jasmine."

Ranger looked stumped.

"And Ash," Paul added.

Ranger immediately perked up. "Oh, yeah! I remember you! Let me put these away and I'll just show you inside real quick," Ranger said, entering the building.

"Ash is his weed supplier," Paul whispered to Mickey. "More on that later."

"You know, when I first heard you were settling in the desert, I pictured you living next to a golf course in Palm Springs riding around on a golf cart and dating rich, too-tan widows, living the life of Reilly. Not the life of Hunter S. Thompson for chrissakes!"

Ranger popped his head out the door, "Come on in!"

Ranger gave them a short tour of the lower-level displays with a rapid rundown of the Venusian plans, energy vortex, universal UFO beacon, shady Giant Rock connection, and sound bath full-body vibration chamber.

Mickey looked as though he was listening to a lying defendant in court.

"I'd love to give you guys the full tour, but I've got some secret celebrities coming in later for a sound bath and I have to get the place ready," Ranger said, leading them to the door.

"No problem, thanks so much for the look-see," Paul said, waving goodbye as they headed for the car.

"Secret celebrities. Yeah, like who? Gomer and Goober?" Mickey said, dripping with skepticism and ridicule.

"You wouldn't believe who's already been here: Oprah, Robert Plant, Moby…."

"Here? Out here in the middle of the Sea of Tranquility on the moon?"

"Yup."

"What else you got? You know I've only got today, really. I gotta get back to Vegas in the morning."

"Okay. We're going to a couple of neighborhood parks."

The next several hours were spent with Mickey's jaw dropped and eyes wide open as they checked out the giant oversized Jesus and bible icons in Desert Christ Park, and the magical miles seen while rolling through Joshua Tree National Park, from the Joshua tree forest to the Ocotillo pastures to the vistas rivaled only by pictures sent back from Mars by *Viking*.

"I feel like an idiot," Mickey said, standing near the edge of a high roadside turnout in Joshua Tree National Park. "I didn't know any of this existed. You could just picture a herd of brontosaurus walking through here. How could something so ancient be so surprising and new? It's like a secret world revealed. A revelation."

"Didn't they write a book in the Bible about that?" Asked Paul.

"What's that?"

"The Book of Revelations."

They were both exhausted and relaxing after showers and late-afternoon cups of tea. It was a long day's journey from UFO headquarters to Venus and Mars and then on to dinosaur fields and through to biblical times.

Paul made arrangements for Tracy, Heidi, and Kate to meet up at Pappy and Harriet's for dinner. It's a local roadhouse in the middle of the nearby Pioneertown, an historic western town built by Hollywood cowboys as a working movie set in the Fifties.

Still intact, it has been converted into a hipster tourist destination compete with post-modern art galleries, alternative music recording studios, and staged Old West gunfights complete with shotgun blasts, pistol packin' mammas, and instant justice from quick-shooting sheriffs.

The drive to Pappy and Harriet's was yet another awe-inspiring experience for Mickey. The sun was setting, casting long shadows across the gold and purple rocky landscape as the two-lane blacktop road rolled, swayed, and wound its way past horse ranches, mobile homes with big rigs parked in the front yard, geodesic dome homes, and assorted Santa Fe style southwest mansions perched on rocky hilltops.

"It just keeps going and going, doesn't it?" Mickey wondered.

"Off to the right, which actually hooks over to my property, this road goes up almost fifty miles to Big Bear, which is a winter ski resort town. And just about all of that land is Federal property. The BLM. Bureau of Land Management."

"It's called BLM?"

"Yeah. Bureau of Land Management. Why?"

"Who was protesting that night you snapped and retired faster than a politician caught in a sex scandal?"

"Black Lives Matter. Oh. BLM. I get it."

"And why did you buy that piece of property you own. Because it's next to the...?"

"BLM. Yeah, and?"

"I'm just saying. So it's protected land?"

"Yup. It will look like this forever. That is why I bought where I bought. It's what makes this little piece of the earth magical."

Paul pulled in to the Pappy and Harriet's parking lot and noticed Heidi's pickup just behind them.

"Mickey, I told you we're meeting Tracy and her friend. But there's more to it."

"More to it? Are we are on some kind of undercover op or something?"

"It's not just Tracy's friend."

"Yeah, go on."

"It's her fiancée?"

"Hey, mazel tov! Since you retired, Jeanie Espinoza and Kitty O'Brien married each other. Nobody in the entire precinct even suspected they were dating. Oh yeah, remember Ryan? He dropped dead. Retired for all of three weeks. They were packing the van for the move to Lauderdale, and *phhht*. Dead."

"It seems like yesterday, we were underage trying to sneak into bars. And now, they're calling our row for last stop. Let's go meet the girls."

"I think the last time I saw Tracy was at graduation from grade school when you and I drove up there."

"I've only seen her a handful of times since then myself, up until very recently."

Paul was always interested in Mickey's reactions to things. Whether it was a bet on a horse, *It says it's going to rain tomorrow in Miami, is he a mudder?* or if he should wear a wire on an undercover drug sting *It's 80 degrees out! How the hell you think you're gonna conceal a wire?* or whether or not he should get married? *If you want a kid, get married. Otherwise fughedaboudit.* Sometimes it was just a look Mickey had that told Paul if he was doing something that would end in a laugh or a trip to the ER. So Paul was thrilled when Mickey, Tracy, and Heidi exchanged loving bear hugs with laughs, smiles, and some tears between Mickey and Tracy. With just the ambient light from some beer signs in the windows, Tracy resembled her mom so much that Paul couldn't help but be yanked back to those crazy days of bar trips, softball games in Van Cortlandt Park, and wild summer group-home parties in the Hamptons when couples started pairing off. These were soon followed by wedding after wedding, then christening after christening, in a grand parade marching down the avenue of life. It seemed that new marriages, babies, and careers would lead to nothing but better days. Until the parade and parties ended, and everyone went back to their three-room, four-story walk-up apartments, and started balancing check books on Formica kitchen tabletops with up-all-night babies and moms and overnight-shift dads and crappy cars that wouldn't start. Then reality really kicked in.

"It does my heart good to see you two back together again," Mickey said, putting his arms around Tracy and Paul.

Tracy motioned for Heidi to get between her and Paul. "They say when one door closes another opens. But sometimes, one door closes, and you have to knock down a wall or two to get on your way," Paul said.

Paul had been meaning to check out Pappy and Harriet's since he arrived. He knew they had live country music most nights, an outdoor barbeque pit, and an Old West theme, but had no idea that this roadhouse in what looked like the middle of a moonscape was packed to the rafters from the first breakfast Bloody Mary to last call. They got on a wait list and stood at a crowded bar for the next available table.

"Here she is!" Paul said, seeing Kate pushing through the crowd towards them.

Kate was resplendent in a gauzy pink cotton dress that went below her knees, and embroidered denim jacket. "Sorry I'm late! My shift replacement wasn't on time. Again."

Introductions and hello kisses on the cheek went around, as Paul watched and waited as Kate and Mickey interacted.

With his arm around Kate, Mickey chortled, "Kate says Paul's a sweetheart! So, I told her how you must've changed a lot since moving here!"

The crowd was growing around their group at the bar. Paul and Mickey wound up standing at the bar, while the ladies stood behind them chatting and laughing with non-alcoholic drinks in hand.

"Am I the only one drinking? That makes me nervous," Mickey said, taking a gulp of Jack Daniels.

"I stopped drinking just recently. And I don't even know how or why I did it," Paul said taking a sip of his club soda with lime.

"How long have we been here?" Mickey asked. "Ten, fifteen minutes?"

"Yeah, so. What, you never waited for a table before?"

"Look around. What do you see?"

"Okay, Mr. Observant. Clue me in," Paul said in anticipation.

"This group at the pool table? They look like they just came from a Hell's Angels hazing party. That table over there. Those four look like the winners of the Crosby, Stills, Nash and Young look-alike contest. Then across the room, I see a long table of Marines in t-shirts and jeans with their girlfriends, who could probably take out an ISIS base with some baseball bats. And this group behind us is speaking some language from who-knows-istan."

"So what's your point?"

"Paulie, this place is like St. Mark's Lounge. Back in the day! Don't you see it? All the different factions. The bikers, the artists, the immigrants, the tourists, the military. Before every bar, every neighborhood in New York was taken over, gentrified, homogenized, and sterilized."

"These are the people who live around here."

"Exactly!"

"It's like an ancient, pre-urban, East Village."

"Excuse me, but your table is ready," said a seventysomething bartender with a Polish accent.

The hum of the crowed was getting louder as the evening wore on. A band was setting-up on stage in front of a huge tie-dye banner. Its members looked like they got their style from looking at album covers in the psychedelic bin of a used vinyl store.

The food and service were good, and there was an electricity in the air, as if the crowd felt they knew they were part of something new in this last frontier of open space and freedom. It would take decades for this place to be ruined by urban planners.

Paul got a kick out of Mickey bantering back and forth with the girls. It reminded him of the old days, when they were single and on the prowl. Obviously there was nothing sexual about Mickey's hilarious storytelling of Keystone cop-like NYPD escapades to three beautiful girls in a noisy bar. And neither Mickey nor Paul had any kind of a look about them that would attract young ladies. It was just pure enjoyment to watch Mickey's personality and charm in full swing with eager-to-listen friends who haven't heard these stories before. Or lived them, like Paul had.

"Dad, we've got something we want to tell you," Tracy said in a quiet moment when Mickey got up to hit the head.

"Oh, would you like me hit the powder room, so you could have some privacy?" Kate asked.

"Not at all. Please stay," Heidi said reassuringly.

"I've been doing some thinking. We've been doing some thinking. And we decided it's not a good idea for two people in a relationship to be in the military at the same time. There are just too many variables."

Paul closed his eyes and gave a sigh of relief, but tried not to be too obvious. He remembered those around him who advised him against being a cop, but he wouldn't have any of it. In fact, hearing those naysayers bleat on made him want to be a cop even more. And he knew there was a lot of himself in Tracy.

Mickey came back to the table and sensed there had been a change of mood. "You want me to go outside and have a smoke?"

"You don't smoke!" Paul said.

"I could start."

"Sit down!"

Mickey sat. "Go ahead, I'll be good."

"I was just telling dad that I'm not joining the Marines, because it's too difficult for both parents to be serving…."

"Whoah! Parents? You didn't say *parents* before!" Paul said excitedly, spilling some of his club soda.

"Oops. I'm having a baby," Tracy said, as Heidi put her arm around her.

"That's fantastic!" Paul said, then stopped dead. He closed his eyes, and saw his wife Marcy's smiling face. He flashed on his departed mom and dad, and how happy they would have been to hold their first grandchild. He opened his eyes and for a moment saw Marcy, but it was Tracy, crying with Heidi and Kate.

"There's more," Tracy said, wiping her tears with a paper napkin. "I'm going back to school to become an RN."

"Your mother would be so proud, Tracy," Paul said, holding her hands, as their eyes locked.

"You know dad, I had a strange dream last night. I dreamt that I was a toddler, back in our old Bronx apartment. Mom was busy in the kitchen. It was sweltering hot, and for some reason, I was out on the fire escape all by myself. Did we have a fire escape? I don't even remember the apartment, really. We moved when I was, how old?"

"About two. Yes, we had a fire escape," Paul said, looking at Mickey and giving a very subtle wink.

"I was out on the fire escape, holding onto the bars, leaning out, and then in slow motion I slipped through and fell, how many stories were there?"

"Six," Mickey and Paul said in unison.

"But it felt like fifty. And I was falling in slow motion down, and I looked down and below there was a police officer, standing there, with his arms open. And he was calling my name, *It's okay Tracy, It's okay, I got you.* And as I got closer I could see it was grandpa."

"Her mom's father was a cop," Paul interjected.

"Of course I remember the picture of him in his police uniform, which was always displayed on our wall at home. But I don't remember meeting him. And I wasn't even scared. I landed in his arms with a thump. And when I looked up at his face, it wasn't grandpa at all. It was an African-American cop. Then I woke up."

Paul turned pale. His face ashen and disturbed. He turned to Mickey. "Did you tell her?"

"I swear. Never," Mickey said, just as shaken as Paul.

Now Tracy, Heidi, and Kate had worried looks on their faces, as glances and perplexed expressions shot around the table while the band began tuning up their instruments.

"It's getting noisy in here," Paul said, picking up the check. "Let's meet out by my car and we'll talk."

Tracy, Heidi, and Kate got up and left Mickey and Paul at the table.

"You didn't say anything? She has no idea?" Mickey asked.

"Well, I guess, her mom or grandma could have said something."

"Yeah, that's probably it. You know how the mind can block things out. I can't remember where I parked my car half the time."

"But you'll never forget the time Joseph Greeley threw up on Danny Daly's back during morning prayers in seventh grade," Paul said stone-faced.

"Of course not."

"You don't forget the big stuff."

It was a surreal scene outside. The car was parked at the end of the bar's parking lot, right next to the start of the Old West TV town, underneath another starry desert sky. There were a few bare light bulbs on some storefronts, putting the entire length of the faux town in view as if a backdrop for a *Twilight Zone* episode.

"Tracy, do you know anything about a story where you fell out of a window?" Paul asked.

"No. Should I?"

"You fell off the fire escape when you were about 18 months old. You got out there when your mom turned away for a second. You fell six stories."

Tracy got chills as she hugged herself tightly. "Oh my God. What happened? Tell me!"

"A cop just happened to see you who was walking by. He caught you. He was a black guy."

The band could be heard playing their first song in the distance. But that was the only sound that could be heard. All were silent.

Paul absentmindedly kicked some dirt. "And there's something else. Your grandfather had died about a week before this happened. Dropped dead of a massive heart attack."

"It was one of those dreams that felt so real. So vivid," Tracy said, her alabaster skin given a glow from the bright full moon. "But I wasn't scared as I fell. It was like I knew everything was going to be alright. Why didn't anyone ever tell me about this?"

Paul and Mickey looked at each other, in what could be described as shame. "Well, your mom was home alone at the time. And we wanted as few people to know about what happened as possible."

"Was mom…drinking at that time?"

"Yeah. And I was working a lot. I was new on the job and couldn't turn down the hours. It wasn't long after that incident that your mom and I separated, and you moved upstate to move into grandma's house. It was best for you."

"I don't know why your generation doesn't talk about these things. Why is everything so secretive?"

Kate took the few steps to be by Paul's side and put her arm around him. "It's not that they're secrets. It's denial," she said.

"My husband died from drugs and alcohol abuse, and I know I was in denial. He'd stop for a few weeks or a month or two, and I'd tell myself everything was going to be fine. He'd get better. I called AA one time and was asking a bunch of questions about treatment. They guy on the phone said, 'Lady, are you calling for yourself? Because if you're calling for somebody else, you're just wasting your time. He needs to be the one to pick up the phone and dial.' It was shortly after that I started going to Al Anon."

"Grandma and I went a bunch of times. That's where we learned that Serenity Prayer."

"Oh yeah," Mickey chimed in. "That Serenity Prayer is on more refrigerators than Homer Simpson. I heard a good joke at an AA meeting," Mickey said, trying to lighten up the mood. "A pompous monsignor is in the rectory and gets a warning on the radio about a flood coming, but he thinks, 'No need to worry. The good Lord will take care of me.' So the street's flooded, and a guy in a 4x4 Jeep honks and yells, 'Hey monsignor, come on out, I'll take you to higher ground.' 'No need,' said the monsignor. 'The Lord will take care of me.' Then the waters rise above the first story, and he's on the second floor, and a boat comes by, and the guy yells, 'Hey monsignor, hop in!' 'No need,' he answers. 'The Lord will take care of me. So now the flood's up to the roof, and he's up there by the chimney. A helicopter flies overhead and a guy drops a ladder and yells, 'Come on Monsignor, it's your last chance.' 'No need. The good Lord will protect me.' So of course he drowns, and next thing you know, he's at the gates of heaven, and in a huff he asks Saint Peter, 'Why didn't the Lord help me?' Saint Peter goes through his notes and says, 'Are you kidding me? It says here we sent a Jeep, a boat, *and* a freakin' helicopter!'"

They all laughed, and when the laughter starts to die down, Paul asks, "What about the UFO?"

"What UFO?" Mickey asks.

"I thought I remembered hearing that joke but there was also a UFO sent."

They all looked at Paul like he was nuts.

"Yeah, there was a UFO, and then something about the Serenity Prayer...," Paul said, eyes squinting, head turning as though he's trying to force himself to recall something important.

"I think this high desert high is getting to you," Mickey said laughing. "Earth to Paulie! Earth to Paulie!"

"Okay, Okay, so I'm a little tired. Let's call it a night," Paul said, exchanging hugs and goodbyes.

Paul decided to take some back roads home, rather than the two-lane blacktop. The moon was full and the rocky landscape looked more like an actual moonscape in the brightness of the moon's glow. The road was winding and undulating, creating almost a hypnotic effect.

"Do you believe in UFO's?" Mickey asked, gazing on the strange scenery passing by.

"Oh boy. Here it comes."

"What? I'm just asking," Mickey said.

Paul keeps his eyes on the road. "Something happened to me out in the desert one night. I thought I saw a UFO and I was chasing it down. I crashed the car, wound up in the hospital for a day or two and it's a long story."

"I got time."

Back at the house Mickey was sipping whiskey in a comfortable chair facing Paul as he told the story of the night he chased a UFO, crashed, thought he was slipped a mickey, got busted screaming at giant statues of Jesus, was almost committed to a mental ward, and was on his way to have a shoot-out at the O.K. Corral with Ash until his car conked out and he blacked out.

"Are you sure you're okay? I mean, we've all had crazy shit happen, but it looks like you're the steel ball in a pinball machine."

"But who's pushing the flipper buttons?" Paul said, digging into his pocket. "Look at this," he said, unfolding a small paper and handing it to Mickey.

"Serenity Prayer," he read, looking at the unremarkable scrap of paper. "Yeah, and?"

"I found that in my pocket. I don't remember putting it there. And that's not my handwriting."

"And who's exactly do you think it is?" Mickey asked, cautiously.

"I thought it was Tracy's," Paul said, waiting for a reaction from Mickey, which didn't happen. "I think it might be Marcy's handwriting."

"You mean, like from years ago?"

"No."

"You mean like, maybe it was something you picked up in her house when you were cleaning it out?"

"No."

Mickey jumped up out of his chair and walked over to the refrigerator. "You have any ice water in here? I need a cool dose of reality."

"I don't know, Mickey, there's something really weird going on. But even though I was almost thrown in a loony bin, since I found that piece of paper shoved in my pocket, I've...."

"You've what?"

"I just feel different. Like, at peace or something."

"Okay, Paulie. You were hitting the gin mills up here before you went on the wagon, right? And you were meeting people. Who the hell do you think goes to bars? Alcoholics! What's on the wall behind every lectern that's hung up before every meeting? The Serenity Prayer! Somebody you met, probably a female with nice penmanship, thought you could use some words of wisdom and gave this to you."

"Nope. I found it the day after my car conked out and I blacked out."

"That's when you *found* it! You could have stuck it there weeks ago and just didn't know it."

"I guess you're right," Paul said, slouching in the couch, crestfallen. "I don't know why, but I think it means something more. There's something more to this...whole journey. I'm not the only one, either. I mean look at Salvation Mountain."

"You got me on that one. Did we see it today?"

"Nah, too far. It's this mountain in the middle of nowhere...."

"Isn't everything out here in the middle of nowhere?"

"Way out. In a place called Slab City, where desert-rat squatters have lived for decades, off the grid, before there was a grid. This mechanic built this, mountain...I've got a flyer somewhere. It's crazy. He built an actual mountain out of hay bales, wire, and a gazillion gallons of paint," he said, rifling through piles of paper on the table, through drawers, in the magazine stand, the refrigerator magnets, and on the bookshelves.

"Ah! Here it is! I never would have found this. I stuck it in this Kerouac book, *Some of the Dharma*, as a book mark." Paul unfolded the Salvation Mountain flyer and began reading it. "Holy jumpin' shit," Paul said in a deep, low voice, jaw drooping, eyes focused like a laser beam on the page.

"What? What? You look like you saw a ghost!"

Paul reached into his pocket and pulled the Serenity Prayer scrap out again. He held up the Salvation Mountain flyer, hands shaking, revealing the missing corner of the flyer. He placed the scrap next to the missing corner. "The missing piece of the puzzle."

"Now you're freaking me out."

"I went to Salvation Mountain the morning of the day when my car conked out and I blacked out. So this piece of paper proves that it came from that day. That's the day this scrap of paper was written on and given to me. And that's the day I woke up after my car, my phone, and my flashlight wouldn't work. And my gun almost set my pants on fire!"

"I didn't hear *this* part."

"The reason I was on that road was I was in a red-eyed Hulk rage and was probably going to blow this guy Ash away."

"Are you out of you mind?"

"Was. I *was* out of my mind."

"And my gun started heating up like a freakin' iron set on linen, to the point where I had to get it out of my pocket so fast, I threw it somewhere and couldn't find it. Then….."

"Yeah, then what? What?"

"I blacked out. And when I awoke. I put my gun in the trunk. Walked to this guy Ash's house, had a chat, and he thanked me for being a good cop."

"Paulie, you've been under a lot of strain, I'm gonna hit the sack. I gotta get up early and get back to Vegas."

"Yeah. Okay. I'm gonna read a little and then crash out. Do me a favor?"

"Anything you want, brother."

"Keep all this under your hat."

"Scout's honor. But Paulie, listen," Mickey got up and put both hands on Paul's shoulders, going right in his face, his steely blue eyes penetrating Paul's dark eyes. "You blacked out how many times? Got into a wreck. Got picked up by the cops. Almost got into a gunfight at the O.K. Corral, and that's just the stuff you told me about. They're could be something serious going on. I mean...medically. Or mentally."

Paul smiled and tapped Mickey on the cheek. "That's the thing. Since that last blackout I feel great. I don't know what it is, but I feel fantastic all of a sudden. Like, I flipped a switch."

"Promise me, if you black out or try to take on Twentynine Palms Marine base, you'll check yourself in and get help."

"Scout's honor."

"Wait a minute," Mickey said, relaxing his hold, "we weren't even Boy Scouts!"

"Okay, Buckeye honor!" Paul shouted.

"Buckeye honor."

"By the way, speaking of the old neighborhood, how's Brielle? I haven't heard from her."

"You won't believe this. After she took over your apartment, she started hanging out with us deplorables, in The Buckeye after-hours when she got off work downtown at St. Mark's Lounge."

"Really? Brielle?"

"Yeah, and she's engaged. To a fireman, that rookie Ramirez, from Review Place. He moved in with her."

"A fireman! Where did I go wrong?" Paul laughed. "Say hi for me when you see her."

"You're really not coming back?"

295

"Nah. This is it. I got that high desert high. I'm beat. I'll make coffee in the morning. Nightie-night."

There was no time for a long good-bye. Mickey scarfed down some coffee and toast, took a shower, and left a dust trail behind him as he sped down the dirt road, next stop Las Vegas. Paul waved good-bye and watched the dust swirling behind the car until it dissipated and melded in with the rest of the dirt, dust, and hardscrabble left behind. A roadrunner came from under a creosote bush and rushed towards Paul. He stopped short, just a few feet away, head darting back and forth as he checked out Paul, standing there, statue-like. It seemed the less movement you made, whether standing or sitting in the yard or the park or taking a break on a hike, the more likely a critter would appear seemingly from nowhere. They had an extended staring contest, and in those seconds, or maybe minute or two, Paul felt like he deserved to stand close by this beautiful bird.

Chapter Eleven

It wasn't unusual to see people on horseback come down his long driveway, but even from a distance he could see that Mabel's horse was trotting – instead of doing its normal slow walk – and that meant something was up. Paul stepped out to the front porch, morning coffee in hand.

Before the horse even stopped, she was talking. "Just found out we've got a problem, and I just don't know what to do."

"Come inside and grab some coffee," Paul said, as Mabel dismounted and tied the horse to the porch post. Paul poured a cup and pointed for Mabel to sit. "Tell me about it."

"You know those godawful ginormous windmills down by the freeway in Palm Springs?"

"How could you not?"

"Well, some giant energy conglomerate from up in Washington State got hundreds of millions of grant money for so-called 'clean energy' and is going to put them up here," Mabel said, her hands shaking slightly.

"Calm down. What do you mean up here?"

"Here in the BLM. Across all these hills, these washes, these Joshua tree pastures. Everywhere. It will ruin everything."

"Those things are the worst! Every study shows they don't even offset their carbon footprint for their own life expectancy."

"They will destroy everything. Our birds, our bats, our wildlife, our sacred lands."

"Not to mention our real estate values, those scumbags."

"What do we do?"

"You want some milk?"

"Yes, please," Mabel said, already looking defeated.

As Paul went to open the refrigerator, he looked at the Serenity Prayer magnet on the door for the ten-millionth time since he discovered it in his pocket after that fateful night. His eyes zeroed in on the word *courage*.

"Mabel, I went through this once before. Not here, but back in New York City."

"They have windmills in New York City?"

"No. But they have scumbag politicians and crooks who'll do anything to make a buck. Even risking the lives of more than birds, bats, and the landscape. They just bulldoze through and destroy everything in their path. It ain't gonna happen here. You know that community center in town? We're going to have a meeting there. There's no way they're getting away with this again. Not on my watch."

"You're a good man, Paul."

"I'm trying."

Mabel hopped on her horse and they slowly walked up the driveway and down the dirt road.

Paul didn't want to screw this evening up. It was going to be just Kate and him. He had all the veggies, all the tofu, all the yogurt, all the ground flax seed, and several kinds of olive oils and vinegars. There would be music, candles, even incense! The outdoor fire pit was stocked with wood for an evening fire and the chaise lounges were in line with the Milky Way for optimum stargazing. He even set up a telescope that was already aiming at Saturn, so the rings would already be in the eyepiece without having to search.

Paul had been taking Beast on long hikes through the BLM, sometimes for hours. And most times, they wouldn't run into another human the entire time. There were plenty of critters along the way, slinking, darting, staring, and sometimes it seemed like they were performing for them. Once in a while, one or two people might pass by on horseback, which always made Paul think about how not much had changed around here for centuries, if not thousands of years. These boulders, these Joshua trees, and these hundreds of years old creosote trees were here when Native Americans had never seen a white man. Before there were guns, and internal combustion engines, and smartphones. Paul tried hard to imagine he was traveling back in time when he was on those hikes. And as he breathed in the arid air, shared some water with Beast, and sat on the shady side of a boulder it was getting easier to do. He couldn't believe how or why he got so lucky. He felt great for the first time in years and he was grateful.

Kate looked incredible when she stepped into the living room, lit by candlelight. The soft light danced off her silver earrings, necklace, and belt buckle. Her eyes twinkled like Milky Way stars. Gram Parsons was singing "Return of the Grievous Angel" on the CD player. Paul looked at Beast on his dog bed, and he could swear he was nodding his head, as if to tell him to get close to Kate. He did.

"Kate. I just realized something about us."

Kate laughed. "Really? About us?"

"Yeah. I mean, I haven't dated for decades."

"Is that what this is? A date?"

"I mean, I guess…."

"Paul," Kate said, holding out her hands, palms up. "Give me your hands."

Paul did.

She pulled Paul close to her and they kissed a kiss as lovers do.

Kate whispered, "Did you feel anything?"

"Wow. Yeah. I haven't felt that in a long time."

"Good. So did I. Shall we eat?"

As they ate, engaged in small talk, laughed, smiled, and flirted, Paul tried to remember when he felt so comfortable with a woman. He knew it was those early days with Marcy, when young love was magic. And the future seemed like a far-off dream.

"I thought we'd do some stargazing, then maybe afterwards light the fire outside," Paul said, standing behind Kate's chair and placing his hands on her shoulders.

She turned, reached for his hand and kissed it. "Sounds perfect."

Suddenly, the music stopped, and all the power in the house was lost.

"At least we have candles," Paul said. He grabbed a few candles, and lit them. "Let's go outside and see if the lights are out everywhere."

They stepped out the door, and Paul looked up in the sky. "Do you see that?"

"Yes, I do."

Directly above them, high in the sky, was a bright, shiny object, slightly larger than a star, wobbling, but not twinkling like a star.

"Look at that," Paul said, holding Kate's hand.

The bright object, moved to the left, the right, then shot straight up, and seemed to burst into a million bits of starlight and become part of the Milky Way.

"What in God's name...?" Kate whispered.

Paul dropped to his knees, head bowed, clutching his heart.

"Are you okay, Paul? What's happening?"

"I don't know. I got this tingling in my whole body."

"Like a sharp pain? Should I call 911?"

"No. It felt...pleasant."

"That was weird," Kate said, helping Paul up.

"Did you ever hear that when a shooting star goes up, not down, it means something?" Paul whispered.

"Something? Like what?"

"It means that someone in purgatory was just promoted to heaven."

"Like every time a bell rings an angel gets his wings?" Kate asked, perplexed, but smiling.

"Wait. I know. Hold the flashlight and follow me."

Paul rushed over to the Escape, and began emptying out everything from the rear cargo area.

"What are you doing?" Kate said.

Paul lifted the spare tire and took out a cardboard box. "I've got it. Don't think I'm insane."

"What is that?"

"It should contain my ex-wife's ashes."

"*Okaaaay.*"

"Only, I'm not sure if they're in there."

"'And why would that be?"

"I had this dream. And in the dream, my wife, Marcy, told me that purgatory is an actual place. Out there in the universe. And when you're in purgatory you have to earn your way to heaven to leave the physical world behind."

Paul opened the box, and there was a metal container inside. He shook it and it sounded like there were ashes in there.

"Let's go back inside and have some tea."

"Wait. Hold the flashlight steady."

Kate held the flashlight on the container. It had a small plaque on it that read "Marcy Santo."

"Are you sure you want to do this?"

"Positive," Paul said, holding the lid. He pulled it open and he was shocked at what he was saw.

"Look! See that! Those are her ashes." Paul said, hands shaking.

"Of course they are." Kate said, mystified. "What else would they be?"

"After my car accident, I noticed after it was fixed that some of this spilled out." Paul's eyes widened in the harsh light of the flashlight. "When it spilled it was rocks and dirt. It wasn't her ashes. I didn't know what to do at the time. I didn't understand. I didn't want to know."

Paul closed the lid, placed the container in the box, and put it back under the spare.

"Now I know. This is what's left of her body. She's made her transition. We just saw it. I just felt it. I know it. Let's keep this between us."

"I don't know how or why, but I believe you."

Paul closed up the Escape and they went back to the darkened house. As soon as they stepped inside the kitchen, the lights came back on and the Gram Parsons CD began playing again on the boom box.

Paul and Kate stared at each other, not saying a word for a good minute.

Paul closed the door behind them and locked it.

"Would you like to stay?"

"Yes, I would, Paulie." Kate said, smiling.

They turned out the lights, blew out the candles and walked hand-in-hand to the bedroom, with Beast right behind them, wagging his tail.